OPEN MIKE

Gregory Petersen

Martin Sisters Publishing

Published by

Martin Sisters Publishing, LLC

www. martinsisterspublishing. com

In memory of Gregg Rocca

CHAPTER ONE

His name would be called soon. Any minute now, perhaps any second. The host had probably been on stage for his allotted time already. Michael didn't know. He'd never met the emcee, didn't know his routine, and did not have a clue when to go on. Plus, he wasn't paying much attention. He had missed out on the customary run-through pleasantries while throwing up in the men's room. Either anxiety or his fifth gin and tonic could explain that. Neither sounded like an acceptable excuse—especially on a night like this—so he planned to blame some sort of stomach bug. But even if he truly had been sick, he doubted anyone would believe it. Regardless, nobody seemed to notice.

Half a bottle of Budweiser replaced one vile taste for another. He'd always hated beer. Not only was it bitter, but it took too long to drink to cause any inebriation. Whiskey was a better choice. Now *that* was a man's drink. But at least the Bud was slightly more palatable than the vomit, and certainly more predictable than Jack Daniels. His newest fear was that the spotlight would trigger a new wave of nausea and create a performance nobody would ever forget.

Yeah, sure, some may laugh immediately, at least those out of harm's way. And his friends, if any were left, would find the secondhand telling piss-your-pants funny. What was the point of trying to be clever, or, on a good night maybe even witty, if all it took to bring down the house was to bring up the beer?

Up on stage, the emcee, who looked young enough to be proud of his peach fuzz goatee, continued. *What the hell is that guy's name?* Michael thought. He should probably know since it had always been the drill to thank him by name from the stage and tell the audience to keep the applause going. He peeked over the the soundboard guy's shoulder and saw the name, Brandon McMahon. That must be it. Hopefully there hadn't been a last-minute change. That could be embarrassing but played off easily. He looked at the list. Brandon McMahon, Michael Clover, and Drew Greene. He certainly was closer to the emcee on the food chain than to Drew, who could soon see theater shows, but it was fun to be along for the ride.

He tried to listen, but his mind kept wandering, only catching a word here or there. It didn't matter; he could tell this McMahon kid probably still had a way to go.

Either it was a tough crowd or this guy couldn't get a laugh with a dick joke. It was a Thursday, and except for the real drunks, everyone was either stone sober or bored stiff. Whatever the case, it could be a tough night.

He had pictured this night differently. His first show featuring in a real comedy club should have been preceded by a bells and whistles package. Of course he had only himself to blame for its absence. This was not the time for regrets.

Whining on stage might coax a laugh, but he could feel no real regret. Whatever *real* meant.

Michael had been quick to remind anyone he'd told about this new gig that featuring was just a glorified way of saying opening act. Headlining was the real goal. Or maybe it was just the dream. Maybe it would remain only that. What's another dashed hope or unmet expectation? People like pain. They aren't interested until someone starts to bleed.

Hell, maybe I can capitalize on it.

He also knew that landing top billing was close to impossible without being on the under card at some time. Half an hour on stage tonight. He'd done that and more back at Captain Riley's, but this, of course, was different. This was a place he couldn't screw up.

Just get to that first laugh; the rest will fall into place. That was the first advice he'd ever been given when he'd decided to take up comedy. So far it had worked. But this was a long way from Captain Riley's.

If he were to ever join the elite crowd, he'd better have more solid material. Even his half-hour set had its lulls. He reached into his jeans pocket and pulled out a small wad of paper. On a crumbled sheet, next to a thought he'd written the other day, he began to scrawl.

I used to be my own worst critic. Then I got married. He cringed.

I used to be my own worst critic, then I applied for a job at that boutique? Own worst critic, then my fly was down at the church picnic?

He sighed. Years ago he'd been told that ninety percent of what he would write would be complete shit, but that ten percent would make it all worth it, so keep writing. If he only came up with one good bit a week, he'd soon have one hell of a routine.

There was still a little more clear space on the paper. *I used to be my own worst critic, then I went back home to visit Mom.* He cringed again.

Ah, yes. No place like unresolved maternal anger to find an easy laugh.

Know what it's like to hurt on the inside? he continued to write. *No, but it's funny to watch from the outside.*

Too corny? Perhaps, Michael thought, allowing a brief smile. People liked corny, though. At least he hoped that was the case. Otherwise he was set to commit career suicide.

The emcee began to remind the crowd to tip the excellent wait staff, and that there would be half-price drinks and free billiards at the bar next door, also owned by the proprietor of the club. It would soon be his turn.

His calves tightened. The tendons behind his knees felt like a strand of string as a kite catches a gust of wind and sends it into a spiraling flutter. His spine took on a life of its own with constant spasms, while his throat grew dry, head ached.

Just get that first laugh. Just get that first laugh.

At least the beer was a liquid. Bottled water was probably a wiser choice, but the beer would do more than just lubricate his throat. Maybe it would lubricate his self-confidence, maybe even the crowd's.

All he saw of the silhouettes that would soon be his audience were stagnant figures, a few laughing here or there. The small candles inside the tempered glass centerpieces gave little more than a flickering image. As he looked closer he saw that a few were laughing, and some drinking out of the long-neck bottles that never caught on with Dasani or Aquafina. That was a good start; he wasn't drinking alone.

"Okay," Brandon McMahon said. Michael prayed that was the right name. Ready or not, this was it. Life was about to change.

"You've heard enough out of me," he continued, and Michael saw more than one nod of agreement, "so please join me in welcoming tonight's feature act, Michael Clover!"

The obligatory applause was louder than he expected and felt unspeakably good. His feet carried him toward the stage, zigzagging through the tight quarters of small tables, chairs, and patrons. A slight half-jog, driven by pure adrenaline, and then up the three steps leading to the stage. Never mistaken as sure-footed, he was just glad he didn't trip. While that would have certainly earned a heartier laugh than vomiting everywhere, he still held hopes of creating a name for himself in a more conventional way.

The emcee continued to lead the applause and made certain the microphone was back in the stand, stage center. During Michael's open mic days, he had been on stages like this, but tonight the spotlight blinded him. He closed his eyes, and countless purple squiggles floated across his frame of reference. While his eyes hurt, he could see that he was now onstage alone, and the applause was starting to die down.

"Hi, I'm Michael Clover," he said. "But you should still be clapping for tonight's emcee, Brandon McMahon. Funny young fellow."

The audience complied, and he took a second to adjust the microphone stand slightly. Even if it had been in the perfect spot, changing the height was his usual if not compulsive habit.

"Now," he said and paused, "have you ever been so horny you fantasize about your own wife?"

Right from the beginning he got a few belly laughs. And all he had worried about was that first joke. His vision cleared, and the spotlight felt more friendly than frightening.

Yes, he thought, *it's time for the show.*

CHAPTER TWO

Twenty-Two Years Earlier

The dinner table was cluttered with Jessie's art project, family bills, and a few leftover dishes. Nobody was motivated enough to put anything in its proper place. Both parents worked late, Jessie had painting class, and Michael was in detention. So at the end of all that, when Dad walked in with pizza, the day was redeemed.

It was generally against the rules, at least Mom's rules, but she was too tired to clear the table or have anyone else do it, which was more work. It was almost eight o'clock, and even though she couldn't understand it, both her kids and husband loved the laugh track-driven sitcoms that were about to start. Exceptions could be made, even though one had been made yesterday as well. Maybe the next day would see them at least look like a traditional family. There would be no bets on that, of course.

"Mikey," she said, during a commercial, "did you get all your homework finished? You should have had time during detention."

"Had to wait until after that, too. Mr. Koehlner said that's what study hall is for. We have to sit and be quiet for an hour. And they're called JUGS now."

"What in the hell are you talking about, Michael?" his father asked.

"Detention," Jessie said. She didn't look up, just stared at the television. "I got all my homework done already in case you were going to ask."

"Yeah, well you could have cleaned a little," Mom said.

"But I'm still the good one, right?"

"More by default. But what's this jugs talk?" Dad asked.

"Detention," Michael answered. "St. Stevens calls them JUGS now. Judgment Under God."

"So this Catholic school here isn't being self-righteous whatsoever," Dad said.

"That would be their understanding."

Jessie turned around. "Michael was actually the first to get one. They had a school assembly to announce the new name. The first time they said JUGS, he and Patrick Maguire laughed so hard Father Wilfong's face got redder than his hair. I laughed a little too, I'm sorry to say. But not as much as the sixth graders. It's kind of sad that fourth graders show so much more maturity."

"Well, Michael, just remember, if you get five detentions— or JUGS—not only will you look like a mutant cow, you'll get suspended. And it won't be the week's vacation that we got when I was younger. You have to serve yours in school, sitting outside the principal's office from open to close."

"You don't have to rub it in, Dad."

"Just fair warning. That's all. I'm just saying don't be a dumb ass."

"Sound advice there, Pop."

"Timothy Franklin Clover," Mom said. "I try to instill at least a little couth into our children. Are you trying to dismantle that in just one dinner?"

"Suzie, everyone's little angel can fall a little short sometimes. That's your cue to smile, Mikey."

Michael looked up and gave his best innocent smile.

"Okay, now go back to watching the idiot box."

"Yes, sir," Michael said and turned around as the laugh track signaled the return of the show.

"But the integrity of a man is measured in how you pick up the pieces," Timothy continued.

"And where did you pick up that little pearl of wisdom?" Suzie asked.

"Last night from that housekeeping dad on *Who's the Boss?*"

"Well," she said, "if I've learned one thing, it's never argue with the wisdom of Tony Danza."

The laugh track sounded again. Nobody in the family laughed, but they sat contented enough in front of the television, absently eating pizza. At the next commercial break, Timothy turned to his son. "You are going to try harder now, aren't you?"

"Absolutely. And trying is the most important thing. Unless it's algebra. Then trying means about as much as tits on a nun."

"Michael Arnold Clover," his mother said. "Is that gray matter up there completely dead?" She tried to go back to watching the television, but it was still far from captivating. No real escape there.

"That's how he got his last detention, when it was still under the old name," Jessie said. "In religion class he said, 'Balls on a priest are as useful as tits on a nun.'"

"Oh, dear God," Dad said. "And who, pray tell, did you say that to?"

"Mister Flannery. He's also a basketball coach. He teaches religion because the school must figure he can't screw that up too bad."

"So you didn't say this to a priest."

"Right," Michael answered.

"Well, at least you're not going to hell. I guess an hour detention isn't so bad after all."

"JUGS, Dad. Remember?" Jessie said.

"Yeah. How could I forget?" He went back to watching television with the rest of the family. As the laugh track sounded again, over an inexcusably contrived joke, Timothy laughed way harder than the show merited. "I'm sorry, but JUGS is just pretty damn funny."

CHAPTER THREE

By the time 4:30 AM rolled around, Dana was barely awake enough to count her money for the night. When she reached six-hundred dollars, and the roll of singles left to thumb through wouldn't bring the grand total past another fifty, she didn't see a need to go any further.

By just about any standards, it was a good night. Not much else going on around Ann Arbor, Michigan, so there was little competition for the money. Three bachelor parties came through, two former professional baseball players, as well as a few businessmen, and several ringless husbands, were nearly enough to pay the month's rent in a single night. She had changed out of her G-string and sequined bra and into her University of Michigan sweatsuit. While she'd never stepped foot on their campus, it was traditional, if not mandatory, clothing for just about anything in "Wolverine Country."

Most of the other dancers were long gone. They were also more familiar with the routine at Whispers. After changing the singles for more manageable bills, most just wore a full-length coat over their work attire and left. This caused Dana to wonder if their workday was ending or starting again as they left the club, but honestly she didn't care. She hadn't become a stripper to look down on other people. But the money was good, the dancing kept her in shape, and she was never too proud or bashful.

"Did good out there tonight, Angel. Worked the crowd real nice," said Elijah Martin, the owner, fill-in disc jockey, and professional dirty old man. She didn't hear him walk in, and if she weren't so tired, he may have startled her. Elijah just had a way of silently showing up.

"Oh," she said. "Yeah, it was a good night." She wasn't used to the name. Angel. During her interview for the job at Whispers, which had consisted of her undressing and twirling on the pole for about a minute, one of the regular DJs said she danced like an angel. He went by the name of Buster Hyman and probably thought that was still funny, even though he'd been there ten years now. When she revealed that she used to dance at a club called Alison's Angels, the name stuck.

She'd never made more than two hundred a night there. Plus they had to keep the G-strings and pasties on as well. Somehow that protected family values, but it didn't bring in the dollars. And there was no draw for the really big spenders or parties. The girls weren't exactly pin-up material. Somewhere along the way the club earned itself the moniker of "toothless and topless." But what the dancers lacked in looks, they made up for in hard work. A blow job in the back room was the great equalizer, and Dana was not going down that road. She may have been a lot of awful things, but she was no prostitute.

At least this place was an improvement over Alison's. It took her a while to get used to the totally nude part, but the more she thought about it, the more she figured if she was going to be exposed, she might as well go all the way. Creepy owners just seemed to go with the territory. Elijah must have thought that the industrial-strength breath mints and cologne he used sufficiently masked the cigarettes. And his teeth were artificially white. Dana also suspected that Elijah was the type of guy who at one point had tried a spray-on tan.

"Good work down there, too." He pointed down at her crotch. "Most guys like some hair, but they don't want it to look like you got a hedgehog guarding the pink gates. Know what I'm saying? And the completely shaved? I don't know about that. Makes me think pedophiles are getting off on that shit. Or when the razor burn starts, well, it ain't pretty and won't help you on tips. But your cunt looks really good."

"Uh, yeah. Thanks."

"But pussy's pussy. Am I right?"

"Yes, I suppose you are," she said, surprised that her fake smile may have looked genuine.

She had realized long ago that, in this profession, it was not smart to examine where her feelings lead her. And perhaps she was just fatigued and suddenly sensitive, but even though she had shown every square inch of her body, there was no need to talk about it now. Especially so crudely.

Earlier in the night, one of the other strippers had complimented her on how loud some patrons got when she took off her top. At the time, that was not a bad thing. It meant more money and, in this context, was good for the self-esteem. Perhaps that made more sense while "Girls, Girls, Girls" by Mötley Crüe was playing.

Elijah laughed like he had just reinvented wit. Dana was surprised he didn't slap her ass on his way out. Maybe he was still too impressed with himself. She grabbed her purse, an off-brand from Target, made sure she had her makeup, gum, keys, and money, and then she left.

It was dark outside. The sun still was not due for a couple of hours. *It's always darkest before the dawn*, she thought.

There were still several cars in the parking lot, mostly left by those too drunk to drive. Elijah had probably paid for cabs. He was not about to let his best customers wrap themselves around telephone poles. Dana looked back over her shoulder. The bodyguard was still watching. It dawned on her that he probably had less interest in her and more in finding a reason to beat somebody to a bloody pulp. At least he was on her side. Somebody needed to be.

She opened her car door and nodded in his direction. He, however, did not return a wave until she was driving past. There was never any of that type of security at Alison's Angels, and those in those positions, makeshift as they were, filled her with more fear than comfort.

The only rock station her radio could pick up was broadcasting its morning show's highlights from the previous week. After AC/DC's "Thunderstruck"—a song which Cinnamon, a fellow dancer, always chose for her stage time—a comedian who must have been plugging his show from earlier in the week was having his routine replayed. Something about his nagging wife. Dana didn't know. She was too exhausted to notice much of anything. She was also hungry. At about ten o'clock, more than seven hours ago now, she'd eaten a granola bar. If she wasn't going to be a stereotypical stripper prostitute, she wasn't going anorexic either.

McDonalds was open. She pulled into the drive-thru for an Egg McMuffin and a Diet Coke. She paid for them with a few singles from the stack of uncounted bills and started driving home. Her apartment was less than two miles away, so she put the bag on the seat next to her, the drink in the cup holder, and left for home. In no way could she attempt the multi-tasking of eating and driving, even though the roads were empty. It was too late for die-hard partiers, and too early for the most insane joggers.

She pulled into the parking lot of her small apartment complex and was lucky to find an empty spot. The building had exactly the same amount of parking places as it had units. With no reserved spaces, and apparently no accounting for roommates or freeloaders, it was a good day when she didn't have to park a block away. But what could she expect for such cheap rent?

The inside of the basement apartment was dark, pitch black, and she liked it like that. Dana hoped to fall asleep before the sun started to shine through the thick drapes. She unwrapped the Egg McMuffin and realized she had left the Diet Coke in the car. That was okay. Although she had long since claimed immunity to caffeine, right then she just wanted sleep. After three bites of her sandwich, she quickly lost the taste for it and tossed the rest in the garbage.

She scrubbed her teeth, and since she was already wearing something comfortable, rested her head on the pillow and slipped under the covers. While she didn't usually wear sweats to bed, she had been naked enough already.

The bright red glare of the alarm clock showed it was somehow six o'clock already. No matter how hard she tried, she could not account for the lost hour. Time to sleep. She closed her eyes and felt herself drift, but not very far.

Soon, the sun was up.

CHAPTER FOUR

Life on the road was far from the American romance Michael envisioned when he began to tour with Drew Greene. While Drew was definitely a consistent draw, and his name was getting bigger with each sold-out show, there were no private jets or fanfare. It was a tough gig and never one mistaken for the life of a rock star. Some comedy clubs provided limousine service from the hotels, and that was a nice touch, but city to city for a long weekend and then off again, they saw a lot of endless roads and featureless sky.

Drew liked to drive. That was just part of his personality, which was fine with Michael. That may have been what helped him relate to his audience so well. While Drew made his way, handling the directions and weaving past the tractor-trailers, Michael was free to daydream. He didn't write during those times. For one, it made him nauseated just to read in the car, but it would have been too nerve-wracking to write in front of Drew. Writing was his private time. It was his world, and when he wrote he felt bold and powerful. Even if he was just scribbling on scraps of paper, he knew he was creating something greater. Drew merely asking what he was working on would further rattle his unsteady nerves.

He didn't want to bother him by announcing that he had to take a leak or wanted a bite to eat. Quite literally, he was along for the ride. If Drew wanted to stop for any reason, including a roadside attraction featuring the world's largest prairie dog off Interstate 70 in Kansas, he just pulled off and announced he was stopping as he put the car in park. Maybe he was just being funny. Michael never asked. After they'd been on the road for about a month, performing in Shreveport, Topeka, and Little Rock, Drew had started to talk a little. Never about comedy, though. His brain was not open for the picking. Comedy was his job, and he was serious about it. He paid for gas and meticulously placed the receipts in his glove compartment for safekeeping come tax time. It was probably a wet dream of the IRS to audit a comedian. Drew never critiqued Michael's portion of the show. Maybe it was because he never paid any attention to it, and that was another question not to ask.

Michael also realized that he spent very little time thinking about home, though all home meant was a small apartment that was largely unfurnished and completely undecorated. His fifteen-year- old but surprisingly reliable car was parked in the lot behind the building, and Michael could not even remember if he locked the doors to it. There was nothing in it to steal anyway. He never even kept spare change in the ashtray, so if anyone were ever tempted to break in, Michael would feel more pity than rage.

And there was no wife there. Not anymore.

The landlord, Alan, a loner who never talked much, broke his normal silence when he heard that Michael would be out on the road doing comedy. In fact, he was more excited about it than Michael was. He said that he wouldn't charge the majority of the rent while he was gone. Alan never brought up the fact that he had been unable to rent out the other vacant units, but this became one less concern out on the road.

He still had to wonder how he'd gotten here. On a drunken bet with a complete stranger, he'd signed up for an open mic night at a comedy club. It went well enough, so he decided to try it again. The laughter became contagious, and he wanted more of it. A dive bar, Captain Riley's, just north of his Cincinnati home, let him become a regular on its comedy night. He struggled at those shows initially because he had to fight harder for the crowd's attention in a bar. But once he got comfortable, the audience was his.

Somehow, someone who worked with Drew Greene stopped by, exchanged contact information with Michael, and after just a few surreal phone calls, he was signed on to tour with a real comedian. It always seemed too good to be true, so he tried not to think about it. The money got deposited into his account, and while it was not much, he had no responsibilities or debt.

The hotels were usually fairly nice. Perhaps not by Drew's standards, but Michael would not have complained about a Motel 6 or anything with sheets that looked close enough to clean. He was not going to examine them with a black light, so he could remain blissful in his ignorance. Drew's hotel room was always on a higher floor or in the more expensive wing. If there was a hot tub option, he usually had it, even if he had no plan to use it.

A couple of places had what was affectionately referred to as a *comedy condo*, which was an efficiency apartment above the club. The closest Michael had ever come to complaining was after the third night on a trundle bed.

With each exit they passed, Michael imagined life there. He dreamed of being a stranger in those towns, finding a place to live, and planting roots. He'd be a man with no story, no baggage. Just an empty page in the middle of nowhere. That could even be the retirement dream. Property values could not be all that outrageous, and even the high rent district in Bald Knob, Arkansas, might still fall within his budget. One day, that was. For now, he was just suckling milk from Drew.

Until then, there were many more miles to go. A lot more silence, time for his mind to wander, and a road that he did not have to navigate. He stared out the window until he fell asleep.

CHAPTER FIVE

The day after detention was pretty uneventful, at least during school hours. Michael almost paid attention in most of his classes, passed a history quiz with a C plus when he thought he should have failed, and one of the hot girls actually laughed at one of his jokes. That was reason enough to put a gold star on the day.

But after school, and before he could even think about watching more TV with the family, he and his buddy KJ Uggla—Ugh to just about everyone—were running faster than they thought possible. Twice he nearly fell, and once he looked back to see if Ugh had fallen more than a half-step behind. He hadn't and knew he couldn't. While they didn't hear any sirens over their gasps for breath, they knew they couldn't slow down until they got to the other side of Crawford Field.

And perhaps if they heard any sirens they would be for something else entirely. But there was no need for reasoning now, just running. Boys ran all the time; it didn't have to be suspicious. Sirens disrupted neighborhoods with their din constantly. There was nothing unusual about it. Only a few people looked their way, and old people were always staring, so there was no need for paranoia.

Michael slowed to a trot as Ugh passed him and walked into the clearing on the other side of Crawford. Just last week they had tried to look cool back here, smoking Marlboros and learning to drink beer without making horrid faces. They were both out of breath and started to laugh, but their sides hurt and legs felt incapable of holding them up any longer.

Ugh sat on a log they had dragged from the other side of the field about two years back because it looked like a wood couch. It had been a big deal at the time. This was a place where they could go and shut out the outside world. That day it felt like it was going to find them. There was no longer sanctuary.

"What are we going to tell them?" Ugh asked.

More out breath than he realized, Michael paused. "Nothing. We're not going to tell them anything."

"But we really didn't do anything wrong."

"Exactly. So there's nothing to say."

"My uncle's a cop," Ugh said. "And he said the stuff you see on cop shows is all wrong. Dusting for fingerprints or technology is not how anyone gets caught. It's the dipshit that can't keep his mouth shut who ends up fucked."

"And we didn't do anything wrong. Not really."

"But I think we should go home," Ugh said.

Michael nodded again. "Yeah, but different directions. And no running. Not now. Just walk. I'll go around Pinehollow to McHenry. You go down the hill, past Forsythe and Pawnee. Understand?"

"And if someone says something?"

"Who would say anything? Nobody is going to say a word. Starting with you."

Ugh raised an eyebrow.

"And me, of course," Michael said.

"Call you later?"

"Not a good idea. See you tomorrow on the way to school."

They both nodded. The walk home was slow. Michael assumed Ugh would walk a little quicker, but it was never in his nature to rush. What was better was that his mind was pretty calm. Perhaps fun with spray paint and hurling eggs was a good rush, but in the end, was it worth it? Probably not, so why did he keep doing it? Guidance counselors and teachers thought he acted up because he was trying to fill some type of void. He always knew what they were asking about when talking about something else, but he knew very early on that being smarter than the counselors at his school was no major accomplishment. He was never great at sports, but when it came to manipulating a situation, he sure knew how to play that game.

He knew never to tell someone that Mom or Dad was the problem. Such a bold proclamation always brought the wrong type of suspicion. The better idea was to lead someone to that conclusion without driving them there personally. It's all about what is not said. If someone thinks they've made some grand discovery about the root of a deeper problem, suddenly they are sympathetic and holding his hand. The only difference between being a victim and a complete asshole is the spin you put on it. And it's even better if someone does that for you.

But those were all just thoughts that wouldn't matter. The only thing he ever really knew about his grandfather was that he was a poker player. The old man was never one to give advice, at least any that should be followed, but he did say that he must always have his hands covered. And if the shit was going to hit the fan, then he'd better prepare to do something other than just get covered in it.

Plus, his father had been out of town, monitoring the process of fixing copier parts. Perhaps that was important. Leaving town all the time sounded fun, but Michael figured places like Toledo and Fort Wayne weren't the destinations that brought bragging rights. Maybe he'd be home tonight. But sometimes when he did come home he wasn't quite himself any longer. He often said that the strain of travel and job pressures caught up with him, but that was just a case of adults saying something that meant something else entirely. And he was starting to figure that out.

Then there were those days when his father was in town—at least that's what everybody assumed—but his work kept him from being any type of a presence. When Michael caught the chicken pox a year ago, he was up itching all night. He got up, not knowing what time it was, only aware that he was so tired the world was surreal. On the way back from the bathroom he saw his mother sitting on the couch, staring out the window.

"Tim, is that you? How long have you been home?" she asked.

Michael looked around like he was waking from a dream.

"Tim? Tim, what are you doing?"

"No, it's just me Mom."

"Mikey, what are you doing up?"

"Bathroom. I'm still off school tomorrow, right?" Michael answered.

"Is tomorrow Saturday?" she asked.

"No, Thursday."

"Oh," she said. "I guess. Chicken pox is usually a full week off school."

Michael nodded yes, though he doubted his mother would be able to see, even if she were looking in his direction. He thought he heard her begin to speak something else, but her voice trailed off so drastically, he wasn't sure she had said anything at all.

"Can I sit with you?" he asked.

"Shouldn't you be in bed? Shouldn't—" Her voice faded again. "Okay, come here."

He walked to the couch and plopped down, landing hard on her ankle, but she made no gesture of pain or anything else. She just moved the blanket so he would have enough room. Before he could remember anything else, he was awake and his father was cooking eggs. His mother had left him on the couch and at some point and had gone to bed. In fact, she did not wake until mid-afternoon, and by that time his father was gone again. Michael could not remember where he went, probably something work related, but that night Michael slept on the couch with his mother again.

He didn't know why he remembered that moment again. It had been so long ago, but he had been alone with his thoughts for longer than he wanted now. Maybe if he needed an excuse or diversion, it could be a story that just somehow slipped out.

***

When he walked into the house, his father was cooking. Spaghetti with more meat than sauce, something simple, yet he was proud of it and called it a specialty.

"Here comes trouble," his father said.

Michael just stared blankly.

"No detention today?"

"Uh, no."

"That's good, because the posted school zone speed limit ends at three. If you've got some kind of JUGS situation, then the drivers are allowed to drive twice as fast at that time. If you ask me, that's not fair to the bad kids."

"You tell 'em, Dad."

"Well, get your homework done now. At least pretend to. ALF is on for a whole hour tonight. Say what you will, but I think that's the best show ever about a puppet alien from Melmac."

"Agreed."

"Now go get started. I'd help you, but since I really can't do third grade math, I'm not even going to look at that algebra book."

"Okay." He ran up the steps, opened his book, copied the odd answers out of the back, tried to mimic the pattern from the even ones, and was confident that he may have had a solid "C" homework. If he went back downstairs so soon, it would look suspicious, so he decided that he should just do nothing for half an hour. After about two minutes, he realized that would be impossible. He flipped through the *Playboy* hidden under his bed, then had to throw it back under when Jessie walked past.

"Busted," she said, making no effort to conceal her grin.

"Shut up," he replied and went back downstairs to help with dinner.

"You should probably wash your hands before you go down there."

CHAPTER SIX

It was not that Dana didn't want to work on a Tuesday afternoon. She just found it sad that Whispers was open. Stripping was not supposed to be a day job. The club was about a quarter full. They had a lunch special. She found it hard to look sexy while there was some guy lusting over her with pulled pork falling off his chin. A few regulars were there to see their favorite dancers. Dana didn't have any of those yet, at least none that she knew of, and was happy about that. Those were the guys who tended to be the stalkers. A little extra attention from a stripper was just a way to get more money out of each titty jiggle, but not every guy knew that. And the sexual predator psychopaths were probably more likely to show up during the daytime than the peak hours. She had no statistics on this, but from what she'd seen, she was convinced of it.

It was easier to dance when the room had some patrons there. But during the daytime it was a quieter place. Guys sitting by themselves at small tables usually didn't give much more than customary applause at the end of each dance. The hooting and hollering were what usually told her that she had done a good job. Well, that and a wad of cash.

Pandora was onstage, dancing to "Magdelena" by A Perfect Circle. Dana thought she missed the point of the song by dancing to it, but what did she really care? It all came down to getting paid, and Pandora probably brought in more money than anyone there. Some of her *fans* tipped tens and twenties, where others offered singles. Dana thought Pandora was the perfect name for a stripper. She wondered if anybody else there appreciated the joke.

Probably not. When guys had pussy on their minds, not much else mattered.

The applause for Pandora was louder than the rest, probably from her appreciative stalkers, but Dana envied it. She also felt sick for feeling the jealousy.

"Let's give it up for Pandora," Buster Hyman said. "And now as a special treat, for the next hour, private dances are only ten dollars. Plus tip, of course. So if you see your favorite dancer, it will take less cash for her to give you a show you'll never forget. Up close and personal."

The other five dancers quickly took away five patrons, shaving the medium-sized crowd down to a sparse gathering. Dana hated these small rooms. Not only were there fewer dollars being sent her way, but she didn't like a crowd that could be called intimate. That and she was not getting much response. She could do some of the pole tricks, but what was the point if it would go unappreciated? Just show them what they paid to see, and her job would be done.

A few dollars came her way, but she was certain they were singles. The only guy who seemed to be enjoying himself was more into her song choice than her increasingly naked body.

Rob Zombie's "Dragula" was apparently rocking this guy's world. Of all the ways guys tried to impress a stripper, knowing all the words to a song ranked slightly below pathetic. If her body didn't give him an erection, then maybe her second song, "Living Dead Girl," would. Perhaps he'd tip on that alone.

When her second song had finished, she picked up the few remaining singles, her bra and G-string, and put on her robe so she could walk into the back room to get dressed, only to take it all off again. The job wasn't complicated; this was just the routine.

A guy who had just walked in motioned for her. She walked over to his table, put her hands palms down on the table, and leaned closer. "Something I can do for you, sugar?"

It still sounded artificial and painfully forced, like she was living up to a horrible stereotype. The patron didn't seem to mind, and she would have been shocked if he did. She could have said just about anything, and it would not have changed what she was selling.

"Yeah, uh, well," he began.

"What is it, sweetheart?"

"I was just wondering if that private dance thing—" he paused again. "I was wondering if a private dance was still ten dollars."

Dana pinched his cheek. "Anything for you."

He nodded.

"I'll be right back. You'll wait for me, won't you?"

"Uh, yeah. Yes. I will."

"Well, you better." She smiled and walked into the back. The shy, insecure guys normally tipped the best. They couldn't talk a big game, so they had to make up for it some way, and Dana was completely okay with that.

When she came back, she saw him trying to discretely look over his shoulder. If there was one thing this guy could not do, it was play coy. He pulled a ten dollar bill out of his wallet and held it in his trembling fingers.

"Just hold onto that for now, sugar," she told him and led him to the private dance area that management called the VIP section.

She positioned him on the bench and adjusted the back of her bra strap. Morgana's first song was coming to a close. Her next track was usually Christina Agualera's "Fighter," and Dana could live with that. She would do this meek fellow's private dance to that.

As that song started, the guy began to squirm.

"What's your name, hon?"

"Troy."

"Well, sit on your hands, Troy. I can touch you, but you can't touch me. Understand?"

"Yes, ma'am, I do."

She turned around and started shaking her ass in his direction. She peered over her shoulder as she did so. When he saw her glance, even the dim lights of the VIP section could not conceal his blushing face.

"You're cute when you're embarrassed," she said and pinched his cheek.

He squirmed as he sat on his hands. *This guy is going to tip big time*, she thought as she unfastened her bra and let it fall to the ground. She leaned in, putting her hand on his knees and shook her breasts close to his nose. The almost impossible hue in his face deepened. She pinched his other cheek.

Just as the song's refrain repeated, she wiggled out of her G-string. His previous fidgeting was tame by comparison. Easy money. She was looking up at the lights dancing off the charcoal-colored drop ceiling, as was part of her routine, when she felt his hand move from behind him and grab her crotch. He was quicker than she was, because before she could react he was already pushing for her clitoris. The pain was immediate and nauseating.

Dana wanted to vomit as, for the first time, this guy, this fucking pervert, was looking *her* in the eyes. Somehow it felt like an equal violation. With more strength than she thought she possessed, she pushed his head into the back wall. While it certainly must have hurt him, it was nowhere near enough. The security that had watched every inch of the place before was distracted by the attention Pandora got for stripping at bargain basement prices.

"Get the fuck out of here," she said calmly.

"I'm sorry," he answered, grabbing his wallet. "Was it ten dollars?"

"I said get the fuck out of here."

Troy blushed again. The ten dollar bill shook in his hand, then he dropped it on the ground by her high-heeled boots, the only clothing she wore.

"Just leave." Dana turned and saw that security was now looking in her direction again. Bruce, the guy with the giant biceps and perfectly shaven head, was now watching with more than just a curious glance. Why hadn't he been there before? Maybe things would have happened differently. Maybe they would not have happened at all. There was no way anyone could have been quick enough to keep this pervert from touching her, but it may have kept her from having to look at him now. In fact, right now she could be watching the motherfucker scramble to pick his teeth off the floor. Yeah, that would be better. That would be much better.

"I'm sorry," he whimpered. "Don't know what happened."

"Go. Please."

He put his wallet back in his pocket and walked out. As he was about to go out the door, he stopped and turned around. There was obviously something he wanted to say but couldn't. And even if he could, Dana doubted she would be able to hear it. He walked out.

She cursed herself for being so weak. For saying *please*. Why the hell would she say that? She had every right to rip his eyes out. Instead, she just went with playing nice.

"You okay, Angel?" Bruce asked, startling her. "Want me to take care of someone for you?"

"No. No need."

"Okay."

She nodded, grabbed her few strands of clothes she called a uniform, and walked into the strippers' dressing room. That was always her favorite oxymoron, but no one else there thought it was funny. Now she understood why. Nothing seemed funny. The other girls who were back there, fixing their makeup, counting money, and getting ready for a smoke break all wore that empty stone expression, and Dana knew she looked the same.

But there was no time to think about anything like that. She knew it would not lead to anything good. And maybe being angry was a good thing right now. Hell, she knew she should, and it felt like self-preservation. And worse, it was almost time to go back to work.

CHAPTER SEVEN

The laughter was nice, and he decided the crowds in Toledo were better than anywhere else. A throwaway joke about being the capital of karaoke bars landed huge appreciation. The audience seemed to like him, and he began to feel at home on stage. For the most part, he did not deviate from his routine, but he was feeling brave enough to try.

Most of his sets had gone smoothly, but it always still seemed like Drew Greene was left with some work before he had the crowd where he wanted them. Tonight they would be primed. And if the delusions continued in Michael's head, maybe Drew would be a bit of a letdown after this warm up.

The audience laughed harder than he'd expected at his last joke. This was a crude crowd, and he could work with that. A story about a fart in church was good enough, but adding the details of a wooden pew and superior acoustics took this audience over the edge, and thank God for that.

"So," he said after taking a second to drink from his now lukewarm beer. "This is the part of the show where I try to give something back."

It was also the part of his set that felt the least polished and left him uneasy. Yeah, the jokes were in there, but he had yet to chisel them out sufficiently.

"This is the time where I tell you how to fuck a stripper." He got some chuckles out of this, but not many. "Now, I know what most of you are probably thinking. *Isn't that like shooting fish in a barrel?* You may think that. Hell, I thought that, but it didn't really work out for me. Come on, guys. Let's be honest. Most of us here are years past the ol' sexual peak, and the body mass index ain't dropping any time soon. So what you need to do here is outsmart the stripper. And really, I would like to think that most of you are at least capable of that. Because exotic dancers, as you may know, are good for some things, but a partner in Trivial Pursuit ain't one of them.

"This is what you need to do. Pay for a private dance. Most places, it's twenty to thirty bucks. That's really just a minimal cost when it comes down to it. Now, if you're not familiar with a private dance, it means you're with a date and wisely acting stupid. If so, well played.

"What happens in these encounters is the girl strips for you, and you're the only one in her audience. It's usually in an exotic place, like a cubicle. When the song starts, she undresses. Herein lies the difficult part. Stop her. This may violate the code of every Y chromosome ever, but hear me out. This will pay off. Trust me.

"Tell her you just like the way she moves. Tell her she's a good dancer. See, what you have to understand here is that the only thing that keeps her from taking a bath with a toaster is the delusion that she's not really a stripper. She is a dancer."

A guy in the audience, probably one without a date, blurted out, "Hell yeah!" A few people snickered.

Michael turned in his direction. "See, brother? I am here for you."

His timing was thrown off, and this would have terrified him before, but tonight he was completely comfortable in the spotlight. And comfort was not something he had been able to find much of before. Things were looking up.

"But nobody ever saw that in her. That is, until you waltz in there with just enough money for the cover charge and an additional twenty bucks. You see her as something more than just a stripper. You see her artistry."

He was grateful to get a laugh from the audience because it helped with his pacing.

"Next thing you know, she's doing a private pole dance for you. And the best part? You don't even know one another's real names. I'll even add a money-back guarantee."

With only about two minutes left in his allotted time, Michael was already despondent that the white-hot blistering light would be turned over to Drew. Soon, center stage would be his much longer. Could this dream really be coming true?

A smile crossed his face as he got ready to close his set.

CHAPTER EIGHT

There was just something about eating dinner while watching television at the Clover household that seemed to make everything okay. Timothy, without fail, turned on a situation comedy during these times. Even on the most delusional of days, they knew they were far from ideal, but maybe watching perfect families filmed on artificial and controlled sets with canned laughter to boot might somehow rub off through the screen.

The reruns were okay as well. Something familiar, formulaic, and an excuse to turn off all cognitive function. The real world was out there. Just a short trip out the front door or a flip of the channel proved that, but there was no need to do anything like that today.

The matriarch of the Clover clan agreed for a change. It probably defied what her therapist had instructed before, but at that point she could not remember what advice had been doled out. It just felt therapeutic to talk to someone who would listen, even if she had to pay an ungodly amount to do so. And wasn't laughter supposed to be the best medicine? The rest of the family was cackling hysterically, and she at least enjoyed the sound of that. Even if the product they were watching was an insult to just about anyone's intelligence.

"Your art project done, sweetheart?" Timothy asked Jessie during a commercial.

"Finished it in homeroom last week. It's not due until Friday. Already got it graded."

"And how'd you do?" her mother asked, not surprised her husband had not immediately followed up with such an obvious question.

"Well of course I got an A. It is my work after all."

"Good job, darling," Timothy said, still looking at the television screen. He finally turned to look at his daughter. "I'm proud of you, Jess."

Her smile was wide, immediate, and more genuine than anything she'd felt in quite some time.

"Shut up, cherished family members," Michael chimed in. "The regularly scheduled programming is set to resume."

"Yeah, as for you boy," Timothy began, "guess we won't see you until later tomorrow evening. You still trying out for football?"

"Yeah, I guess."

"Coach Lautner is an old friend of mine. He said even though you've never played before, you could probably get on with special teams. You won't be the smallest kid out there, and the workouts will buff you a bit."

"Okay," Michael replied.

"The girls will like that."

"Don't need any help there."

"Yeah, you don't need muscles with inflatables," Jessie said, impressed with herself. It didn't help that her mother immediately laughed.

"Suzie," Timothy said. "That probably wasn't real good for the boy's self-esteem."

"Speaking of muscles," Jessie added, barely able to keep air in her lungs from her growing giggles, "if I'm not mistaken, Michael's right arm looks a lot stronger than his left."

Mom laughed again, another blow to the ego. This time Dad joined in.

"Sorry, Mikey," she said.

"What can I say?" he answered. "Guess we're just one big zany family."

CHAPTER NINE

An off day was worse than having to go to work. Rent a movie? Order a pizza? Drink herself into a stupor? The third option sounded best, and if she were to do that, she might as well get some of the good stuff. A bottle or two of a hard-to-pronounce wine sounded like a flawless plan, but she hated the stinging hangover that always followed the wine drinking nights. Beer always left her feeling bloated, and that tended to last for at least a few days, which was worse than the headache.

There was always the option of going to the bar. A simple flirtation would land her a few margaritas or whatever else she fancied. She found herself leaning toward going out, but if she had been vulnerable while sober in a facility with security, what chance did she have while out alone and as drunk as she wanted to be?

Maybe she could get online and waste the rest of the day signing up for one of those social networking sites. She was never one for Facebook or anything like that, and hell, she spent most of her time under an assumed name anyway. And how loose was the definition of "friend" when it came to those sites? With most people, how many of their online pals would actually pick up the phone or show up at the door to reach out to a friend in need? No, the most these sanctimonious fucks would do is respond to some bullshit status update with more bullshit.

She sat on the couch and thought, *Why so angry?* Then, knowing the exact reason, the exact moment, she found herself uncontrollably furious.

That motherfucker. Who does he think I am? *What* does he think I am? How fucking desperate. How fucking lonely. How pathetic must *that* be?

Her crotch felt like the damn pervert had left a squirming insect burrowed inside her, and there was no way to get it out and feel clean again. She shuddered. It became all too apparent how often she'd been feeling this way the past twenty-four hours.

Had she felt it before? If not, why?

The only clear thing was that she had to get out of her apartment. Being alone with her thoughts was a truly bad idea. And she was not entirely without friends. There was no need to go online when there were a few people she would be able to call. If need be, that was.

But the need was there. She knew it sounded stupid, but it was like she needed someone to save her from herself. Any previous notion of independence was fading away. How she hated the thought that she needed someone. She was strong. Damn it, she knew that was true, but the phone just felt so heavy.

It wasn't like she was about to tell someone what had happened. A strange man copping a feel on her should not just be a job hazard, but fully expected. She cursed herself for not being prepared, for choosing to be a victim.

Almost in spite of herself, she picked up the phone. Her friend Randi was the first number on her speed dial's short list. It surprised Dana that the phone was ringing already. She was surprised all the more when Randi answered.

"Well, I guess I can call off the missing person's search," Randi said.

"Randi?"

"You called me. Were you expecting someone else?"

"No. Guess not."

"So you're still ditzy as hell," Randi said. "When are you free to go out some night?"

"Tonight?"

"Do you really think I'm so pitiful that I don't need at least a week's notice?"

"Well, I wasn't—"

"You were right. And not only am I free, I have good news. Sort of. I kicked my boyfriend to the curb."

"Was it James?"

"No," Randi said. "You are really, really out of touch. I got rid of that useless son of a bitch a long time ago and replaced him with another."

"I'm so sorry."

"Why? For calling out of the blue to remind me of my heartache? Not a problem. But Kirk, my newest ex, had plans for us tonight. I've got a reservation for two at the comedy club. But I'm only one. Want to go with me? Tickets are already paid for. Courtesy of an otherwise useless man."

"Okay. Sounds fun." And for Dana, it really did. It had been so long since she'd looked forward to something, the

47

experience was almost foreign. She could drink, laugh, and escape, all within perfectly normal situations.

"Do you know where the club is?" Randi asked. "If you Google it or use a GPS, that might be better. I'm bad with directions, and I won't be blamed if something happens to you along the way."

"I know where it is. I'll assume the risk."

"It will be good to see you, though. What have you been up to?"

Dana was quiet for a few seconds, and Randi was either insightful or impatient because she said, "Probably nothing too good. Otherwise you wouldn't have called."

"You're reading me like a book."

"Dane, I'm reading you like an index card. Meet me outside the club at seven."

She had not spoken with Randi in a long time. She couldn't even remember the last time. Probably six months, maybe a year. Dana was just relieved Randi didn't feel any resentment. That would be hard to swallow right now.

When Dana hung up the phone, she looked at the clock. It was only a quarter past one. Still a long while before it was time to go out, but that was okay. At least she had some place to go that did not involve her undressing for singles. Better yet, she was not on the market and had no intent on meeting anyone. She was not even curious enough to look. Tonight, for a change, she could be herself.

CHAPTER TEN

Some dreams recur so frequently and become so familiar, they break the barrier into daylight. Michael knew this one so well that he was aware he was dreaming. He even knew where he was. And if he had opened his eyes and rolled over, he would have realized his wake-up call would be coming within half an hour. Even better, since he was staying at a semi-nice hotel, when the phone was to ring, it would not just be a buzzing din on the other end.

But here inside his own head, even though it felt like it was coming from someplace else, he was back on the frozen lake. Despite the warm air, the ice was solid, showing no sign of cracking, nor was it slick enough to make it slippery. In fact, there was a strange stability beneath his feet and an unexplained euphoria that gave him the unforgettable sensation of walking on air.

As he always did, ever since this dream had started repeating years ago, he turned around to see how far from the shore he had ventured. Each time, the shore faded farther away. This time he could barely see it on the horizon. Not even a beacon or flicker of life back there. But there had to be something. There had to be some way to get back home. And waking up had always been that method, although something inside Michael told him that was cheating.

Ahead of him was a blaze, right there on the unaffected ice. Like a controlled campfire hissing and crackling, its heat penetrated every inch of him. Michael supposed that was why he always woke up sweating after visiting this dream, but once awake, he usually gave it little thought. To his right was a hole in the ice, the water slowly lapping out as frigid as the fire was hot.

And behind him, as always, came the footsteps. They were light and slow but unwavering and directed right at him. There could be no delusion that this other person was simply passing through. No, whoever this was clearly had come for him.

As he turned around to finally see what was coming his way, he woke again in the hotel room, so alert he wondered if he'd really been asleep. The now unnecessary wake-up call would be coming within a matter of minutes. Soon he'd have to be showered, dressed, and ready for the night's show.

There were a few folded-up pieces of paper on the nightstand. One day he just might own that headline billing, so he needed to write a few more jokes. The other week, while in a remarkably similar hotel room, he was bored enough to watch a segment on television about some guy named Dr. Oz, who got famous because he was one of Oprah Winfrey's temporary gurus.

But this Dr. Oz had apparently said that for every thirty-five pounds a man loses, he adds an inch to his penis. Now if there was not a joke there, Michael thought he might as well quit and flip burgers for a living.

50

He began to write. *So did you all hear that for every 35 pounds a guy loses, he adds an inch to his dick? You, sir, you would be able to poke me in the eye from where you're sitting if you'd just start hitting the gym.*

There were other ways to go with that. A joke about a rise in male anorexia or, "You'll have some dumb son of a bitch who thinks cutting off his legs at the knees would be a surefire way of dropping some weight, and therefore give him that extra inch or two."

Ah, yes, the dick jokes. Can't get enough of those.

The phone rang. Already awake and knowing it would just be an automated message, he picked up the phone and dropped it back on the cradle. A couple of seconds later, it rang again.

"Hello," Michael said.

"You know, I don't like to play the star card very often, but it isn't wise to hang up on me," Drew Greene said.

"I, uh, thought it was the wake-up call."

"Well, wake up and get to the club early. We have something to talk about. This is important. Understand?"

"Okay," Michael said. "Getting in the shower now."

There was a delay in Drew's answer. A wave of dizziness hit Michael. Oh, dear God, please don't let him kick me off the tour. I haven't upstaged him. Hell, I couldn't have upstaged him. Maybe that was the problem.

"Okay," Drew said faintly. Michael now realized he was talking to someone else. "Yeah, so I need you to come down earlier."

Michael could not be sure if Drew was talking to him or if his attention had been pulled away again. If he said something, he might interrupt a more important conversation. If he said nothing, he'd appear nervous and stupid. Hopefully that truth wasn't too apparent.

"Okay, so you coming?" Drew asked, no patience found in his voice.

"Um, yeah. Yes. On my way."

If Drew said anything before hanging up, Michael didn't hear it. That was okay. Nerves were part of the job, but since the tour started, this was the first time they felt this heavy. Not heavy, but paralyzing. And the idea of getting up, showering, and walking three blocks to the comedy club felt like too much.

Michael swung his legs around and put his feet on the ground. Standing was an awkward accomplishment, but he could do at least that. It was like being drunk, only without that annoying buzz.

***

More than halfway through the set, Michael was at the point of shifting gears. He normally referred to this as a jump cut. One of the things that had always irritated him was the constant need some comics found for a clever segue. When it synched it worked, but when it was forced it wasn't funny. People didn't pay for that trite shit. If no place else, he should be professional there.

"Now, I feel like I need to apologize for this next bit," he told the audience after he took a sip of his Corona. Not his favorite drink, but a hell of a lot better than most beers. "I know you all like the dick jokes—"

One woman screamed louder than the rest and brought hearty laughter to the room.

Michael looked over in her direction. "I think I love you."

He stepped back and paused, knowing his transition was going more smoothly than he'd expected. In fact, he was surprised he could be anything close to relaxed. When he'd gotten to the club, Drew could not be found. Michael saw him just before he went onstage, but Drew said that they'd talk before the night was over. And, of course, decent luck. *Break a leg* was too cliché, and good luck was not the type of thing Drew Greene would ever say.

There was no time to think about anything like that right now. If he were to be fired, at least he'd had a good run. But it did make going into the next part of his set far more difficult. He didn't have stage fright, but eventually having to step away from the spotlight terrified him.

"I'm not surprised that it was a woman screaming out," he said. "Guys, I'm going to let you in on a secret here. The woman folk, well, they're a little more vocal than we are.

"Seriously. This is scientific fact. Apparently someone got a government research grant to tell us that women talk a lot."

Michael waited a second to see if the audience would stay with him on a joke that took a while to unfold. He suspected they would. If not, he had a backup plan.

"Know how many words the average guy says in a day? Anyone?" A few people blurted out things he couldn't hear. "We manage to say about two thousand.

"Now, on to the women," he said, hearing a few chuckles, certainly nothing more, but that was okay. So far things were going well. "They beat us by a bit. Yep. Seven thousand. Women say, on average, seven thousand words a day. Yeah. They're packing some serious heat, dude. How is this possible? Don't ask me, I don't listen to most of it. My intake can only about double the output, so after a woman's four-thousandth word, I'm tapped out."

That got him one belly laugh, and while certainly alcohol-induced, it was good for the show.

"So guys, if you ever get into an argument with a woman and she gets in the last word, just remember she had a very clear statistical advantage."

A few more laughs gave him the courage to continue with the set. This part always felt shaky, but since he felt far from confident with himself at that moment, he figured he might as well just go for it. Having to jettison material would likely just take him down a few more notches.

"And there is a word in the female vocabulary that may tip the scales a little more.

"Have you ever been shopping with a woman? When they're looking at clothes, they're not exactly a thesaurus. I went to a department store recently because, believe it or not, I do have to dress myself, and I saw this guy and, well, my heart really went out to him. He was out with his wife shopping for baby clothes. Eliminate the word *cute* from a woman's vocabulary, and see how the scales tip.

"Here's this chick pulling clothes off the rack." Michael mocked the motions. "And all she can seem to say is, 'Cute. Cute. Too cute. Oh, this is cute. Cute. How cute is this? So cute. Cute. Unbelievably cute. Classically cute. Historically cute. So, so, so cute. And this one might be even cuter.'"

Michael took a sip of the beer, which got an unintentional laugh. It took him a few seconds to realize that they were laughing because he was playing the role of the guy who desperately needed a drink. He'd have to keep that in the set.

"Then the woman holds an outfit for her unfortunate shopping companion. 'What do you think of this one?'"

Michael stood in the middle of the stage pretending to hold an outfit with a wide-eyed, what-do-you-think look.

"Uh," he said, playing the part of the clueless man, "it's…cute?"

Now Michael forced a wide, glassy-eyed smile and made his voice go up a few octaves. "'I know! It's so cute, and this is cute, and this is cute, and this is super cute. And this is from The Planet Cute.'"

He stopped for just a beat. "So then this chick stops playing fair and holds up three outfits. 'What do you think of these?'"

Doing his best deer-in-the-headlights gaze, Michael felt the audience with him and was okay with the brief silence before playing the guy's response. "Cute, cuter, and cutest."

"'Oh. Do you really think so? Because I definitely think this one is cuter than that one. So yeah, you are right, this certainly is cuter, but this one is so cute it makes this other cute one look not cute at all.'"

Michael sighed. "This poor bastard had one word to work with, and he still fucked it up."

While the bit seemed to work for him, he couldn't get much mileage out of it. The observational humor thing wouldn't work for him, and he certainly was not a Seinfeld type. Plus, Jerry Seinfeld would not have used the word fuck, but it felt like what would work best for Michael at that time.

And since he was immature by nature, it seemed like the wise thing to do would be to play into those strengths. Not everything had to be for all audiences. The blue material was what people liked. Well, maybe that wasn't always true. But the dirtier stuff was what people who Michael liked usually liked. And that would be this next bit, so he could relax. At least until he had to talk with Drew.

"Okay. Now is the part of the show where you're going to learn something. I am going to give something back. I am going to teach you fellas out there how to fuck a stripper."

Most of the audience laughed; a few groaned and rolled their eyes. In the back corner, stage right, one woman cackled heartily, the other nervously.

#

So much for the carefree night out, Dana thought.

At least Randi was having a good time. And she would probably bust a gut when Dana finally got around to confessing what she did for a living. While trying to get the attention of the waitress, Dana barely heard what was said onstage.

"Isn't that like shooting fish in a barrel? You may think that. Hell, I thought that, but it didn't really work out for me."

Okay, so he's not calling all strippers whores. There had to be some comfort in that. Not much, but enough to go on for now.

"Come on, guys. Let's be honest. Most of us here are years past the ol' sexual peak, and the body mass index ain't dropping any time soon. So what you need to do here is outsmart the stripper. And I'd like to think that most of you are capable of at least that. Because exotic dancers, as you may know, are good for some things. But a partner in Trivial Pursuit is not one of them."

Now Dana seemed to be the only person not laughing. That was, except for Michael, who kept glancing at the clock.

"This is what you need to do. Pay for a private dance. Most places, it's about twenty to thirty bucks. That's really a minimal cost when it comes down to it."

She tuned him out a little more, faked laughter when it seemed appropriate, and hoped the damn waitress would finally ask about another drink. Randi looked over.

"You okay?" she whispered to Dana.

Dana nodded, but Randi kept looking over, obviously knowing better.

"Just tell her you like the way she moves. Tell her she's a good dancer. See, what you have to understand here is that the only thing that keeps her from taking a bath with a toaster is the delusion that she's not really a stripper. She's a dancer."

"Really. I'm okay," Dana said to Randi. "We'll talk later."

"But nobody ever saw that in her," Michael said. "That is, until you waltz in there with just enough money for the cover charge and an additional twenty or so. You see her as something more than just a stripper. You see her artistry."

Dana just shook her head. Things were looking ugly for her right now. Hell, the guy was just a warm-up comedian, not the one anyone came here to see, so why bother with what he had to say? He was probably just a loser who hung out in strip clubs, acting like he was above it all, just there to get material. No need to be bothered with guys like that. Or anyone else for that matter.

"Next thing you know," Michael said, "she's doing a private pole dance for you. And the best part? You don't even know one another's real names."

"In your wildest dreams," Dana whispered to herself, but more audibly than she intended.

"What was that, hon?" Randi asked.

"Nothing. I'll tell you that later, too."

Randi smiled and shook her head.

"Now, know what I find funny?" Michael asked. He paused while the audience remained silent. Before he could get any response, he answered his own question. "I know this may sound insensitive, but it's bulimia."

He waited for a few people to laugh. A little. "I'm sorry, but the very idea of a woman trying to increase her sex appeal through continuous vomiting is hysterical. Then her teeth start to rot out, and she gets this whole Third World sickly thing going."

Dana looked over to see Randi getting a little uncomfortable. What a wonderful night this had become. It was like this asshole was positioning the spotlight on people just trying to have a good, carefree time. At least Dana had always been one who could handle a little humiliation.

"And the funny part? Most guys would still tap that, just like they would have when she carried a few extra pounds. Ladies, your problem in life is that you're working way too hard to please an easy audience."

Most of the room laughed, and a few applauded. Dana could barely hear Randi say, "Well, at least that's true."

"And speaking of audiences. You've been beautiful. My name's Michael Clover, and Drew Greene will be up here in just a few minutes."

The audience clapped, either for Michael's performance, or for the mention of the star of the show. The host, an old man who reminded Dana of her boss, was now set to ramble on, enjoying his undeserved spotlight for a few more minutes.

"Michael Clover, everyone!" the host said as more applause came.

#

Michael waved as he weaved through the tables. His eyes had not adjusted to being out of the spotlight when he bumped into Drew.

"We'll talk after the show," Drew said. "Meet me at the bar next door. Wish me luck."

"I wish you luck."

"Ladies and gentlemen," the host said, "join me in welcoming to the stage your headliner for the night, Dreeeew Greene!"

The applause coming from the audience was twice as loud as anything Michael had gotten. He could attribute a lot of that to name recognition alone, but it also showed him just how far he was from landing the headline spot. Oh, well. Relatively speaking, he was early on in his journey. He could not fault himself for dreaming.

"And good luck to you, too," Drew said and made his effortless jog to the stage.

Michael's shoulders dropped. That was the last thing he wanted to hear. *Good luck?* What the hell did that mean? Good luck with all your future endeavors? Hope this comedy thing works out for you? In this context, the only thing good luck could mean is farewell.

While he knew Drew's set better than anyone by now, he looked up on the stage and heard nothing he said. All he knew was that the people who had been laughing for him just a few minutes ago had quickly turned their attention to a more deserving comedian. But hell, It had been a fun ride this far, so no need to mourn already. The party didn't have to end.

"Jack on the rocks," he said to the waitress. "I need it."

"Good show tonight, Mr. Clover."

He nodded.

"You okay?" she asked.

"I just need a drink. Badly."

"I've got something better."

Michael raised an eyebrow.

"Not like that. Come with me, though."

He shrugged and followed the waitress into the back. Somehow the laughter he heard from whatever joke Drew had just told sounded like it was coming from someplace else.

CHAPTER ELEVEN

Of all the telltale signs of trouble in the Clover household, having dinner at the table had to rank right near the top. Jessie screaming that she was on fire or Mom sleeping with the garbage man's unemployed little brother probably would have distressed Michael less. He had just told Ugh he'd copy his math homework in the morning for two bucks, which freed him up to watch TV with the family. Apparently that wasn't going to happen.

"Uh oh," he said. "Dinner on the table. What's the occasion? The Pope stopping over for a visit?"

Mom was wringing her hands. This was certainly not uncommon for her, but her knuckles popped audibly as she tugged on her fingers. "We're a family, and families eat at the table. Not just on TV."

"Are we going to wait for Dad?" Jessie asked.

"Might as well wait for breakfast then," Michael said.

"Michael, that is very disrespectful to your father. There are just things," his mother began with no idea on how to finish the thought. "Just things."

"Do you want me to set the table, Mom?" Jessie asked.

She nodded.

Jessie went into the kitchen.

"Mikey, you can do the dishes after dinner," his mother said. "You can get your homework started now."

"Already got that taken care of."

"Then you can help Jess set the table."

"Ah, that sucks, Mom."

"Don't you backtalk me, or—" she began, but before she could finish the threat, the side door opened.

"Huh-nee, I'm home," Timothy said, dragging out the last syllable like he was waiting for some imaginary studio audience to finish their clapping. And from the smell of him, the rest of the family could tell he was indeed in some fantasy land. The whiskey permeated the room, and his eyes were dilated. No closer inspection needed there.

"Hi, Daddy," Jessie said and ran into his waiting arms. "Did you have a good day at work?"

Suzie left the room, but her pacing took her right back in. "The office called for you earlier."

"And what did you say?"

"Nothing. Just took a message."

"Great," Timothy said. "Now what's for dinner?"

"Meatloaf."

"Then I'll run like a bat out of hell upstairs to get washed up," he said, laughed loudly at his own joke, and left the kitchen. He giggled all the way up the steps.

"I don't get it," Jessie said.

"That's okay. It wasn't funny," Michael told her.

"Come on, kids," their mother whispered. "If you haven't washed your hands, do that now. Then sit at the table." Her voice was artificially loud as she tried to hide the trembling beneath.

Michael and Jessie took silent turns washing their hands, then sat at the table.

"Should we wait for him?" Jessie asked as she sat down.

"That would be the polite thing to do."

It took their father another twenty minutes before he came back downstairs. Now they missed the corny jokes. Now they missed the unexplained laughter. He sat in his chair, took two bites of mashed potatoes, and dropped his fork on the plate, making a loud clang.

"Ever since I bought your mother that damn microwave, the woman forgot how to cook. The shit's cold."

"We were waiting for you," Jessie said, barely above a whisper.

"I know, sweetheart," he answered. "And I just had some stuff to take care of first. Now don't learn from your dear old mom how to backtalk." Timothy put his elbow on the table and leaned in to give an awkward wink, face flushed, breathing heavy. "Just a little fatherly advice."

The family ate in silence for a few minutes before Jessie said, "This is good, Mom."

Suzie forced a close-lipped smile, like she was trying to swallow the corners of her mouth, and nodded.

"So, Mike," Timothy said. "I talked to Coach Lautner today."

"Yeah, he said I can try out again next year," Michael answered.

"But to try out, you actually have to try. And that's always been the problem with you. You don't try. You want things handed to you like you're one of those useless welfare bastards pulling at my paycheck. But you take more than them and do less."

"My forty-yard dash was decent. I thought I'd make the team."

"Decent? The best you can do is decent? How fucking embarrassing is it for me to have a son who can't make a junior high football team? And they let just about anyone on. I'm going to have to hang my head in shame and apologize to the coach for you. Since you're not man enough to do it. Hell, you'll never be man enough to do anything. Is that the legacy you're going to leave?"

"No," Michael said.

"Well, you sure could have fucking fooled me. You failed, and you're comfortable with it. And that, my boy, is the greatest of failures. Your type falls down and just stays on the ground. I don't blame the coach for cutting you. In fact, you're lucky. If he let you on the team because he likes me, and you cost the team a game, well there would be no forgetting that. He cut you because you're soft. You're fucking soft."

The room was quiet for another minute before Timothy started scratching his back like an anthill had just released an entire colony between his shoulder blades. The rest of the family wouldn't have been surprised if he'd opened the skin and was now bleeding down his back. Nobody said anything as long as he was quiet.

Timothy broke the silence. "Mike, I think it would be best if you excused yourself from the table. I'm sick of looking at you."

Without saying a word, Michael picked up his plate and left the table.

"Thank your mother."

"Thanks, Mom."

"Jess, sweetie," Timothy said, "if you're finished, you may be excused as well. You're always so polite."

Jessie did not look down at her plate, which was full except for two bites, as she carried it into the kitchen. "Thanks, Dad. Thanks, Mom."

With the kids gone from the table, Timothy and Suzie ate in silence. Suzie didn't eat much more than a couple of peas and a corner of the meat. Timothy didn't eat anything; he just looked at the plate.

"I understand why you wouldn't want to eat," he told her. "I don't mean to complain, but this tastes like a sick horse's diarrhea. Not your best work, I must say."

She nodded and under her breath said, "Asshole."

Timothy's chair slid back and fell to the ground as he stood. He stared at her with his wide eyes. His pupils had all but encompassed the green iris. "What did you say?"

"Nothing. I'm sorry."

"Well why would you be sorry if you said nothing?"

She shrugged.

"See, that doesn't make any sense. And that tells me that you did say something."

"I'm sorry," Suzie said.

"You're sorry? Is that because you called me an asshole? I'd hate to think I was delusional and just imagined it. But I would hate even more to know I'm married to a woman who would call me an asshole. Because I am pretty sure that's what you said." He stepped closer to her. "Is that what you said?"

"I'm sorry."

"Saying you're sorry doesn't answer the fucking question. You called me an asshole, didn't you?"

65

She nodded.

"So that is what you said."

"Yes."

"Now, an asshole is someone who would push you out of your seat," he said and pushed her to the ground, knocking her chair over as well. "I didn't want to do that, but if you are calling for an asshole, then I'm going to have to be an asshole."

Timothy reached down for her hair. Before he could grab it, Michael ran into the room and took a swing at his father. Timothy saw him and started to turn his head, but that only allowed Michael's fist to land squarely in his ear. It dazed him, and he staggered back a few steps. Before he could brace himself again, Michael punched him in the side of the chin. The sound from his head snapping to the side was nauseating. Michael's next punch landed directly in his father's nose, sending blood across his mother's face and six feet up the wall.

"Michael, no! Stop it!" his mother yelled. But her screams turned to tears and then deep sobs.

"Who's soft now, Dad? Who's fucking soft now?"

In the other room Jessie was crying as well, and Michael thought he heard her dialing the phone. Michael saw his father was still breathing as he stood over him.

"Who's soft now?"

CHAPTER TWELVE

Michael walked back into the comedy club. Drew was still onstage, and the laughter filled the room, louder than before, but everything was so intense. His eyes darted around the room to the people rocking back and forth in their seats, and it was okay with him, even if he was about to be fired.

"So—ever have one of those days? Well, I'm having one of those lives," Drew said in his signature neurotic character. Michael sat in the back next to the sound booth. He didn't know how long he sat there, but he was aware of his wide and distant smile. And who would have thought he didn't even fuck that girl? As far as he knew, the waitress wasn't even interested in men, but who cares? She had an eight ball and showed generosity with it. She was probably even the one who put the fresh glass of whiskey in front of him. That would likely wash away the numb and bitter sensation in the back of his throat. Hell, that was probably what made his father drink. *Holy shit.* The revelation came to him. It hadn't been his fault. It was the cocaine. Dad was really on to something there.

"It took a long time for me to get that day job thing behind me. I worked in an office where I was seriously outnumbered by the ladies," Drew said. One guy hollered in the back. Drew looked over at him. "Yeah, it sounds good. But women in their natural element are foul creatures. And I think you know what I'm talking about. Those same women you take out on a date and who order a side salad as an entrée. When they aren't out with you, well, they eat like refugees. I've seen the fairer sex shovel in more calories in a single mouthful than is the daily recommended allotment for the average sumo wrestler.

"Then there's that ever-so-lovely discussion about menstrual cycles, which wouldn't be so bad, but do you really need to be so candid about tiny blood clots? I was in the lunch room trying to eat my Spaghetti-O's at the time."

There were more groans than laughter, which was normally the goal with the gross-out jokes. Michael smiled in the back when the waitress walked up to him and said, "Smile wider. Show some teeth."

When he complied, she rubbed his gum line with her pinky finger. He felt a little of the powder fall to his tongue immediately, making that numb as well. Somehow it felt better than the lines he had just taken up his nose. He'd heard so much about the stuff and had joked that he was the only drug-free comedian, but every now and then it was good to be a lemming. This was definitely one of those moments. And while his heart raced, he felt content, relaxed. How long had it been since he'd felt anything close to that? And how amazing is it that he could feel like that right before his dreams were set to crash and burn?

The waitress patted his cheek, sending strange waves all the way to the back of his head, and left to bring a couple of bottles of beer to another table. What a beautiful, twisted angel she was.

"So," Drew continued on stage, "when I was in a meeting at work, in a room of about twenty people, and I was the only guy there, I didn't really think anything of it. That was until some broad let loose a cloud so toxic I'm surprised the fire department wasn't called. Seriously, the smell was so bad it could have gagged a vulture eating a pustule-covered, rotting corpse. That stench could have caused a sewer rat to call PETA and report animal abuse. It was the biggest tearjerker this side of *The Notebook*. And it certainly wasn't going unnoticed. But since I was the only guy in the room, guess who got blamed?"

A few people laughed hysterically. Fart jokes always had a faithful following.

"It wasn't me. I swear. But given the accusatory stares from everyone in that room, they were suspecting me of dropping a deuce in my drawers.

"Why was I blamed? Women fart, too. And if you ask me, jumping to the conclusion that I was the offending party is a clear-cut case of profiling. Women have been allowed to vote since the 1920s, they can run corporations and countries and households, yet when it comes to owning up to a pungent emission of gas, suddenly that's a man's job. Why does feminism end there?"

Michael got up to leave. He was supposed to at least make an appearance at the bar next door. Drew's set didn't have much longer to go, and Michael had become too fidgety to sit any longer. Unfortunately that bar didn't have free pool, which was always a good activity when he didn't know what else to do. He wasn't any good, but he never played for money.

But if he left the comedy club now, he'd already have a few more drinks in him when he talked to Drew. And he didn't want to just walk in, get fired, then turn around and walk back out. Getting drunk, getting fired, then staggering out sounded like a much better plan.

The bar had a cover charge unless you were coming in after the show, which, Michael discovered, was the same in most places he'd gone recently. Laugh, then drink. Sounds like a good evening.

Nobody guarded the door when Michael walked into the bar. The crowd from the club had yet to filter in, and there were only a few people in the place. But even though the crowd was sparse, the coin-operated pool tables were occupied by guys who knew how to play and were cocky about it. Not surprisingly, none had dates with them.

Michael sat at a table in the darkest part of the bar and pulled out crumbled pieces of paper. His pen was low on ink and did little more than create light gray indentations. He didn't feel like writing, but it was part of the job after all.

In what little light he had, he wrote, *Grew up Catholic. That explains a lot. I loved that this church had a one-drink minimum, but I could've done without the cover charge.*

He left the paper on the table as the waitress came over.

"You expecting more in your party?" she asked in her sweet southern accent.

"No. Well, I don't know. I hope not."

"Know what you're drinking?"

"Um, Long Island iced tea."

"Anything from the kitchen? Appetizers half price. Best fried pickles in the state," she said. She probably made a fortune on her suggestions.

"No, thanks. Just booze."

"As you wish."

Michael started to write again as she left. Thoughts weren't coming his way, and he started to panic. He wrote, *I was recently called a loser by a guy who is in three fantasy football leagues. Now that was a real blow to the ego.*

Yeah, he thought, goofing on fantasy sports could work if he put it together. But later. Everything could be done later. And maybe that waitress from the comedy club would come back with just a little more. Not much, of course, just a little.

The waitress approached with his drink. She put a small square napkin down and placed the drink perfectly in the center. "Now, can I get you anything else?"

"Probably a second here in a few minutes."

"Don't you want to finish that one first?"

"I doubt that will be a problem," he told her.

"You're not driving, are you?"

He shook his head no.

"Then I'll bring you that second drink."

Michael nodded and gazed about the room. Soon it would be full of people there for two-dollar drafts and whatever drink special they decided to run. The room would get louder, and he wouldn't be able to hear Tom Petty playing on the jukebox like he could right now. The constant chatter of the room would become one big din. Things were so much nicer when it was quiet.

When the sweet southern waitress brought him another drink, he realized his first was already empty. He didn't know how long she had been gone, but it couldn't have been too long. The song had only changed once that he could remember, now on to The Scorpions.

"Getcha anything else?" she asked.

"I'm good."

She nodded and left. But it was true. He was good. He felt really good. The numbness in his mouth had subsided, but everything else felt so vibrant and real. Whatever was to come his way, he could handle it. If it was bad news, then it would undoubtedly temper what he felt right now, but that was all part of the ride. There would be ups, there would be downs, but nothing could beat the knowledge that right now life was good, and that was certainly better than what he had expected.

He finished the second drink and was brought another.

The crowd from the club started to pour in. Apparently the talk about no cover charge was a ruse because it looked like that was always waived. Nobody on staff went to the front door to see if those coming in qualified for free admission. There was only some guy with arms that looked like cartoon muscles inspecting ID's.

He could no longer hear the jukebox, and his glass was empty again. The sweet southern waitress signaled from across the room that she would be with him in just a minute. Her workload had just increased exponentially. While he could not make out much of the conversation around him, not that he had any real desire to do so, quite a few were talking about Drew Greene. A room full of unintelligible sounds with the words *Drew* and *Greene* bouncing around it.

"So I guess you think you're funny," a female voice said. He was startled by how close and clear it sounded.

"If I could just find somebody who agrees, I'd be okay."

He looked up too quickly and remembered how many Long Island iced teas he had. Or tried to remember.

"I'll agree with you. My friend's in the bathroom. Can I sit with you?" She sat before he could answer. "My guess is that she's puking because she ate half her dinner earlier. Do you find that funny?"

Michael shrugged.

"And I'm a stripper, but I do have half a brain, so I won't fall for your cunning mind tricks."

"Fantastic. A Mensa stripper. And to whom do I owe the pleasure?"

"Dana. My name's Dana."

"Well, pleased to meet you, Dana," he said, his voice not slurred, but definitely slower.

"Don't know. You just made me feel awkward before. Thought you should know."

"And you should know that I just play an asshole character up there. In real life I'm a different kind of asshole. Excuse me for a second." Michael grabbed his tattered paper and wrote something close to legible. *If you call someone a dick or if you call someone an asshole, it's basically the same insult. But if you call someone a pussy and you call someone a cunt, it's completely different.* He put the paper back in his pocket.

Dana looked at him and shrugged her shoulders.

"You must inspire me," Michael said. "So where were we?"

The sweet southern waitress walked up. "So I see you have company. What can I get your lady friend here?"

"I'll take another," he told her.

"The only thing better than a Long Island iced tea is five more," the waitress said. Without the accent she might have sounded condescending.

"Really?" Michael asked.

"Yep. Just telling you now so you won't be too surprised when I bring your bill. And if you throw up on the floor, you'd better tip big. What can I get for the lady?"

"Vodka tonic."

"What a high falutin' table we have here. Should I put hers on your tab?"

"Might as well. Won't make much difference now."

The waitress nodded and went back to another table.

"Was that your way of getting me to buy you a drink?" Michael asked. "Because if so, that was smooth."

"And what would you know about smooth?"

"Nothing. I used to watch a lot of TV."

"A couch potato who drinks a lot. Now there's every lady's dream."

"I'm a recovering couch potato," he told her.

Randi walked up to Dana. "There you are. I was looking all over. Thought you may have ditched me already."

"This is Randi," Dana said, and then pointed at Michael, "and this is the warm-up act."

"Michael Clover," he said, extending his hand. "Can I get you a breath mint?"

"You're an asshole," Dana said.

"I thought that was already established."

Randi sat at the table close to Dana. "Oh, yeah," she said to Michael. "You were the second guy up there."

"Yep."

"So you know Drew Greene."

"We've met."

"What's he like?" Randi said, leaning closer.

"Brunettes. You're in luck."

"Do you ever take a day off?" Dana asked. "I mean, the spotlight ain't on you anymore."

"Guess I'll just have to get used to that."

"But is Drew as miserable as you? No offense, of course." Dana sat back and smiled.

"He's nice. Above average hygiene. I should know more, but I don't have it in me to write his unauthorized tell-all biography."

"Ah," Randi said and started looking around the room.

"He should be here in a little bit."

"Really?" Randi asked. She started looking around the room for him.

"I can introduce you," Michael said. "I just need some help remembering your names. As you can see I'm intensely popular here, and I can't keep all my fans' names straight. Such is my curse."

"Yeah, and this place is crawling with tabloid reporters," Dana said.

Michael smiled as he looked at her. "You don't like me very much, do you?"

"No. But I can handle people I don't like. I know what to expect."

Randi turned to Dana. "Dane, I think I just saw someone I worked with a way's back. Can you excuse me for just a minute?"

"Sure," Dana said. As soon as Randi was out of earshot, she turned to Michael and asked, "She just abandoned me, didn't she?"

"I've never been such a close third-party witness to that before. It was kind of fun, to be perfectly honest."

Michael leaned back in his chair. He still didn't see Drew, not that he expected to right away. And before he'd be able to see him, there would be a decent amount of people moving in that direction. A lot of the other patrons would also turn to see what the commotion was. Drew was pretty well known but certainly no Robin Williams. There'd be a lot of handshakes, pats on the back, and one or two autographs. Those usually came from the most faithful of the comedy followers, or from the drunken imbeciles who thought they were being funny. But whatever the reason, it was still a nice stroke of the ego.

He found himself missing Captain Riley's. The place was a dump, the sound system hadn't been updated much since the 1980's, and most of the crowd was too dense to pick up on most jokes. But he liked the people. Being alone on the road had its advantages, but he missed a place where he was known.

The theme song to *Cheers* rolled through his head. His father had loved some horrible sitcoms, but that was a good one. He remembered genuinely laughing then. It may have been the first time he'd started to understand the grown-up jokes. Sometimes he pretended like what was said on TV went over his head. A subtle smirk told his father otherwise, and that was okay. Just as long as Mom didn't know. It was their little secret. Sometimes the best dad is the imperfect one. Unfortunately, some dads take imperfection to a whole new level. However, there were those moments when everything was perfect, and enough of them to keep from continuous moping.

"So I guess what you said is true," Dana said, interrupting Michael's thoughts.

"What's that?"

"That women do talk a lot more than men."

"They stopped paying me to talk long ago," he said.

76

"So you hanging out here is—"

"Dangerous."

Michael started to feel his eyes get heavy as Dana turned around suddenly. He was startled as he looked up.

"Damn, Mike. It looks like you picked up the pertiest thing in here," Drew Greene said.

"She picked me up. I'm a stud."

"No doubt. No doubt. Care if I run her off for just a minute?" Drew turned to Dana. "Can you give us five minutes?"

It wasn't comfort sinking Michael into his chair now. As he'd heard Tom Petty extol earlier, "The waiting is the hardest part." Maybe Tom wasn't right about that. Shitty news could be the hardest part.

"Sorry, Mike. Things were busy before. I need to get famous so I can hire someone to do the administrative shit one day."

Michael sighed.

"Are you playing a solitaire version of a drinking game?"

"Well, you chased off my lady. I miss what's her name."

"Okay, here's what's going on with the tour. Slight change of plans."

"Okay," he answered, eyes blank.

Drew took a long look at Michael. "You didn't ask what they were."

"Probably something about my replacement?"

"Why? Are you quitting?"

"No. I thought I was fired."

"No. Even if I were firing you, I wouldn't have to fret too much over it. There are other schleps out there."

"Good to know."

"I take it you're not too good at guessing games," Drew said, "so I'll get to the point. I got a call from an old friend, Charlie. He books The Mac and Mark Morning Show."

Michael nodded.

"They're based out of Cincinnati for some reason, but they're syndicated, and you're an Ohio boy, so it will be a homecoming. Then we'll resume in St. Louis. Thursday, Friday, Saturday, and Sunday."

Again Michael nodded. He'd dreamed of this many times over. At one point, and again recently, he would have been happy just to intern on that radio show. He couldn't admit that now.

"Now," Drew said, "you'll just be sitting in studio, may not have much air time, if any, probably not any at all really, but be prepared. And you always need some radio-friendly shit. They may give you a mic if things go well at the end. You can get your name mentioned. Probably. And there likely won't be much time for you. Maybe enough for a quip or two."

"Wow."

"I know. I haven't done that show in a long time. Well, I'm supposed to make friendly with folks here, hopefully especially friendly with some. Then I'm turning in. See you tomorrow."

Michael sat in silence for a moment when the sweet southern waitress came up. "Anything else, sweetheart?"

He shook his head no, and she left. His head started to feel heavy, and he couldn't wait to get back to the hotel room. Maybe paying for a cab to take him a couple of blocks was a good idea.

Dana stood by his table. "You okay?" she asked.

"I think so," he said. "I'm going home."

CHAPTER THIRTEEN

It did not take long for the police to show up. With Jessie's hysterical cries, and the proximity of a police cruiser, two uniformed cops were at the house within minutes of the call. Shortly after, two more cars came to unnecessary screeching halts outside. It also did not take long for the rest of the neighborhood to start viewing the spectacle.

The only female officer took turns with Suzie and Jessie. She planned on interviewing them together later, just to see how close the stories were. Michael was led to his room while Timothy was in the dining room. All four Clovers were separated.

An unending strobe of blue and red from the police cars penetrated the closed drapes and danced on the ceiling. It just added to the spectacle of a usually quiet house.

The female officer introduced herself as Officer Jen, while the rest of the squad used their last names. Officers Lofland, Dineen, Kaspar, Renfrow, and Sergeant Beck. None of them seemed to have any interest in playing the good cop role. It was an otherwise slow day in the district, and domestic abuse situations were usually time for some justified ass whipping.

Michael tried so hard not to cry. For the most part he was able to fend off the full brunt of emotions, but they flooded back when he saw the sergeant point his finger directly in his father's face before Lofland closed the door. Timothy showed less control over himself as his voice cracked with each *yes, sir*.

Holding the numbers advantage of six to four, Sergeant Beck stood with Officer Renfrow in the front doorway, while Lofland talked with Michael in his room, Jen with Jessie in the living room, Dad with Kaspar in the dining room, and Mom with Dineen in the office that was never used for office-type functions. Jen talked with Mom as well, but the majority of the time she spent with the girl.

Officer Jen started chatting with Jessie about school, sports, and what music she liked. Jessie tried to engage in conversation, if only to be polite, but she also knew exactly what the purpose of the talk was. One wrong word out of her mouth and her father and brother would be gone for more than just a vacation.

Ever since Michael's first misstep at school, the running joke had always been that he was getting ready for full-time juvenile detention. Now talking about juvie grew beyond stressful.

And while Officer Jen was good with people, especially those at the awkward age that Jessie felt get all the more painful by the moment, she also would have been ready to pull her gun from the holster and use it if the situation were to present itself. And the way she talked, she was prepared to shoot Timothy now.

"I don't really know what happened," Jessie answered, and immediately she knew that was the wrong thing to say.

"You're not in trouble here."

"I know."

"But tell me what you do know," Jen said.

"They just started fighting."

"Your father and your brother?"

Jessie nodded.

"What started this?"

"We were eating dinner, and then after I was excused, I heard them fighting. It was scary and loud. That's why I called."

"So there was nothing out of the ordinary before that? Nobody had said anything or was acting funny? You were all just having supper, and then your brother started hitting your dad?"

Jessie shook her head no. That was when the tears came rolling down her cheeks again with no way to stop them.

"What happened, Jessie? We want to make sure it never happens again. I want to keep you safe."

"It was—" Jessie began, dragging her words. "It was not a good day for Dad. He came home happy. Really, really happy. Then he wasn't."

The officer nodded. "So he was happy, then all of a sudden he got mean?"

Jessie sighed. Something deep inside told her not to say any more, that she wanted to talk to a lawyer, or whatever they said on TV. But she was more afraid of being silent. "No. He went upstairs. He was up there for a while. When he came back down, he was different."

"Different?"

"Yeah. After that he didn't like the dinner. And he talked about Michael not making the football team."

Jen nodded.

"It's like none of that would have bothered him before. But then he was, well, as I said, different."

"Agitated?"

"I guess." The officer looked at Jessie like she might not understand the word. She knew what it meant, and yes it was fitting, but she could not give her the satisfaction of instant agreement.

"And you said he was upstairs?"

"Yeah."

Officer Jen patted Jessie on the back. "I'll be right back. Everything is going to be okay."

While Jessie was only in the fourth grade, she knew that whenever someone told her that everything was going to be okay, it wouldn't be. And it was hard to imagine things ever being okay again. The police were in her house, and she'd brought them there. They were standing around where she did her artwork, talked on the phone, and ate dinner. She could feel violation creeping into the walls. Some things could never be made right again.

When the officer returned, she brought Jessie's mother with her. Suzie's nose was a bright red from all the tissues she'd gone through in the past half hour. Oh, how great it would be if someone robbed the neighborhood bank and pulled their attention away.

"You both know that we can't let this slide," Officer Jen said. "And it's not a real man who abuses people, or other things."

Jessie and her mother shared nervous expressions.

"I don't care if you play dumb with me. Just don't do it with yourselves," Jen said. Jessie couldn't tell if she sounded concerned or patronizing.

Sergeant Beck and Officer Renfrow went upstairs. Within two minutes they came back down. "Yeah, there's paraphernalia as well," Officer Renfrow told the rest of the huddled cops in a heavy whisper.

"Okay," Sergeant Beck said. "Cuff him. Take him down to the station. Get him processed. We don't need to see more. Take the boy to see that social worker. He may have beat the shit out of his dad, but I just wish he'd given me the chance to do it."

"We don't know what the fuck really happened," Officer Kaspar said with a humorless chuckle. "Let the courts figure it out."

The rest nodded.

Sergeant Beck was in complete agreement. "And we do have to get the boy out of here. Get him to talk to Lavonne at Children's Services. And do it now. If something goes wrong here tonight, well, we have a political nightmare. And the boy did just mop the floor with his old man. We have to protect this family. I doubt he's going to do the same with mom and sis, but we can't take the chance."

And just as quickly as they'd arrived, they were gone. The neighbors tried not to gawk, but there was a good show being provided by the Clovers. Officer Jen stayed to talk for a few minutes, long enough for Mom to try to sound authentic enough to convince the police that Timothy had never actually physically assaulted her. Suzie agreed, most certainly, that he was out of line, but he did not cross into fist meeting face. Maybe this would just scare him. Keep him clean. It could be nothing more than just one crazy wake-up call. He was having a bad day, and it became the worst of days. It was the worst day for the entire family, and she saw it as her responsibility to keep it from going any further. Sometimes that was what a mother had to do.

"But you were on the ground," Officer Jen said. "That is what you said."

"Yes."

"How did you get on the ground?"

"We were arguing. It got heated," she said. And suddenly Michael's face came to mind. It would be so easy to blame him. He would not have this marring his permanent record, and maybe this could scare him straight, too. There was no doubt he needed it. Sending a twelve-year-old to a program of the strictest discipline could be a good thing, and it would make parenting him when he got home a hell of a lot easier. But could she just dump all this on her son? What were the options?

"So how would you sum up what happened?" Officer Jen asked Suzie.

"An argument that got out of hand. A scared little girl. And a big embarrassing evening."

"And you, Jessie?"

"Yeah."

"Yeah what?"

"That's what happened," Jessie said.

"That's what happened?"

"Yeah. That's what happened. I'm sorry for bringing everyone out here."

The officer looked her in the eyes. Jessie dropped her head. "I'm going to leave you two here. Your father and your brother are going to figure things out. We're going to help with that. I'll be back to follow up."

"Okay," Suzie said with a nod.

Jessie only nodded.

"And you," Jen said as her gaze remained on Jessie. "I never want to hear you say you're sorry about this. No part of this was your fault. Do you understand me? None of this was your fault. Do *not* say you're sorry."

She still could only nod.

Jen stood up and turned to mom. "You have all our information. Call. We'll be here, or we'll talk you through it and explain what happens next."

"I will."

Since Jen was not a woman who needed an invitation into a house, she didn't act like she needed one to leave. "We'll be in touch." She shut the door behind her.

Jessie sat on the couch and stared into space. She didn't think she could feel anything if she tried. She was tired but knew she couldn't sleep. She was hungry, but the idea of food nauseated her. All she wanted was to be someone else, anywhere else.

Her mother stood up, turned toward her, and slapped her so hard she fell off the chair. Now she felt something. She bit her tongue and immediately tasted blood. Her vision turned into a blinding white for a moment. Closing her eyes only took the edge away. As she was lying on the ground, constant streams of tears rolling down her face, she heard her mother walk up the stairs and slam her bedroom door.

"I'm sorry, Mom!" she screamed. "I am sorry!"

CHAPTER FOURTEEN

The walk back to the hotel should not have taken as long as it did. For every step he took forward, he staggered off to the side a little more. He had to reposition himself twice to keep from stumbling into the street, but he was just glad he didn't fall or get lost. At this point he easily could have been robbed with nothing more than a plastic fork.

When he reached the hotel lobby, the girl at the front desk got the assistant manager to help him to his room. Michael was barely aware of the presence next to him, even though the assistant manager was talking to him, and as far as he could tell, he was responding.

"Here's your room, Mr. Clover. Should you need anything at all, please call us. We're down there twenty-four hours a day."

Michael nodded and allowed the assistant manager to guide him into the room. "Okay. Good to know. Thanks."

"No, thank you."

"And by the way, I can hold my liquor, so you can tell the maid I won't puke on the floor."

"Good to know. Good night, Mr. Clover."

"Yeah," he said with a dismissive wave.

The door shut behind him, and Michael sat at the edge of the bed. He wasn't fired, but he didn't feel better. And there was so much to do. He'd better keep writing if this dream coming true were to continue. This didn't feel like the time to do anything, but he did not want to give up. Goals that seemed like they would remain dreams were close at hand. Something was happening, and he was more than just along for the ride.

Maybe he was just happy he hadn't been kicked off the tour. Or perhaps it was because he was drunk. Regardless of the reason, he felt euphoria and didn't want to let it go.

But was he really going home again? Who should he call? Would they be happy to hear from him? As he played each possible scenario over in his head, he could not imagine many genuine smiles or hugs. But not calling or notifying anyone that he was coming would be much worse. Wasn't this supposed to be a good thing?

He picked up the pen and scrawled on a piece of paper. *I went to see a psychiatrist. He told me my problem was that I had low self-esteem. But not to worry, since I have damn good reason for it.*

Yeah, that type of joke usually worked. And mental health gave such good material. He began to write again. *I went to a discount therapist. He wasn't cheaper than anyone else. He just discounted everything I said. "Issues with your mother, how's that working out? Next!"*

He put the paper in his suitcase, which was now more paper than clothes. He wore the same things over and over, and laundromats were good places to sit and write. There was nothing else to do there. And the *people-watching* done there could only be rivaled by flea markets and Wal-Mart at three in the morning.

What he needed more than anything was sleep. That was the most important thing, but it felt next to impossible. For one thing, he was terrified of dreaming. Maybe he would see who those footsteps belonged to, but it seemed like a better idea just to let that remain a mystery. For tonight at least. Just for one more day.

Eventually he would fall asleep. He had to. His body would make him when it became physically impossible to stay awake any longer. While he didn't feel high from the drugs any longer, the alcohol was still steering the wagon. He'd heard cocaine would keep you awake, and boy, was that ever the case. Maybe a few more good ideas would come his way. Or maybe some bad ones, but that would be fine. That would just make room for more good ones. That might make sense in the morning.

He picked up the remote control and turned on the TV. Absently flipping through the stations could land him on something interesting. Sports, news, three channels dedicated to nothing but weather, and a station advertising all the hotel's amenities. He sighed and stopped at a commercial. Maybe when regular programming resumed, it would be something decent.

Michael didn't realize he was still watching the television when the show resumed. It was instantly familiar, and he'd seen this old sitcom rerun at least twice. The artificial laugh track from the set filled the small room. And sitting on the edge of the bed, Michael cried.

CHAPTER FIFTEEN

Some toxicology reports stun even the most jaded medical staff. After the police found cocaine and a medley of pills to sort though, Timothy was ordered to piss in a cup. From there it went to the lab for the technician to wonder how one body could consume so much.

He was charged with two counts of felonious drug possession and given a court date. Until that time, he had been settled in a holding cell and left alone with his thoughts.

***

Nearby, Michael sat in a much more padded but equally uncomfortable chair. He had sufficiently tuned out all the small, getting-to-know-you conversation. When it got to be his turn to talk, he had no idea what he would say. Should he step up and be a man? After all, he had just sucker punched, then continued to beat the shit out of his father. Hell, he could have killed him with another punch or two.

Lavonne Baker's wall was covered with degrees, awards, and recognitions. There was a framed newspaper with the headline about a missing boy who had been found. Michael was certain her picture was on that page, but he didn't feel like looking any closer.

"Are you comfortable talking with me?" Lavonne asked.

He shrugged.

"Because if you would feel better talking with one of the male counselors, I will gladly get one."

"Doesn't matter, Ms. Baker."

"It's Lavonne."

Michael shrugged again.

"You're not betraying any confidences here. And the more you tell me, the more I can help you."

He found himself shifting in the chair and immediately tried to stop. *It must be part of their job to make their guests wiggle*, Michael thought.

"Do you want to tell me what happened?"

"Well, see, Dad was painting an orphanage for these poor, underprivileged children. He was working so hard he forgot to eat and the paint fumes got to him. It was an honest mistake, could have happened to anyone."

Lavonne stared at him, flipped through her file folder, held it up to her face, adjusted her glasses, and put it down. "Is that why you punched him?"

"I don't like paint fumes."

"Were you aware of your father's drug use?"

"What he gave me for show-and-tell day was awkward."

"Has he ever hit you?"

"No."

"Has he ever hit your mother?"

Michael stared back.

"Has he ever hit your mother?"

A staring competition with Lavonne Baker was not going to work out. He just wanted to say he was sorry and go home. What would even be going on at home?

"Michael, has he ever hit your mother?"

"I don't know. If you want an honest answer, it's that I don't know. I thought he was going to and—" He stopped himself, but it was too late.

Lavonne's pen was burning a hole through the paper. He thought he saw a slight smile make its way onto her face. "So you were protecting your mom?"

Not another word. He knew he couldn't continue to talk.

She stared at him for a few more seconds, but instead of asking another horrid question, she stood and walked toward the door.

"Are we done?" he asked.

"I'll be right back."

The door shut behind her with a quiet click. The room was silent. Whatever *right back* meant would probably have to be drawn into question. There were no mirrors, so there were no cops watching him sweat it out as they laughed with their coffee and doughnuts.

It was late. There were also no clocks on any walls or on the desk. What time could it be? How long ago had he punched his father? How long ago had the police taken them away?

If there was no two-way mirror, maybe there was a camera. Michael strained his neck to look around when the door opened, and Lavonne walked back in. She didn't comment on him looking around. She probably expected it.

"Michael, do you want to stay here tonight?"

"No."

"It's," she said and looked at her watch. "It's almost 2:30. We have a place. And clothes if you want."

"I want to go home."

"I know. But with it being so late, and—"

"This has nothing to do with the time."

"Perhaps not. I'm not going to talk to you like you're stupid. And you're not in trouble, either. We have people to sort out what is going to happen with your father. I don't know yet. I'm not lying to you about that."

He nodded.

"And we're not keeping you here as a prisoner. You need to sleep. You'll go home in the morning. I'll stop by later myself."

Michael could only say, "That's fine."

She led him to a room and closed the door. He was by himself again. And while she had said he was not a prisoner, he was captive, and he had never missed home like he did now.

CHAPTER SIXTEEN

Shortly after Michael left, Dana was ready to take off as well. Randi introduced her to her friends, and they seemed nice enough, but it did not take long before she was left out of the conversation. Occasionally someone in Randi's new entourage would explain what something meant to Dana, either in context or definition.

Dana needed neither. Everyone there worked in commercial sales. The idea of being out on the town and still talking about the detergent, deodorant, and whatever the hell else their company made was sad. More than sad, it was unhealthy, Dana thought. She'd heard of major corporations having a cult-like setting, and it suddenly made sense to her. These poor people were worshipping those products.

Earlier in the evening, Dana had hoped to confess a little to Randi about what she did for a living and how she was feeling now. But none of that seemed appropriate. Randi had corporate friends who looked down on people who used the wrong type of antiperspirant. What would they think of someone who took off their clothes for a living?

But at the same time, what was the difference? They were both selling an image, enticing someone to believe something that wasn't real. What separated Dana from them was that she knew what she was doing was just to pay the bills. Those bastards actually believed what they were saying. Perhaps that was just survival. Believing that what you do is important can get you through the day. And these heroes were saving the world, one fabric-softening sheet at a time.

The remaining problem was this: what kind of spin could she put on her life? That asshole Michael had put things in perspective for her. And the bottom line was that strippers are an easy target. They can be used and reused and then when they get too old there aren't a whole lot of other options out there.

Maybe she wasn't too old. The early thirties weren't when people began collecting social security, but it was a crucial time for her. Going out and filling out an application would be humiliating. When it got to the previous work history section, what would she write? Entertainer? Undressing specialist?

"You okay, Dane?" Randi asked.

"Oh, uh, yeah." She was surprised to hear from her.

"Just checking. If you need to go outside and talk..."

"Nah, I'm good. Thinking. Usually isn't a good idea."

"Hope you don't think I abandoned you. I just haven't seen so many of these people since I transferred out of the downtown office. But I want to catch up with you as well."

"I understand."

"What have you been up to?" Randi asked.

"Mostly temp work. Nothing of interest to put in the annual Christmas letter."

Once a few drinks were in her, apparently Randi was no longer such a keen observer. Either that or she didn't care. It was too much to think about.

"If you're looking for something a little more permanent, a little more stable, I could get you to talk with Bryan. Most everything would be entry-level, but he might be able to help you."

"Don't know. Maybe."

"Bryan," Randi said above the bar noise. "Come over here."

A short guy in a golf shirt walked over. His hair was cropped close to his head, perfectly exaggerating his satellite dish ears. As she looked closer, with no surprise, she saw his shirt had the company's emblem.

"Bryan, this is my dear friend Dana."

He immediately put out his hand, and Dana shook it. She could tell he'd practiced the art of the handshake. Probably part of his job. "Nice to meet you, Dana."

"Dana might be interested in a career change." Randi looked over, prompting a smile and a nod.

"Fantastic. But are you sure you'd want to join this crazy bunch? We're quite the crew," he said and laughed.

If this was his attempt at sounding casual or conversational, then talking to him would be a soul-dragging experience. He probably said things like *she's such a card* or *watch out for him, he's a real character*. Maybe that was how everyone talked there. And she would be, at best, the white trash chick who wouldn't know which fork to use at a fancy restaurant because she never went anywhere that didn't use plastic sporks. That is, if they'd even think of hiring her. And sooner or later, her past job would come to light and be gossip for anyone. Either it would be leaked out of human resources, or someone would have recognized her, said that someone else had seen her there, and the whispers would be loud enough for her to hear. Not that anyone cared. Discretion was reserved for those who deserved it. And she didn't need to be reminded of where she didn't belong.

"Well, Randi had the thought for me."

"Oh, that Randi. Gotta keep an eye on that one." He winked and with his thumb and index finger shot at her. Even with the jukebox and other conversations everywhere, his accompanying clicking sound registered, forcing Dana to conceal her shudder. At least that was something she did well.

"You're such a kidder, Bryan," Randi said.

Dana could taste the bile building up in the back of her throat.

"So what are you looking for? Do you have any special talents, skills?" he asked.

"I was hoping that wasn't necessary."

"Heck, sometimes we prefer it that way. It might be better to start off learning things with our method."

"That's true," Randi said to Bryan. "Remember that girl from General Mills? It took a long time to get her reprogrammed."

"Yeah." He laughed way louder than seemed merited. "It was like we had to de-frag the whole system from all the junk they put in there."

This time Randi laughed unnaturally. Dana cringed. That Michael guy was a jackass, but when he made her laugh, it was real. At least on stage. So did Drew Greene and whoever that host was. Too bad Michael had to leave. She hoped he'd made it back to wherever he was going. He wasn't looking so good. Either too much to drink or bad news. All Dana knew was that he was gone, and she wished he were still here. Instead she stayed to talk with the plastic people.

"I'm a quick learner," Dana said. "Maybe I need a change of scenery."

Bryan handed her his card. He looked like he always had one ready. It didn't take much for some guys to feel important. Handing out a business card put a wry smile on his face. She took it and put it in her purse without looking at it.

"Give me a call Monday or Tuesday morning. Tell my secretary, Ashley, that you talked to me and she'll bump you up on the schedule."

Dana nodded.

"Get your résumé together, references, preferably someone other than Randi," he said and did the same index finger and thumb shooting motion with the obligatory click. "I don't know what we have, but even entry-level with us is better than just about anywhere else."

She nodded again. He was probably right, but every part of this felt so wrong. And while trying not to think about it, she felt herself stammering just to say, "Thanks."

"No. Thank you. And thank Randi. If we can find a place for you, I think that would make you very happy."

Randi put her arm around Dana. "See? This is turning out to be a good night."

Dana smiled. She knew there was no chance in hell of getting a job with no skills or reputable job experience. But for a while, she could dream a dream of something she didn't even want. She was also ready to go home.

CHAPTER SEVENTEEN

When he was talking with the police, social workers, and people from the drug-awareness progress, all Michael could think about was going home. Now that it was time, he was not ready. Having to sit and wait only to wait some more before he told the same story became a painful routine. And all he knew about what was going on with his father was that there was plenty to prosecute and no need for the family to testify, but a plea could be reached depending on certain decisions.

What that would mean, and what his father would actually do were complete mysteries to him. Children's Services seemed to like the mystery, just waiting for him to give them that "aha" moment. Every time they told him he was not going to betray any confidence, he knew exactly what that meant.

He was also reminded many times over that he was not at fault. Like that was supposed to supply some relief. But for as much as he hated his father, and with all the justifications presented before him, he was not about to hand over that final nail for them to pound into his coffin. Every tragedy has its resolution, and he could see the family coming to grips with the fact that he beat up his father; there could be peace about Jessie calling the cops or even the addiction that had brought on the rest of the shit storm, but if he were to betray him now, that would be unforgivable.

Michael had grown tired of the kid-friendly environment. Since he had a while to go before that magical eighteenth year, he sat in rooms designed to make the younger crowd feel at home. Faded pictures of Mickey Mouse and Dalmatians had been painted on the walls. The dolls where the kids were supposed to show where they had been touched were probably somewhere in there as well. There were smaller chairs, tables, and Legos.

As the day wore on, Michael thought about playing with those, but if he did, it would undoubtedly speak volumes to the next person trying to tap into his mind. And all he wanted to do was reduce his boredom.

Finally the door opened. He heard muffled voices before anyone appeared. Trying to look uninterested, he stared at the pictures on the wall. It had not been long ago that Jessie had begged for a Dalmatian. She watched that movie at least three or four times a week and acted each time like it was the first time she'd ever seen it. And since she was Daddy's Little Girl, she'd almost gotten it. Not until the cost and upkeep were explained was the final no spoken. Even then she hinted at what great dogs they were. Michael was still surprised she didn't get one after that.

Lavonne Baker walked into the room. She barely looked at him as she sat. "What do you want?"

"I want to go home," he answered with little sincerity.

"Well, yeah. We're not going to keep you here forever."

Michael was silent. Lavonne didn't even look in his direction. Probably another method in her observation.

"So. Home, you said?"

"Yeah," he answered. "Is there some other option I don't know about?"

"If the conditions are not right for you, or because of you, other arrangements are sometimes made."

"Is this one of those times?"

"No."

He had grown tired of this place long ago and knew they liked to keep him squirming. Even if he had not shown anything, they would read into whatever they wanted.

"I'll drive you home," she said.

He nodded.

"What are you waiting for? Get your stuff together, and we'll get you back to Mom and sister."

He didn't have anything to take with him. Some helpful hints written on government paper they gave him to read, a toothbrush, and small travel-size toothpaste were the extent of what he had. It seemed like he'd been there for a long time, but it had been less than twenty-four hours. A lot can happen overnight though, he had learned.

She led him to the car, a white Ford with the State of Ohio seal on the driver-side door. It looked like a cop car, and the neighbors were going to be on high alert looking for another. At least this would not be accompanied with lights and sirens. There may be some chance to sneak in unnoticed.

Lavonne remained silent for the entire ride, except for telling him to put on his seat belt. It was not a far drive and not long until they reached his neighborhood. He knew every street, nearly every house, but today it seemed only vaguely familiar. The sky looked like it wanted to rain, but it held off, leaving a heavy feeling in the air. When the sun made its appearance through the clouds, it was immediately blinding. Michael felt like another storm was coming.

The car pulled into the driveway. "Welcome home," she said as she unfastened her seatbelt and stepped out of the car.

Michael didn't move.

"You coming?" she asked.

He nodded, sat there for a moment, and opened the door. He didn't realize the seatbelt was still fastened, and it pulled him back. Lavonne didn't laugh, she didn't smile, she just waited patiently for him to perform a simple task. When he finally got out of the car and up the front steps, she was right next to him. It didn't seem like she feared he was a flight risk; this was just a difficult time for him.

Lavonne knocked on the front door. Michael felt awkward having to wait to be let into his own house. And what if nobody was home? Would he have to go back? If so, where? Wasn't this supposed to be his home? Why didn't it feel like it?

He heard his mother's footsteps approach the door.

CHAPTER EIGHTEEN

Dana woke up three hours before she had to be out the door. There was plenty of time to get dressed and ready to get undressed again. Plenty of time to kill, and no weapon to use against her own thoughts. Nothing to keep her from focusing on what she had to do today, where she had to go, and how the cycle would continue. Worse, what would happen when that cycle no longer churned? And if she didn't think about it now, when would she?

Long ago, even before she made this career choice, she knew that her mind was a bad neighborhood, and there was no option of moving out. There were really no options at all. Survival made for a good day. If she made good money, then she could find justification in it all.

For a time at least. Then would come a time to re-examine everything again, and see, with sober eyes, how far gone she had become. She would see the lost years that only read as employment gaps. There could be no denying the fact that she was qualified to do nothing. That wasn't to say she did not have the capacity, but that just made her all the sadder. It just put her failure under a brighter spotlight.

But what if *he* came back? In a room full of lust-filled stares, would his be one of them? Did it matter? As long as he did not touch her, then she would be safe. Another thing she could not forget was that all it took for him to taste his own blood running down his throat would be a whisper in a bouncer's ear. Justified brutality was apparently as good as it got.

The clock seemed to remain stuck. All Dana wanted was to get to work, get it over with, come home, and pray to sleep. Maybe something would happen and change everything. There had to be some hope to hold on to; there had to be some other place to look.

Another day would pass, regardless of what she did. If she didn't take off her clothes for singles, then the world would survive. But would she? That was all she had, and for better or worse, it was her world.

With hours until she had to go, Dana sat on the couch and stared intensely at nothing.

CHAPTER NINETEEN

The Sunday night crowd was typically more reserved, and there was never a late show. It usually sold out—with Drew it always did—but Sunday tickets were always available until the week of the performance, and that came from people who saw he was coming to town and figured seeing him the night before they had to go back to work was better than not at all. Most who drank only had one. Iced tea and Diet Coke ended up being the most common orders taken. Fine choice for the working people, but it did not lend itself to a rocking crowd.

It was also Michael's last night before heading back on the road again. Back home. He woke up without a hangover, but that had become the norm. Not since high school, when Wild Irish Rose counted as passable, did he remember being hung over. He had thrown up his fair share throughout the years but had never had that awful, unending pain. This morning did require coffee and Gatorade, though, and that took care of the weariness and dehydration. The rest of the pain came from somewhere else entirely.

The change in plans kept Drew busy, so Michael did not see him before the show started. While that was hardly uncommon, Michael hoped for some reassurance and even thought about vocalizing the need. Of course the idea was stupid, and he would have sounded like a fifteen-year-old girl, but he did not count himself much higher than pathetic. The gin helped a hell of a lot more than a beer, and when his name was called he hopped up the steps and started his set.

It was better than a real job, but it was still work. Something to take seriously, something to improve on. And he knew there was still plenty of that to do. The best comedians could stand on the stage, talk about nothing, and yet manage to captivate a crowd. There wasn't always the firmest reason behind it, but that was what made them great. The ability to deliver a punch line where there wasn't one, and the only reason it was funny was because they said it.

Michael knew that required work. Just because somebody can hit a baseball doesn't make him Babe Ruth. He was in the game, and for now that was good enough. The set was going well.

"I'm sorry," he told the crowd, his shoulders slumped. "I'm just in a bit of a foul mood. You see, my wife left me, and that really hurt."

The audience replied with varying degrees of, "Awww." Some mocking, some sincere.

"Yeah. And then she came back, which was devastating."

The crowd liked that one.

"Guys, you're never going to believe what she said. She said I don't communicate. She said I didn't understand the female perspective. She said that a relationship is a two-way street." He paused and acted like he was thinking. "All I told her was that it would be a whole lot more interesting, and I would get more of that female perspective, if it were a three-way intersection. If not, then how about a six-lane highway? Round about? Dirt road? I'm just trying to understand you, baby."

Michael stepped back from the microphone and looked at the crowd. They actually seemed to be enjoying themselves. If only he could hold on to this moment a little longer. If only he didn't have to go back home. There had to be some way to control his thoughts, but for now he had a calm moment.

"After that, conversation only went one way. Then I decided to go seek counseling. But that was too expensive, so I found a discount therapist.

"He wasn't any cheaper, he just discounted everything I said. 'Alcoholic? Issues with your mother? Co-dependency? How's all that working out for you? Next!'"

A few chuckles.

"Then he goes on to tell me that I have low self-esteem, but that's okay since I have such damn good reason for it."

Some of the newer material was coming together, and it felt good. He would be ready to expand his set soon enough. But his time was almost expired. The blinking light from the sound booth indicated that he had less than a minute left. Not enough time to go through with the bulimia joke ending, so best not start into it. After all, he was still at the place where keeping his time was just as important as being funny.

"But before I go, I want to remind you all to tip your wait staff, stick around for Drew Greene, and always follow your dreams. Even if that means going to work naked and being chased off a cliff by a thousand cannibal midgets.

"I'll be next door. My name's Michael Clover. Thank you."

The applause was becoming addictive. He ran off the stage, shaking a few hands along the way, and ran up to the waitress from the night before.

"Good show," she said.

"Thanks."

"You're not here to talk to me about the show."

"Not really."

"Okay." She led him into the wait staff area. Instead of sitting him on the couch, she led him into the restroom.

"Why back here?"

"It's safer. From here on out I revoke your interrogative privileges, funny boy." She pulled a mirror from her apron and put it on the back of the toilet. Next to that she dropped a small baggie of powder and pulled out a razor blade. Within seconds she had three lines and handed him a straw.

"You first," she said.

Michael put the straw in his left nostril and did the first line, sweeping back and forth for any missed granules. From there he quickly did the second. A shiver ran from the base of his neck down to the soles of his feet.

"Hey, am I not invited to your party?"

"Sorry," he said. "I just, well—"

"You're new to this. Don't worry. But that last one's mine. Remember, I know how to use a blade."

The waitress—Michael decided he didn't want to know her name—bent over and snorted the last line. With her pinky finger she dabbed up the rest and said, "Smile." When he complied she rubbed the remainder on his gum line. He closed his eyes and smiled wider.

"If anyone asks what was going on back here, tell them I wanted to fuck a celebrity. And got confused," she said.

110

A roar of laughter shook the room.

While he had done far more the night before, his heart was racing as fiercely as it had then. His legs shook, and he would count himself lucky if he did not fall. Since it was a Sunday, and not football season, the bar would be pretty empty. He decided to go over a little earlier than he'd originally planned.

The laughter, the lights, the scurrying of people going in and out of the restrooms, all hit him with a new intensity. He didn't want to leave but knew he couldn't stay. Next door would be calmer—for a while at least. Plenty of time to have a few drinks, collect some thoughts, and get ready for tomorrow.

Again there was no enforced cover charge. He walked in with barely a nod to anyone. The jukebox played Tom Petty again, this time "Free Fallin'." With the money he had in his pocket, he could probably play "Achy Breaky Heart" on a continuous loop for the next couple of hours. But that type of thing was only funny in theory.

Highlights of a horse race were being shown on one of the many televisions in the place. Michael would have bet that some bars were in danger of losing their liquor license if they did not have at least seven TV sets. He pulled out a wad of paper and began to write, *I'll bet the best part of being a horse in The Kentucky Derby is the pet midget.*

The sweet southern waitress, who did not seem like she'd be one to work Sundays anyway, was nowhere to be found. A heavily tattooed and ornately pierced girl filled in that role today. Michael found it hard to imagine that the same person hired both employees.

But she served her purpose when she brought him his drinks. Since he'd had gin earlier, it seemed like a good idea to stick with it.

"Drinking alone?" a voice asked.

"Yes. And to quote the great George Thorogood—" he began to say when he saw Dana sit across from him.

"Hey," she said, the casual tone in her voice comforting.

"Hey."

"Good show."

"It was the same as last night. And the night before. And, well, I could go on like this."

"Of that I have no doubt," she said.

"Get you something?"

"Those Long Islands you had yesterday have been running through my head."

"And they're still running through my bloodstream, so I can attest that they do indeed work."

She nodded and Michael motioned for the waitress, who was much more polite than he would have guessed. Stereotypes were good for comedy, but not always in real-world functions.

"Hi, my name's Kimmy. What can I get you?"

"A Long Island iced tea. On his tab," Dana said.

"And I'll have another. On my tab. Since I'm not cute enough to have someone buy mine."

"Yeah," Kimmy said. "You need a few more to drown your sorrows."

She went back to get the drinks, leaving Michael and Dana to sit in a silence that was not awkward until noticed.

"Thought the show was supposed to be sold out. But a single girl with big tits can find her way into places."

"I hadn't noticed those before."

"Liar."

"Perhaps," he said. "But it's generally bad form to say, 'Hey, ma'am, nice rack.'"

"I've heard worse."

He nodded and thanked the waitress who brought over the order.

"Want anything else?" Michael asked Dana. "From my understanding, they have the best fried pickles in the state here."

"Not really, but I'll bring you some," Kimmy said.

"I'm good," Dana answered.

Michael nodded, indicating his agreement. The waitress left.

"So what brings you out on consecutive nights?"

"Last night was a girls' night out. Tonight I called off sick. The place will survive without me for a night."

"I'm sure some will be disappointed."

"They'll live."

Michael squeezed the lime into his drink. A splash landed on his shirt. He pretended not to notice. "So did you have a good time with your friends?"

"Oh, it was a blast. Fun-loving bunch."

"I'd never be able to hang with such a crowd."

Dana's eyes began to well. She dabbed them with the square napkin, then blew her nose with it. "It's my off day. I don't have to be sexy."

"I'm not too good in these situations."

"Me neither."

Michael motioned for the waitress to bring him another drink. "Make it two."

Dana laughed and then began to cry again.

"You're killing my buzz."

"Sorry."

"Since I've known you for almost twenty-four hours now, you're just about my oldest friend. Talk to me."

"Those yuppies offered me a job."

"Regular employment brings me to tears as well."

She sniffed back the snot running from her nose. "Those are the worst people on Earth. They love the stuff they sell. Not just really like, they *love* it. Worship it. It's creepy. Apparently, in that world, it matters what kind of dish soap you use."

"Gotta worship something."

"And their whole lives just revolve around their company. But that's not the saddest part."

Michael stared back blankly.

"I wanted what they had," she continued. "They can go out, be respected, enjoy the weekend, and not have to be embarrassed all the time."

"If I went out and talked about dish soap, I'd be embarrassed."

"Even the guy who works in the tampon department boasted about what he does. But what would I have to offer? I'm ashamed and afraid."

"Afraid?"

"More shame."

"But you said afraid."

She dropped her gaze and shook her head. After several false starts she was able to speak again. "I don't even know why I'm telling you this. I don't know you, and you're in the profession of making fun of people."

Michael thought about laughing this off, but somewhere between the high from the drugs and the buzz of the booze, he found himself warming to this strange woman. It didn't hurt that her chest was just as good as she had mentioned, and even if they weren't real, he wasn't in the business of being real to begin with. That wasn't what people wanted, at least out of him, that was. The rest of the world was just a place for him to walk through and pick what he wanted to talk about. Then the lights would fade and it wouldn't matter until he took the stage again.

He was not ready to leave in the morning, especially now. There was more to this girl. More than she knew. The problem now was that anything he would try she could just refer to his routine. It would just go to further his point that strippers are stupid and easy. And yeah, the thought of bringing her back to his hotel room ran through his head in several different ways, but there really was something about her. Or maybe he was just really fucked up. Regardless, he liked what he felt.

"I don't want that world, but I don't like that I can't have it," she continued. Michael was sure that he'd missed some of that, but that was okay. She didn't seem to notice.

The show must have let out, because the bar got loud. The once tranquil haven had turned overwhelming.

"All I know is that I don't want to go home," she said.

"Me neither."

The crowd continued to grow and get louder. Several people walked up to Michael to say things like "good show," or "funny stuff." Nothing major. Nobody was there to try out their own material on him or be a one-on-one heckler. Those were all part of the job, nothing new, but would have felt embarrassing right now, even though he could not put his finger on exactly why.

"How long is your obligation here?"

"About to expire."

Dana hesitated before she spoke. "Does your hotel have free cable?"

"Uh, yeah."

"I'm just looking to hang out. I'm not *that* type of girl."

Drew Greene walked in. The crowd that had come to see him in the club now gravitated there. "Thanks, everyone, but if I had any more funny lines, I would have used them onstage."

He saw Michael and walked over to him, shaking several hands along the way.

"Hey, Mike. I'd like to get an early start. Be ready to go by eight?"

"You're the boss."

Noticing Dana next to Michael, he extended his hand. "Drew Greene."

"I know. Met you yesterday," she answered.

"Oh."

"It meant a lot to me, too."

"Okay, well, if you are any part of the equation, make sure Mike's ready to go early in the morning."

"He'll be there. He's a professional. And I'm not, in case you were wondering."

"Um. Not at all. Carry on."

Michael and Dana walked outside, giggling. It had been a long time since he could remember that type of laughter. And from such an unlikely source.

"I don't think I've ever seen Drew blush like that," he said.

They walked and laughed until they got to the hotel room.

CHAPTER TWENTY

After the police station, spending the night enduring stares and answering the same question at least ten times, the gravity of the situation did not hit him until he stood on his own front porch and had to be let inside. His mother finally unlocked the deadbolt and opened the door. Michael pictured her on the other side, sighing, probably drying her eyes or taking deep breaths, hoping for some sort of stability. Or as long as it looked that way, maybe the inside would catch up with the façade.

Lavonne shifted her weight from one leg to the other. She didn't look like a patient woman, at least when she didn't have to be. When things were on her time, she could wait as long as she wanted. Part of the joy of fishing had to be watching the worm wiggle on the hook.

The door opened.

"Hi, Mikey."

"Hi, Mom."

Instead of leading them in or stepping aside as a welcoming gesture, Suzie stood frozen.

Lavonne sighed. "Are you going to let us in, or are you going to make the neighbors wonder what's going on now?"

This got Suzie's attention, and she opened the door wider. "No. Please. Come in. Sorry. This is all just so...so...well, I don't know."

Michael walked inside. He'd spent nearly all his time over the past twenty-four hours dreaming of coming home. But now that he was there, and that dream had indeed come true, this did not feel right either. Something was missing, and it was more than just his father. That would be too obvious. There had to be something hiding beneath the surface. He was acutely aware of his father's absence and had long since prepared himself for that. If he allowed himself to think about it a little deeper, he would have realized he'd started that process years ago. Perhaps the best preparation was all-out denial.

"Can I offer you something to drink?" Suzie asked.

Lavonne looked back at her like the question ranked somewhere between stupid and offensive. "No, thank you. I don't plan on staying long."

"Okay."

Standing in silence, Lavonne allowed herself a brief smile. This was the type of place where she found her comfort zone.

"You okay, Mikey?" his mother asked.

He nodded his reply.

Jessie's bedroom door creaked when she opened it far enough to peek out. In the silence, everyone's eyes were brought to it. As soon as she realized she had become the center of attention, she closed the door. Suzie grimaced, and that was not the type of thing Lavonne Baker overlooked. Her smile vanished.

"How is your daughter, Mrs. Clover?"

118

"Oh. Jessie?"

"Is there another?"

"No. No, of course not."

"Then yes, I am talking about Jessie. How is she?" Lavonne asked.

"Fine."

"So Jessie can be listed as being fine."

"She's doing well."

Lavonne stepped past Suzie and walked into the dining room. Ground zero, the place where the series of actions had set the wheels in motion and somehow brought them back together with a social worker replacing dear ol' dad. A simple family dinner that ended up with handcuffs and sirens was not all that common, because Lavonne had seen very few families where both parents were present. Even fewer had dinner together.

"Would it be okay if I spoke with her?"

"No," Suzie said, and immediately corrected herself. "I mean yes. It would be no problem. At all. Let me get her for you." She cleared her throat three times before calling up the stairs. "Jess. Jess, hon. Can you come down here, please?"

Michael was certain that Jessie made the same slow sigh that his mother had made on the other side of the door before opening it.

When Jessie emerged from her bedroom, she made every effort to look normal. Everything betrayed her from smile to posture. Each step she made was awkward, and with every eye on her, she began to sweat. During more normal times, a lifetime away, her shoulders would have slumped as her mind drifted in countless daydreams.

"How are you, Jessica?" Lavonne asked.

119

She nodded, barely able to blurt out, "Good."

"I'm glad to hear that. Are you happy to see your brother?"

Her pause was brief yet noticeable. "Of course."

"Mrs. Clover, just to let you know, I will be making my presence known around here. All I ask of you is compliance and honesty. Is that understood?"

"Yes."

"Okay, well, Michael, it looks like it's time for me to check out now, but I do expect to hear from all of you in one form or another."

There were collective nods, nothing more. Lavonne joined in, but her stare did not leave Jessie.

"How old are you, Jessica?"

"I'm eleven."

"Ah, yes. I would never go back to that age, even if you gave me a million dollars. Would you agree, Mrs. Clover?"

"Absolutely."

"That's when I started wearing makeup myself," she said and took a step closer to the girl.

"It's okay," Lavonne said as she looked at her cheek, then, while gently guiding her chin, looked at the other. "Did you apply this yourself?"

"Well, um, my mom was teaching me."

"I see. Because it looks like she had to apply more on this side."

"Adolescent skin can be—"

"I would advise you to speak as little as possible, Mrs. Clover."

She nodded, cheeks flushed.

"It's a little puffy here," Lavonne continued. Must have fallen or something. Clumsy kids. That's why someone would have one swollen side. And must have just happened, because I'm sure I would have seen that in the reports." She emphasized the "s."

With her lip quivering frantically, Jessie only dropped her chin closer to her chest.

"Don't worry, Miss Jessica, you're not on the hook here. And we will be talking. Soon."

Suzie quickly looked away.

Despite her large frame, Lavonne spun easily toward Mom. "We'll be speaking again soon as well. And against my better judgment, I'm leaving now. But did I mention I will be checking in again? If the children lose two parents in as many days, well, I don't think that's going to do much good. I'd be lying if I said I was without reservation, though. A whole hell of a lot of reservation. Make things right. Do it now. Because if you don't, well, as I said, I'll be checking in again."

"I understand," Suzie said.

"Hope so. Now you're probably wondering about Dad," Lavonne said. There was not much body language one way or another. Suzie only closed her eyes. "As you can probably imagine, he's being charged with felonious drug possession. That's the clear-cut part. And since there have been no prior instances, at least that have been made known to us, he will likely have the option of seeking treatment and not face any real time. But this is all just my speculation. Don't confuse it for real lawyer talk. That's coming, and it's coming soon. I think you know quite well that the three of you hold a lot of influence on what we'll call the gray area."

Michael felt like he was ready for more interrogation, and it was so much worse not knowing if or when it was coming.

"I hate to repeat myself so much, but should there be some new information it would be wise for all parties to come forth with it now. If you want to talk just a little later, that's fine as well. Through proper channels, of course. I can be contacted. You know Officer Jen, and there's always somebody on duty. Trouble doesn't take a holiday, and neither do we."

"Yes. We understand," Suzie said.

And with that, Lavonne left. The door clicked shut behind her and left Suzie, Michael, and Jessie in silence with nothing to say. Business cards and official-looking papers stretched across the dining room table. They would certainly be important later, but impossible to look at now. Not yet at least.

The phone rang. The shrill sound of the bell startled them. Jessie's eyes began to water, and she got closer to full weep with each successive ring, until the call went into the answering machine. While nobody said anything, it was generally understood not to pick up the phone. They would hear who was calling shortly, and from there could make a decision.

That was the entire reason they'd bought the contraption, as Timothy had called it, in the first place. But if he were on the line, or somebody on his behalf, would she be able to pick up the phone? She couldn't imagine what to say. Hopefully the call would only pass along some information. Something for her head to comprehend, because her heart could hold on to nothing. Maybe some instinct would kick in, no matter how unlikely that looked.

By the time the sixth ring sounded, Jessie was ready to scream. Timothy's voice on the outgoing message was enough to make Suzie hold her breath. The tears that Jessie held back released and poured down her face. Michael simply closed his eyes. There could be no surprise. This was not the first family-screened call, and they always heard whatever he decided to record. "Thank you for calling the Clover household," Timothy's tinny voice said. "We are standing around the answering machine right now, screening our phone calls. So if we don't pick up when you start talking, you should take it personally."

That was Timothy. The Timothy that Suzie loved. The old Timothy, the man who brought smiles with him wherever he went. But what would she do if New Timothy was on the line?

The long din of a beep finally ended. Suzie looked over to see that Jessie had reached over to hold hands with her brother. She would have thought it was sweet in any other circumstance. Now, just like everything else, it made her nervous.

"Mikey. Mike. Mike," Ugh began. "What's going on, teabagger? People been asking me what's up with you. I made up some really sick things. Let me know if the real story is even better than that. This could help you get laid, by the way. Oh, and if your mom's listening, Hi, Mrs. Clover. Hope all is well with you. Once Michael is done with his chores, which I am certain he will do, may he come out and play?"

Ugh hung up the phone, making the tape rewind, and the flashing red light indicated there was a message. Suzie began to laugh, allowing her children to do the same.

"Deep down inside, he's probably a good kid," Michael said.

"He is," Suzie answered, no sarcasm detected in her voice. "But if you want to go over, I understand."

"Well—"

"Go," she said. "It's okay."

"Okay," Michael answered and went up to his room to get dressed. He couldn't stay in his bedroom very long. Everything in it was familiar, yet somehow off. He just was not able to know what, and every ounce of self-preservation in him prevented further thought. Just get out.

He had to brush his teeth again. While he'd been able to do that during his overnight stay, he'd missed his own toothbrush more than his pillow. The reflection in the mirror, always unflattering from the fluorescent light, showed him how tired he truly was. Staying with the remainder of the family and going to bed early seemed like a better idea, but he needed to get out of the house. For a little longer at least.

As he went to leave the house, he tried his best to act like normalcy had already made its triumphant return. His mother stood by the dining table, exactly where she had before. Jessie, however, had already returned to her room so quietly he had not heard her.

Somehow his mother smiled as she stood there. "Bye, Michael."

He tried to answer, was unable, and left the house. Once he had walked down the front steps, he stopped. Since he had not called Ugh, he was not expected. Instead, he just sat undisturbed on the porch for a while.

CHAPTER TWENTY-ONE

"Wow, what a room," Dana said as she walked inside.

"It even has an ice machine just down the hall."

"And a pool."

"Well, I do have to live like a rock star, don't I?"

She sat down on the chair by the window overlooking the interstate and kicked off her shoes. "I'll bet you can even order room service."

"They probably have the best cheeseburger twelve dollars can buy."

She laughed. "There's too much small-town girl in me to pay that much for something that's on the dollar menu. My father would roll over in his grave at the thought of that."

"So your father's deceased?" Michael asked, surprised by how awkward he sounded. Just like the night before, the coke had him trembling, heart rate beating a tattoo into his chest. He had trouble remaining seated on the edge of the bed. He just knew it would feel better to walk around the room, but it might look like anxiety-driven pacing, and that was certain to have her reaching for the pepper spray.

"Every stripper has some sort of daddy issue. With mine, it just wasn't his fault."

"My bad. I forgot you were a stripper."

Dana smiled and stood up, walked over to Michael, and kissed him on his cheek. "That may be the nicest thing anybody has ever said to me." She sat back on the chair.

"Well, I'm sure that if I'd seen you undress, it would've burned a lasting image in my memory. Just a guess."

"You're sweating."

Michael brushed his forehead, which was indeed wet. "Yeah, well, you know it's my way of releasing pheromones and—"

"And shaking."

"You see, I haven't brought a girl back to my room with me since the last town I was in. And I was surprised they had a comedy club in Haiti to begin with, but then she was insistent as well as—"

"And I do know why."

"See, I thought it was some sort of voodoo thing, too, but that would have been a better circumstance, because after—"

"You shouldn't really mess around with that shit, but I guess you're required because technically you are in showbiz."

"What are you talking about?"

"I know you claim my profession isn't made up of the brightest bunch, but we do know some things."

He just stared back at her.

"Jittery. Dancing eyes," she said. "It's killing you to sit still."

"I'm not good in every situation."

"You don't have to be. And I'm not judging you. Dear God, I'd be the last person to do that. But you're making it a hell of a lot harder when you're lit up."

He smiled and dropped his head.

"How much did you do?"

"Not much. A little. I've never done it before. Before last night, that is. A waitress at the club had some."

"As I said, I ain't judging you."

"Hearing that a second time sounds less convincing."

"I just don't like it," she told him. "Shit, I've done it. Couple of times. But never liked the way it felt. Don't understand dropping that much cash on something that doesn't feel good. Guess I'm too jumpy to begin with. Smoked some weed a way's back. Liked that better. But not into that either."

"I have some red wine."

"Now that's much better."

Michael pulled out the individually wrapped plastic hotel cups and put them on the table. The wine was not so cheap that it could simply be unscrewed, so he had to call down to the front desk for assistance.

He picked up the phone. "Hi, this is Michael Clover. Yes, *the* Michael Clover, and I am in need of a corkscrew." He waited for the response and hung up the phone. "They're bringing it right up."

"I could try my keys if you'd like."

Michael looked at his suitcase and opened the front pocket. He fished around for his keys and left them there. It had been so long since he had needed to use them that he felt the need to make sure he hadn't misplaced them. For so many years it had been a nervous habit to slap his thigh to assure that he'd not lost his keys. Now, after several weeks on the road, with someone else driving every mile and hotels now offering cards instead of traditional metal keys, he had grown accustomed to not having to worry about such simple things.

But eventually the road would end, and on the way it would stop by home. Tomorrow. Back to a place where things like keys were important.

"You okay?" Dana asked. "You're not flipping out on me, are you?"

"I haven't gone nuts on a stranger in my room in over a week. You're safe."

"Should we use the keys?"

"That will result in pieces of cork falling into this fine merlot," he said as he pulled out bottle of *Razorback Red*. "I got this at a truck stop just outside Little Rock."

She reached for the bottle and read the back. "Classy."

"Now we can drink like we're Arkansanians. It's a good thing you're not my sister. I'd be all over that."

"Would that be family bonding?" she asked.

"Say what you will about incest; at least it's convenient." He walked over to the nightstand with all the crumbled pieces of paper, flattened and smoothed a piece, and wrote on it. "May not be a keeper of a line, but who knows?"

Before she could reply, there was a knock at the door. Michael opened it, and a hotel employee handed him the corkscrew. "Delivery for *the* Michael Clover."

Michael took it from him and gave him a dollar. "Everyone's a comedian," he said as the door shut behind him.

"So is this your method?" Dana asked, looking at the pile of wadded paper. "I could buy you a notebook if you'd like."

"I'd lose a notebook. I lose enough of these damn scraps."

"And they're all jokes?"

"Brain droppings, if I may channel Carlin."

"Are you comparing yourself to George Carlin?"

"Now that would be blasphemy," he said and opened the bottle with a loud pop. "Music to my ears."

"Now be careful," she said. "When you're sky high, you're not always aware of how much you're drinking. Sorry to nag or sound like a mom."

"Nah. Mom never gave helpful advice on how much to drink after doing lines of blow."

"There's a whole chapter on that in *What to Expect When You're Expecting*."

"I like you," he said. "Offer you a drink?"

She nodded and Michael poured one of the cups half full and handed it to her. He poured himself one, a little less than half when he noticed how frantically his hands shook, and took a sip. Before he realized it he was pouring another. When that one was empty, he sat on the edge of the bed next to her and flopped back.

"I guess you're probably not too surprised," he said, "but I'm thinking about sleeping with you."

"Well, we are in your hotel room. Guess I'm setting myself up for that."

He breathed deeply, rattling the inside of his rib cage. "Just don't know."

"If you can? How much have you had to drink?"

"I don't know what I'm supposed to do."

"You a virgin?"

"No. I was married once, which means I was involuntarily celibate, but no." His voice trailed off.

"I don't know if I'm ready, either. I mean, I just met you yesterday after all."

"I understand, but that's not your reason."

"Are you calling me a whore?" she said, trying and failing to maintain some jest in her voice.

"No. There's something else."

She shrugged and looked out the window at the fluorescent light shining down on the parking lot. She had not brought anything with her, just her purse, and she could just grab that and go.

"Yes, there is something else," he said.

A faint smile crossed her face. A tear followed. "Some pervert touched my crotch."

Michael nodded and said, "I'm sorry."

She took a long look at him. The last thing she'd expected to hear was something close to empathy. She had set herself up for a crude joke, his livelihood, yet his response was simply *I'm sorry.* "Yeah. Just the other night."

"Well, you're safe here."

Dana smiled. Almost laughed. The funny thing was that she actually felt safe. For only a short space, she thought, but that had to count for something. "I'm afraid."

"You should be. I'm a tiger."

"I'm afraid to go back to work. I'm afraid to see him again."

Michael looked at her. His head still ached, his heart still pounded, but he had no idea what to say, or if he did, how to say it. There was always the option of getting more booze, coke, and end up scaring the hell out of her. But then there was the fear that she'd gravitate to him, and there was nothing like adding to the collection of psycho women he'd met. This one, Dana, seemed different. At least he hoped she was. He just didn't know why he felt this way. There had been nothing to base this on, and if there were, it was so brief or whimsical that it should have been overlooked. Now she sat in his hotel room, and it violated every instinct in him not to want to sleep with her. There was the opportunity, and she certainly qualified as attractive, so there had to be something wrong with him to not jump on her now.

Instead he found himself sweating and drinking another cup of Arkansas wine. With the early morning ahead he knew he should probably try to sleep, but that did not seem possible even if he had been inclined.

"I thought you'd be all over me," she said, breaking into his thoughts.

"I'm not real good with the ladies. That's why I normally kill them first and then have sex with them. It seems to work in everyone's best interest that way."

"Oh."

"That was a stupid thing to say. I'm just nervous, and when I get nervous I just start talking."

"Don't be nervous. And if it's all the same to you, don't talk about killing me and then violating my corpse. I'm not a prude, but that doesn't sit well with me."

"A friend once told me that necrophilia is a victimless crime."

"You should write that on one of your little scraps of paper."

He turned to look at the paper but just shrugged.

"So why are you afraid to go home?" she asked.

"If I told you, you'd laugh."

"Isn't that your business?"

"I'd need a few more drinks for that confession to come through," he said, staring at the blank television.

"That's not the excuse you're looking for."

He breathed deeply, said, "Okay," and before he could stop himself, began speaking.

CHAPTER TWENTY-TWO

Outside of Timothy, none of the Clovers had to go to court. And because of his contagious smile and timely wit, the judge decided that it would be a waste to send such a man to prison. It would also be a waste to let things continue as they had, so it was mandated that he go to intensive outpatient therapy for drug addiction and behavior modification, as well as routine urine tests and a couple of days of community service. Outside of that, he just had to behave himself, because if something else showed up, there was plenty of reason to send him away long enough to wipe that smile off his face permanently.

He was also spared the punishment of having to knock on his own door. His wife went to pick him up and take him home. There were only a few forms to fill out, a treatment plan and things he didn't bother to read but filled out in triplicate none the less. That was it, and he was in the passenger seat, back to see his children.

The drive back was not long, but it was silent. Neither had anything to say. Both looked tired, but they were able to find comfort without speaking. Not even a mention of the grass needing cut or a sale at the grocery store. The only news in the neighborhood had come from the drama at their own household, so there was no idle gossip about what anybody else had done.

A few well-wishing neighbors had come over to offer support, even though they had no idea why. It was just the type of thing to say, along with the trite *we'll be praying for you* line. All they wanted was to gnaw at the meat of the misery while it was still fresh, and then go away with the feeling that they had done some good. Suzie had wanted to scream at them, but that would only result in more police cars. Instead, she gave a thin smile and thanked them for the much-needed prayer.

When the car pulled into the driveway, several of the curtains moved in the neighboring houses. Suzie looked over at her husband, who noticed the onlookers as well. Timothy shrugged and waved to a few who either nervously waved back or hid behind the drapes, trying to maintain some stealth delusion. As soon as he turned away, they resumed their gawking.

He paused at the first stair leading up to the house. Suzie, a half-step behind, stopped immediately as he did, staring at the back of his head.

"I don't have the keys," he said.

She continued to gaze blankly. When he took in a long, deep breath she felt her keys grow warm in her hands. "Oh," she said. "Of course."

Fumbling for the house key, she clenched it tightly and had to try several times to get it to slide into the lock. Her trembling hands made the simple act of entering the house nearly impossible, and she thought about knocking, but that felt wrong. It felt—

She battled a thought from her head she didn't know was there, and then entered her home. Having Timothy right behind her was startling, and she considered not screaming to be a minor victory.

The door opening woke Michael from a dream. A dream that felt familiar but faded immediately. Dreaming in the daylight, Michael missed the comfort that the cover of night provided. Instead he had to go downstairs. Sooner or later he had to face his father, to apologize, accept an apology, or come to an unspoken agreement that there was no need to discuss any part of this ever again.

Michael held onto that hope. Silence had to be the best option. His mother clearly would not speak of this. If his father remained, then things might continue being close to okay. After all, the nightmare had ended. But the residue of something else remained in his head.

Walking on ice, ice that was not cold, and somehow he was not alone. The more he thought about it, the more he needed to leave his room. Plus, the time had come to face his father one again.

He had slept on top of his blankets, even though a chill entered his body as soon as he'd put his head on the pillow.

From the top of the stairs, Michael saw Jessie fall deep into her father's embrace. He kissed the top of her head, and she walked away with a beaming smile. The gleam on her face did not fade as she saw Michael; it only brightened. But then, just as quickly, it was gone. The smile on their mother's face looked artificial, but that had come to be expected.   And Michael didn't blame her for that. After all, what in her life could provide her with hope and promise? Her husband and son had just gotten out of their own age-appropriate jails, and something simply was not right between Jessie and her.

"Mikey, can you come down here? Please." Timothy looked up at Michael and opened his arms. "Please, Michael."

Each step felt faulty, and he had to hold on to the handrail to keep from tumbling over and ruining an otherwise perfect moment with a broken neck. Walking downstairs had never been so arduous, especially now with his father's unwavering expression. While not unkind, it did not look overly friendly. At least not natural. His smile did not agree with his eyes. Lost somewhere in his gaze were too many thoughts and feelings, all swirling around too feverishly to be held on to or recognized with any clarity. It made his smile look like his mouth had simply fallen agape.

"Michael," he said slowly. "I just want to apologize. I just want to—"

When he got to the bottom step, Michael jumped into his father's arms. His reflexes had slowed greatly, and they both nearly toppled over, Michael's face red and wet with tears. When Timothy retained a little composure, he ran his hands through his son's hair and tousled it like he was a toddler again. No complaints came from Michael; he had needed to act too grown up earlier. This simply turned things around. A little balance, a little order, could be restored.

"Welcome home, Dad."

Even with feeble arms, Timothy's embrace nearly suffocated him. Michael had to push back a little as he looked up at his father, whose lips trembled violently.

"I'm sorry, just a little—"

"Not trying to complain. But nothing ruins an emotional family gathering like being choked to death."

136

"My little comedian," Timothy said, and without having to say another word, released Michael.

"Are you home tonight, Daddy?" Jessie asked, falling back into her father's vacated arms.

"Well," Suzie said, "I, um, hope so."

"Not all night. Sorry, sweetie. Got a meeting. Got a lot of meetings coming up. Some are for family, too, and to finish, or graduate, as they put it, I need you all to come. At least once."

"I'll go to help you," Jessie said. "Tonight?"

"Not tonight. But soon. Very soon," Timothy said and turned to Michael. "But I will have time for dinner. Want to help me whip up a specialty?"

"Uh, yeah."

"Well, come on," he said and led Michael into the kitchen and grabbed a plastic garbage bag.

Timothy opened the refrigerator and stared inside. He rolled the plastic bag into a ball and then opened it and smoothed it out. Making sure his son was watching, he pulled out the two bottles of wine dropped them in. The bottles dropped to the bottom with a faint thud as they pulled down on his arms and slightly hit the linoleum floor, their outlines perfectly formed in the otherwise empty bag.

"Did they break?" Michael asked.

"Doesn't look like it. That would be an ironic way to come home and fuck things up."

In the back of the refrigerator were eight cans of Miller Lite. This time he gently placed them in the bag—the plastic was already close to ripping. Timothy reached for the bottle of Crown Royal, held the intricate bottle, and placed that on top of the other alcohol. He tied a big knot and handed it to his son.

"Can you take this outside for me?" Timothy asked. "I know I'm not in the place to ask any favors, but this would help me an awful lot."

Michael felt like he should say something but only picked up the bag and left. It was not until he was halfway through the living room that he realized he had interrupted a conversation between his mother and sister. From the look of disgust on her face, Jessie had resisted a hug from her mom but had given in just to make peace.

They looked at the clear plastic that only put a faint film over its contents and looked away. Jessie tried not to smile, but she could not help herself. She could only temper the enthusiasm that would have been out of place in the Clover house that day.

"That's an expensive load of trash," Suzie said in a very audible whisper.

"Should I—"

"No. Just take it out. Guess it's better that way."

Michael shrugged and took the bag outside. As he passed back through the front door, he looked out at the neighborhood. Dusk had begun to settle in and cast a lilac tint intersected by the stream following two airplanes going in different directions. He stared at the planes, wondering what it must be like to be onboard either of them, on some other course, wherever that might be. He thought about trying to run and catch that plane.

Tomorrow meant back to school, and if having to feign interest in algebra was difficult, having to hear the huddles of assholes giggling about where he'd been and what new rumors had fallen into discourse would be impossible. Was it even his job to correct the lies and exaggerations? If so, how?

He opened the lid of the garbage can and dropped the bag inside. One of the beer cans popped as the bag hit bottom and hissed violently for a few seconds. The sound silenced as he put the lid on the can and started walking back to the house.

There would be no chance of Jessie staying in the living room when he walked back inside. Brothers and sisters often hate each other—at least that's what they say—but in the few moments Michael had spent with his sister since he had returned home, he knew with absolute certainty that his sister abhorred him and may have for a while. It had just taken a tragedy to bring such a truth to light.

He did not think he'd given her some specific reason, at least before he'd beat up her father in front of her. Things were different now. No matter how much everyone might pretend that perfect normalcy had replaced dysfunction, a simple fact remained that some damage simply cannot be undone. Maybe Jessie was still just tired and wounded, but if it were deeper than that, he did not know what he could possibly do about it. Once things settled, or fell into another rut, maybe he would be able to talk to her. But that felt like it would be a long way off.

Michael stopped at the front door and sighed. Too much had been lost, and every healing moment brought with it too much clarity. Would anybody blame him if he opened up that garbage bag and finished off the contents? There would be plenty of excuses and maybe even some misguided sympathy.

When he walked back inside, Jessie had already retreated to her room. His mother looked sadly at him, like she had been able to read his thoughts and disapproved of them.

"Did you walk that all the way to the dump?" she asked.

"Thought I'd give the garbage man a break. Nobody ever seems to care about the garbage man."

"Go help your father."

Michael went back into the kitchen, where Timothy had hamburger meat already browning on the skillet. The pot on the stove was close to boiling and ready for the spaghetti to be dropped in. A jar of Ragu sat next to the sizzling meat. Timothy was always so meticulous in how he poured the sauce onto the unseasoned hamburger.

"I don't have to leave until about 8:30 tonight," Timothy said. "And I don't really like *The Facts of Life* all that much, but your sister does, so can you put extra napkins on the coffee table so we can eat out there?"

"Yeah. Yeah, I can do that."

His mother had left the living room, so Michael got everything ready for a meal in front of the television without having to answer why he did not clear off the dining table. The last thing he wanted to do was tell her he didn't know what to do with all the documents about such lovely topics as domestic disturbance and substance abuse.

For now, he was home, even if he was not entirely sure what that meant, and maybe for a short while, he could sit with his family and pretend.

***

Dinner was uneventful except for the unspoken tension. No talk of homework or chores escaped their mother's mouth, but even that could not be enjoyed. The laugh track on the television served as interaction.

When the closing credits began to roll, Timothy stood up and brought his plate into the kitchen. The rest of the family watched in silence, noticing he had barely taken a bite. He scraped the uneaten portion into the garbage and washed his portion of the dishes.

As he walked back into the living room, the rest of the family shifted like they had not been watching him. They turned their attention back to a commercial.

"Loved ones," he said. "Looks like I'm off to a meeting. Won't be too long, but you might be in bed by the time I get home."

Michael looked at his father. All he saw was a smile too big to be real and eyes too distant to see them. When he shut the door behind him, Suzie turned off the television.

"Is Dad going to one of those meetings?" Jessie asked.

"I hope so."

"Mom," Michael said. When she didn't look his way, he continued. "I'm going upstairs to do some homework. You know me, always reading ahead."

She nodded and left the room. Michael sat quietly next to his sister for a few seconds. All she did was shrug her shoulders as if to say *well, what did you expect?* There was no eye contact, and she left for her room.

He didn't want to sit with her, and he didn't want to be alone. He didn't want to be alone with his thoughts, but worse than that, he knew he wouldn't be able to stand having someone validate what he was thinking. And what if his father had every intention of going to one of those magical meetings, but along the way another thought came his way? And what if that thought pulled more weight than the previous? Or maybe it held more power over him than his own family did. From what Michael could tell, it was probably of greater influence than even his own life.

Things were turning to shit, and there was no way he could deny his part in it. A peaceful end could have been reached at the dinner table the other night. He'd simply chosen not to go that route. Of course the blood from his dying family was on his hands.

Only one of the beer cans had broken outside in the trash. He'd taught himself how to drink it, and right then it sounded really good. The Crown Royal, even better. And if one thing was certain, his mother would not go out and look for him. She was not leaving her room for the night, and he knew he wouldn't see her tomorrow before school. Few things in life were as predictable as her escapes into seclusion.

If his father caught him out there, he couldn't take a higher ground. And if Jessie saw anything, well, she was not talking at all.

Or he could leave. When he'd been sent to the principal's office during class one day, he'd heard his history teacher Mr. Hunley say that the class had just gotten an addition by subtraction. Most of the class laughed, even though Michael was certain some did not get the joke. But maybe that asshole was on to something. Maybe things were just better when he was gone. All could be made right again. His father could focus on what he needed to; at least he'd overheard something similar when he was dipping in a phone conversation with his assigned sponsor. His mother might be able to relax now that she had one less obligation. And Jessie, without a doubt, would be better off. Somehow his thinking felt insane and clear at the same time. If it was all a bad idea, something in his head should have triggered. Instead, there was only his head nodding in agreement and his heart somehow content.

He'd heard about these twelve-step meetings and that prayer they had to recite. He'd also overheard him say, *God, teach me to laugh again, but never let me forget that I cried.*

142

In fact, he had just seen that on one of the countless new papers lying around. He hoped that maybe something could be salvaged. Maybe it wasn't too late.

In the quiet house, he went to his room to prepare for what promised to be a very busy next day.

CHAPTER TWENTY-THREE

The makeshift vacation had done more harm than good. Eventually, Dana would have to return. After all, what else did she have? Apply for the corporate job she could never get and could not do even if they offered the damned thing to her? But with every hour off, with every free moment, her mind had wandered, and that was a dangerous thing. Eventually, her name—back to the horrid Angel—would be called and she'd be naked under the spotlight again.

The art of stripping. Entice the crowd to throw money her way in exchange for an unobstructed view of her breasts and vagina. That, in a nutshell, is what she did for a living. It was who she was, what she had become. A chill overtook her, like she was going to be sick for real this time, unlike when she'd made her voice sound haggard when she called in. It would be consecutive days, so she could call it one instance, not like what she did was so important that absenteeism counted against her. She was climbing a pole after all, not a corporate ladder.

She sat in the car of Whispers' parking lot as the radio aired a commercial for the next show coming to the comedy club.

She turned off the radio and remained in silence. Michael was gone. He'd gone back home, albeit kicking and screaming, and it wasn't like she had his phone number or any contact information. He was probably off meeting some other girl in a hotel room who wouldn't want to just talk. And she couldn't blame him for that. She, perhaps better than anyone, knew how men were.

Yeah, he'd just have sex with some chick without giving Dana a second thought. What reason had she given him to think otherwise?

But as much as she tried to convince herself that she'd made no impact on him, she knew better. Or maybe this was just a fantasy turned around on her for a change. It would have been so easy for them to sleep together, and by most people's standards, it was okay. Instead they'd shared something completely incomprehensible. Intimacy. Thoughts, fears, dreams, and things that just felt more important than anything else imaginable. Of course she had acted like a giddy schoolgirl. Yes, he'd been high and she'd been drunk, but she could not deny there had been something special. She also could not deny that it was over now. Or it was nothing to begin with, which was much more likely.

It was just one night, and while it may not have been special to anyone else, it was to her. Now, if she wanted to survive, she just had to forget about it and let it fade in her memory. She'd done it before, after all. The best thing for her now would be to get back to work at being someone else's temporary fantasy.

Dana stepped out of the car, put her keys in the zipper section of her purse and started to walk in. Guess it was now officially too late to call in sick. One of the security guards saw her coming and opened the door.

"Angel," he said with a nod.

She walked past him and into the dim club. Purple and blue lights flickered off the wall. The smell of Dollar General brand perfume and the residue of cigarette smoke served as an unmistakable reminder that she indeed was back.

Mariah Carey's "Sweet Sweet Fantasy Baby" was coming out of the speakers. That meant Coraline was in her second song. Coraline must have been going for some sort of misdirected sentimental appeal, or more likely, she did not like to dance fast. She was also known for putting excessive amounts of glitter on her chest. Dana was suspect of anyone who needed to bring extra attention to her breasts. Guys were already looking at them, and they didn't give a damn about sparkly confetti.

"Feeling okay there, sugar?" Elijah asked, startling Dana.

"Yeah. You know, one of those things."

"Oh. Well, I get it. If it was a heavy day, you ain't gonna make a whole lot of tips if you bleed all over the stage. Some may like it, but those aren't the ones you want around, if you know what I'm saying. Real weirdos out there. Sick fucks."

"No. It wasn't—" she began and stopped herself. "Glad you understand, Eli."

"Been around a while, kid."

Yes, there were some sick people walking through the doors, but if she was delusional enough to actually believe that things would just somehow magically change, then she was more insane than anyone else. She still had to get dressed and be ready for hours of dancing and begging for dollars. At least she knew she could make the money. That would have to be the lone consoling focus. And maybe it would be a good night and she'd have the next month's rent paid. Sometimes

Wednesdays could be profitable. Guys would come in knowing the week was half over. Dana was surprised Elijah never used a "hump day" promotion. Perhaps he'd never thought of it. She certainly would not feed the idea to him.

"Well, good to see you here."

"Glad to be back," she said

CHAPTER TWENTY-FOUR

This was worse than returning from a summer vacation or a long weekend. Michael rolled over and looked at his alarm clock, knowing he could not avoid what he had to face. Maybe just another day, but if he were to find a way to skip school today, the thought of returning would so fully consume him that he might as well just go.

In less than twenty minutes, the harsh buzz of the alarm would announce that morning had arrived. He didn't need to be told that day. After a night of intermittent napping, he almost welcomed daybreak.

Michael waited until he heard movement from other parts of the house before he did anything. There was still plenty of time to brush his teeth, take a shower, and make it to school well before the bell. The typical morning saw Michael and Ugh running in at the last second. For them that was not only okay, it was the design. But today he had to keep as few eyes on him as possible. There would be no way to avoid the stares and questions. After all, this was the good stuff. This was the type of thing that didn't let up easily. He knew that if he were on the other side, he most certainly would have had all sorts of fun with it. And for a very long time. Against some things there is no defense, and against some enemies there is no white flag.

The only connection between this day and something resembling normal was the silence. Nobody was ever talkative this early, and Michael was already grateful that there would be no attempt at forced conversation. Just the normal routine. That would feel better than anything. If he tried hard enough, he might have been able to pretend nothing had happened. School would be boring, but he'd get through it, and then he would hang out with Ugh and later watch some TV. That would be a dream come true.

For some strange reason, he feared talking to his mother more than his father. He'd seen neither this morning, just rustling behind closed doors. Maybe he figured he had wounded Mom more than Dad, but what about his sister? Who else?

His bladder was close to capacity, and he did not want to start off what promised to be a bad day by pissing all over himself.

***

Once he had taken a leak, showered, and brushed his teeth, it was time to go downstairs and face whoever else was there.

His mother barely looked at him as she sipped her coffee. He was just shocked that she had left her room. Jessie was ready to go with her schoolbag already draped over her right shoulder.

"Your father went to an early meeting," Mom said as Michael looked around for him. "Then off to work, where he has some catch-up and explaining to do."

That was the extent of his conversation with his mother for the day. She took her coffee and went into her room, shutting the door loudly behind her. His mother had a way of closing a door that was not quite slamming it, but hard enough to get attention.

Jessie adjusted the bag on her shoulder and stood upright. She started to walk out the door even though she normally wouldn't have left for another forty-five minutes. He began to ask her why she was planning such an early departure but thought better of it.

He and Ugh usually made it to school on time, always just barely. No merit had ever been handed out for being early. And only tardiness was counted. So as long as he avoided that, he would be okay. Plus, he'd figured while playing on his calculator one day that if he got to school fifteen minutes early every day for an entire school year, that would be nearly an extra forty-eight hours at school. And what was the point of that? He simply could not fathom freely giving up that much time. And if he got an hour detention here or there, he'd still be way ahead on his imaginary scoreboard.

"Hope you're ready for today," Jessie said as she walked out the door.

Even if he had an answer ready, she would not have heard it as the door shut, leaving him standing in the room alone. His mother had already retreated to her room and was not coming out while he was still home, or for all he knew, ever again. His father was off for the day. The house was unnaturally quiet. More so because there were two people in it and no chance of a word being spoken.

Maybe leaving early was a good idea for today. He usually waited for Ugh, but there was the very real chance that his friend might not want to be seen with him. Any number of rumors had certainly popped up, and would Ugh really want to get caught in the middle of something so ugly? Truth did not matter here. There was no counteracting a lie once it had run through the school, so the best thing anyone could do was to simply walk away. Hell, he couldn't even convince himself that he would act differently in reversed roles.

As he stepped onto the front porch, he looked up at the pink sky. The sun was just starting to light the eastern sky and would have been beautiful on another occasion. Wisps of clouds crossed the stratosphere. A light gray semi-covering raced across the sky from a wind Michael could not feel. He was never up this early, and when he was, he never found himself pleasant enough to enjoy such a moment.

But if he left now, would he and Jessie be the only ones at school? The day would be awkward, and she'd certainly left to get away from him, so the last thing she wanted was to see him now. Plus, she had gone through this already. Maybe he could pretend that everything was going to be all right. Maybe he could pretend that Jessie was okay as well.

The second seemed more far-fetched than the previous. What had Jessie endured the day before? And she was so damn sensitive. He always knew that would be some kind of downfall, but he just didn't want it to be his fault.

On an ordinary day he would wait around for Ugh. But the mere thought of anything ordinary somehow made his stomach turn. Everything was still the same, but nothing looked right.

Could he even expect Ugh to walk with him? He would not blame him. Yeah, sure they were friends, but there had been nothing to test that, and he hated all the melodrama around that talk. Either he'd be there or he wouldn't, and no further thought would be needed. But he now had time and reason to think about these things. Nothing is ever promised, especially on school grounds.

Michael stopped on the first step of the front porch. The neighborhood was peaceful. The sky was still rich with color but was beginning to fade as the sun rose in the east. No airplanes crossed the sky, just the jet residue of one that was now likely hundreds of miles away.

Jessie was probably halfway to school already. She had already faced the wolves. Now she was off to face them again. His sensitive sister had likely been tormented, and those bastards would not have stopped until she was crying or bleeding. That was the rule of the schoolyard. Probably universal. He hated that she was in such a position. And it was not like he had ever really been nice to her on other occasions. He was a bully to her, just one that left her alone sometimes. And not because he was being nice—he just didn't want to get in trouble at home as well.

But that was simple survival. He just wished she had understood that earlier. Her life would be so much easier without him. That was as simple as it was undeniable. Michael swore to himself that he would never do anything to hurt her again, but was it too late? Maybe not, but it was damage control time.

It was probably that imbecile Kent Stapleton who started and finished the attack on Jessie. Did she cry in front of everyone, or was she able to hold it in? Was that the only victory she could have?

He began to walk to school. Now he knew he was being watched as a few curtains moved. People never felt the need to be as clandestine when it was a kid in their sights. The same

153

rights didn't apply, apparently. Maybe Jessie had the right idea about getting a head start on everything. She could be pretty smart sometimes.

There would certainly be time to kill when he got to the school grounds. Maybe he could just sit on a picnic table and pretend to read or, depending on what time they opened the building, go to the library. As long as he wasn't loud, he figured he could do whatever he wanted to in there. And it would be safe.

He also was certain that he should walk without Ugh today. If he left now, he knew without a doubt he would walk alone. That part he did not mind. But if he waited, then he might have to wonder. And he had enough to think about already.

CHAPTER TWENTY-FIVE

Waking up on the road with no concept of time or place had become the norm for Michael during his tour with Drew. He had grown accustomed to it rather quickly. But waking up and knowing exactly where he was and how long it would take to get to their destination filled him with unshakable anxiety.

"Welcome home," Drew said, startling Michael.

They were still about an hour outside Cincinnati. He'd slept though Indianapolis and just about everything else. Few landmarks stood between the two nearly identical Midwestern cities. When he was younger the family had visited Indianapolis. Michael had not understood the point. Everything about it looked familiar, and putting the Clovers together in an un-air-conditioned car in August could not lead to anything good.

"Yeah, it's been a while," he answered.

From most of the previous miles they'd traveled, Michael found Drew's quiet nature unsettling. Now he just wanted to suffer in his own silence.

"I've been through Cincy a number of times. Last visit, I had a three-way."

Michael laughed. "If you have a three-way in Cincinnati, you have to worry about cholesterol and not chlamydia."

Now Drew smiled, not something he had shown much of. "If you do a show here, use that. Home cooking line, so to speak."

Michael didn't know where it began, but somewhere, someone had gotten the idea of putting chili, with chocolate as one of its ingredients, over spaghetti, then covering it with cheese. Most stoners he knew wouldn't even try that. And apparently nobody thought anything of calling this cuisine a three-way. Michael found that most people not from the Cincinnati area did not know what to make of the name...or the taste.

"We won't be in town long, but there might be time to hit an open mic. Unless you got some family obligation."

"Not that I know of."

"Your family still lives there, right?"

Michael nodded, not sure if Drew was even looking in his direction. "Childhood house sold long ago in favor of some condo. Not sure if I even have a current address on my sister."

"Ah," Drew said, like all was understood. "Might be good for you just to catch up a bit."

Michael thought that was probably good advice, then he realized he didn't know a thing about Drew. All he knew he'd read off his website's profile. He knew he had been divorced, but that was nothing new or interesting. Michael thought about Tammy, his own ex-wife, which didn't happen often. She might have still lived in Cincinnati. Who knew? He certainly didn't care. A three-month marriage where the majority of the wedded bliss time involved divorce proceedings wasn't much to talk about. It didn't matter. He wanted to have a threesome.

He'd just forgotten to invite his wife, so it had ended up being a sloppy, drunken hookup with the equally sloppy and drunken neighbor. Since Tammy was the breadwinner of the family, or the only one who bothered to get up and seek any type of employment, she felt all the more betrayed. Michael could not remember the last time he'd heard anything from her.

They continued to speed past the endless cornfields, only broken up by the occasional truck stop or mega-church built to have a compelling view of Interstate 74. He didn't want to talk any longer, but if he were rude to Drew Greene, he might not have a friend in the world. Well, maybe except for Dana. And some of the guys back at Captain Riley's. But those were just drinking buddies. As for Dana, well, he found he couldn't think of her very long. At least not right now. And wasn't she just a stripper? What was he thinking? Regardless, he'd probably scared her off.

"So what part of Cincinnati are you from?" Drew asked after they went another mile.

"North College Hill. There's no college there in case you were wondering. Or in College Hill for that matter"

"I see."

"It's about fifteen minutes from downtown. It used to be called the northwest, but they kept building so much more shit up from there that it's just kind of in the middle."

Drew nodded, obviously bored but okay with making some type of small talk. Michael just wondered why he'd started now.

Michael sighed. A few more miles passed before Drew spoke again. "Now is that where we found you?"

The *we* sounded strange. While Michael knew Drew had a manager, he never talked business, and while he had a cell phone, he never used it in the car. All professional matters must have been discussed behind closed hotel room doors. It always looked like Drew was just a man out on his own.

"Well," Michael said, "Woodland Falls is north of Cincinnati, south of Dayton. Worked in a factory, moved into a cheap apartment. Found a dive bar where I could tell jokes, and here we are."

"Why'd you move up there?"

He still didn't know the answer. "It was quiet." This sounded reasonable enough, at least not something to be questioned. "Work wasn't so bad, cheap rent, and, well, after the divorce—"

"That's hard."

"Well, it was a long time ago," Michael answered and cursed where his nervous chatter had led him.

"Still tough. Somehow my parents are still together, still alive and kicking, and only moderately ashamed of what I do for a living. What does your family think of where you are now?"

"Don't know." Michael was surprised he could be so candid with his reply. "Haven't been in touch since I left. Wasn't in touch before that either."

Drew nodded and remained quiet for a few more stretches of farmland. "Now what about that fine little filly you left the bar with?"

"One of the most articulate exotic dancers I ever met."

"Hope she made for a fine evening."

"Actually, nothing happened."

The car swerved slightly as Drew looked over. "You couldn't close the deal with a stripper?"

Michael nodded.

"Now *that's* funny."

CHAPTER TWENTY-SIX

After a few days back on the job, Whispers was beginning to feel comfortable once again. At least as comfortable as it could be. Dana inspected each new face that walked in and found herself sizing up one's capacity for danger. She knew his intentions, of course. There was no hiding that, so why even pretend? Lust paid the bills for her; there was no moral high ground to take here. The more she expected it, the better off she would be.

And once guys stopped turning into knuckle-dragging Neanderthals around her, well, this dream—or whatever it was—ended. Then there would be no livelihood, no survival. She could picture herself as cashier a in a grocery store, with aspirations of one day being a customer service manager who lived for her fifteen-minute cigarette break. She didn't smoke now, but that would end up just being part of her new life.

Maybe she could mix up her song selection, make herself a little more relevant. Not that anyone would notice, but some things she just had to do for herself. It would keep interested, and that in itself was the little pick-me-up she was looking for.

And it could be something to help her get through the day. It would be a minor victory, but damn it, it was her victory.

"Hey, Angel," Buster said. "Same song list?"

She nodded. "Yeah. For now."

"Okay. You're on next."

And she sat on the side of the stage, waiting for her show to start all over once again.

CHAPTER TWENTY-SEVEN

Homeroom wasn't even over by the time Michael wanted to leave. Nobody said much of anything to him as he'd arrived early by anyone's standards, preposterous by his own. Father Wilfong had let him inside even though the school doors had yet to open. Michael wondered if he'd done the same for Jessie but did not want to ask. He was also grateful he was not offered sympathy or wisdom. He didn't think he could handle either right now. Instead, he was perfectly content with sitting silently in the hallway, waiting for the teacher to unlock the classroom where he could take his seat and wait a little longer for her to take attendance.

He got a few strange glances, which was made worse by loud whispers telling the offending party *not* to look. Did they actually believe he would think they weren't talking about him? Subtlety was completely lost on some people.

Ugh waved and gave him a *where-the-hell-were-you-this-morning* glance. That felt better than anything that morning. At least he had looked for him. Michael would apologize later. In that aspect, things were normal.

When Mrs. Foley said, "Michael Clover," for roll call, Andy Kent, another asshole who'd probably sought out Jessie yesterday, called out, "I think he's in prison."

"Mister Kent, march your smart ass to Mr. Krueller's office immediately. You were warned."

Hearing that warnings had been preemptively sent filled Michael with new anxiety. Of course he knew, but he could have gone quite a while without having it confirmed. Couldn't he remain in blissful ignorance until after lunch?

The rest of the class was not going to settle down anytime soon, and if he wanted to say anything, pretend to be some sort of alpha, well, then this was his time. He could act up, threaten, do whatever he wanted in these next few minutes, and then find the justification, but such would not be the case. He couldn't. He wanted to, sure as hell, but all he could do was remain in his seat.

Mrs. Foley was a veteran teacher, or old as the kids put it, and knew better than to fuel their fire. All she had to do was show a little disapproving patience, and soon the feeding frenzy would halt. Suppressing a laugh only gives it new life. Once it was out, it usually had a shorter shelf life. Even in junior high. Discipline would be easier, but sometimes the applecart doesn't need to be any more upset than it already is.

By the time she finished attendance, the bell rang, and they were off to be scattered throughout the building. Now Michael was in no hurry to go anywhere.

"Tough guy coming through," someone said as he walked past. He didn't recognize the voice and never saw a face.

"Jailbird," was spoken by another anonymous passerby.

162

And in a failed theatrical voice, Jamie Baines, unquestionably one of the biggest douche bags in the school, muttered, "Psycho."

By the time he made it to first-period history, he was already exhausted. He'd never prided himself on being a great or even decent student, but he did hope that he'd be able to learn a little something today—about nothing in particular—and be distracted from the side show. He didn't want to be the show any longer. Too much spotlight already.

But for now there was no end in sight. He dreaded lunch. He feared study hall. Maybe he could just run away. Perhaps the circus was hiring.

***

Before he realized it, the day was progressing. Yeah, there were snide comments; he could deal with that. But as he felt himself drifting to sleep in science class, with no interruptions, with no outside influence, something inside hurt. And it hurt so badly he almost found himself crying. Now new fears entered him. What would happen if he actually did start to cry? No damage control in the world could be effective if he sobbed like a baby girl in front of everyone. He doubted that even Jessie did that.

What he found himself hating the most were the looks of sympathy. He didn't know how to deal with that. What would he say? Thanks for your pity? Yes, my life really does suck?

And while he still heard murmurs about *juvie* and jokes about being locked up when the more inane of the bullies tapped their lockers, there was nothing to be upset about any longer. He had nothing to explain. And he still had his family to defend.

***

"Hey, Clover," Kent Stapleton said while he was walking to the final class of the day. "How was jail?"

His piss-poor excuse for an entourage laughed hysterically behind him. There were even high fives after such a clever line.

"It was better for me than for your dad," Michael said loudly enough to gather a crowd. "Felt kinda sorry for him as he got bent over and fucked by all those guys with the misspelled tattoos. But he still said it was better than a night with your mom."

"Fuck you."

"And really? *How was jail?* That's the best you could come up with? How about, *Clover, you're the only guy who gets extra credit in detention?* Or, *Did you get locked up because for you that's career day?*"

Stapleton just stared back.

"Is that the best you got? Are you really that pathetic that you can't think of anything better to say? And the sad thing is, you actually thought this out, ran it by your gang of remedial readers back there, and you still went forward with it. I've always known that you're a fifth-generation inbred idiot who jerks off to the pee-wee football team under the bleachers, but I sadly underestimated how disturbingly stupid you are. I mean, wow!"

"You're dead," Stapleton said.

"See, there you go again. Another cliché. You're even more of a backwoods hick than your uncle who took your sister to homecoming. By the way, congratulations on being related to that genetic concoction."

Stapleton ran at him, but before he got there a school bag flashed across Michael's field of vision and caught Kent directly in the nose. The sound of something like a twig snapping preceded the scream by about a second. He fell down to his knees before crumpling over to the side. The blood flowed out copiously, pouring into his mouth, painting his teeth a light pink as he cried and screamed, attracting the rest of the school and every possible faculty member.

So many yells. Not from just the dipshit with the shattered nose, but from the teachers hollering something to him. He could not hear any of it. He couldn't stop smiling either.

Ugh still held the book bag, which was soon to be Exhibit A, in his hands. Michael hadn't seen him there before, but he was glad to know that he wasn't alone. The only other face he was able to see was Jessie peeking out from between all the other gawkers. Her eyes were vacant, but he did see her lips turned up into something that was probably close to a grin.

Before Michael could get a better look at his sister, he was led to the principal's office by a grip that was bound to leave a bruise. It's always the gym teacher who is first to lead such a march. When Michael looked over, he saw that Ugh was being lead down another hallway. The school nursed raced past them as Kent Stapleton's echoing screams continued.

***

Part of the punishment in being lead to the principal's office was that long wait for justice to be handed down. Today, however, there was no wait and no principal. Father Wilfong walked in and sat in the chair next to him, not behind the desk.

"Bad day?" the priest said.

"Better than yesterday."

Father Wilfong nodded. "I see."

They both remained silent, and Michael avoided any type of eye contact. There was no way of escaping Wilfong's stare.

"Son, now, I don't condone violence. But that kid really did have it coming. Off the record, of course. And I heard what you said to him."

Michael's face turned a bright red.

"Don't worry. I've heard all those words before. You're not going to shock me with that."

Michael nodded.

"But I did notice something. Your words. You've got a gift with them. Especially in someone so young. You misuse that gift. But you misuse a lot of your abilities. I know you don't work hard, not even close. You really don't work at all. And yet you get by at the same level while others are busting their asses. Just hope you don't let that catch up to you one day."

"I guess."

"No. You know. Some kids fall through the cracks. Others choose it. Never choose to fail."

Michael shrugged.

"I know about what happened at home."

"You talked to my sister?"

Now the priest's face turned bright red.

"It's okay, Father. I won't ask about a confidential conversation."

"Okay. Just know two things. My door is always open, and what happened was not your fault."

He barely nodded.

"Don't choose to fail, Michael. Do you understand me? And now I am in the place to hand down some discipline for the fight, and your part in it. Suspension, work detail, JUGS."

Michael started to laugh but made himself stop.

"I still can't believe they named it that either," Wilfong said. "But I send you out and say *go and sin no more*. And I mean it. I would like to talk with you again, but please let it be under different circumstances."

As he got up, he whispered, "Thanks."

"You are welcome. And one more thing."

Michael sighed. He knew it couldn't be that easy.

"Your friend, K.J. Uggla. He was just defending you, right?"

"Yeah. I thought I'd be the one with the broken nose."

"Okay, well, that will be taken into consideration. Go on. The day's almost over. Don't look at yourself as being off the hook. Just know that we have an understanding."

***

Ugh was not there to walk home with Michael. Hopefully he wasn't still at school being held under a JUG, which brought a chuckle when just the thought crossed his mind. Or maybe he'd gotten into another fight with one of Stapleton's goons. Michael tried not to think about it, and with his mind swimming with so much other debris, he was back at the house before he realized it.

He beat Jessie home, which rarely happened. If his mother was still in the house, she was quiet and didn't come out to see how his day was. Probably for the best. He was too tired to make up a story about a good day. When he walked in, he did not check to see if her car was there. The more he thought about it, the more he realized he did not care.

Somehow he'd made it through the day. It had gotten a little close there at the end, but it was something he'd survived. He didn't think he had any homework and couldn't remember any of the coursework for the day. While that wasn't uncommon, he was truly clueless. Instead he walked upstairs to his room, dropped his schoolbag at the door, and before he had a chance to think of anything else, he was asleep.

He woke from a dream. As soon as he recognized it had become frightening, he somehow pulled himself out of it. But now he was more frightened because of it, disorientated and dizzy. He was also sweating, and a chill overtook him.

Someone had brought his dinner up to him and placed it on his nightstand. Finding room for a whole plate must have been the biggest chore. He also didn't know who would have brought it up to him. Maybe they tried to wake him up. While never a sound sleeper, he had also never been so tired.

And what time was it anyway? Midnight? Just before dawn? The alarm clock had been moved to make room for his plate of now cold chicken, rice, and peas, but he liked it better that way. He took a few bites, probably looking like a refugee as he did so, and just as likely spilled some on the bed and floor.

Regardless of the time, he sat up wide awake. Couldn't imagine sleeping. And the residue of the dream still held a haunting grip. He was alert enough to see the clock on the floor. 11:47. He'd been pretty close with the midnight guess, and that helped him restore some of his bearings. Since school had let out at three, and he would have been home within twenty minutes of the final bell, he'd already had a full night's sleep. Although he figured the *early to bed early to rise* axiom was not fitting here.

The television was still on downstairs. He couldn't hear much of anything, and the indecipherable mumble and flickering reflections began to irritate him. Someone probably just left the set on and walked away. Or they were asleep on the couch.

But as Michael began to walk down the stairs, he heard his father laughing. It was muffled, and he did well to contain it.

With the light from the screen, he saw tears streaming down his face.

"Hey, Mikey, shouldn't you be in bed about now?"

"Couldn't sleep anymore."

"I understand. Me neither. Come sit."

Michael went to the other end of the couch. He had to move two video rental boxes but was unable to make out what they were in the darkness.

Timothy laughed again. Michael hadn't seen or heard what was on the TV that caused his father's reaction. He turned to the screen. He recognized Robin Williams, but he knew him more as the guy who played Popeye, which was the first movie he'd seen in the theater. When *Good Morning Vietnam* came out, he begged his mother's permission to see it. In no uncertain terms, that request was denied. Something about foul language, sex, and violence. He didn't see what the big deal was. Nobody ever went broke overestimating the public's desire for any of those things.

He had never seen him in this type of setting before. This was not just a stand-up set with a fake brick wall behind him. He was on a colossal stage by himself with nothing but a microphone.

"I had to stop drinking alcohol," Robin Williams said. "I used to wake up nude in front of my car with my keys up my ass. Not a good thing."

Michael and his father howled. *Wow, that was funny.*

"Need some help? Nah, just flooded," Robin Williams continued.

More cackling. Michael actually snorted when he laughed, which he didn't think he'd ever done before. And before long his eyes watered and his side hurt.

His father continued to laugh while Michael watched intently. How could just one person be so fascinating? And it was so much more than just telling jokes. How brave would you have to be to stand up there by yourself and be funny? That had to be the hardest thing in the world. Suddenly Michael had a new hero.

It was nearly 12:30 when the end credits rolled. It felt even later. By the time Michael's eyes adjusted to the low light, he saw that his father had rented three videos. In addition to *Robin Williams: A Night at the Met*, he had *Richard Pryor: Live from the Sunset Strip* and *George Carlin: A Place for My Stuff*.

Timothy sighed as he looked at the clock. "Guess I would be a really bad father if we watched another one. Probably shouldn't have even let you watch that one, but, well, that could be our own little secret, right? If your mother doesn't know already—we weren't very quiet—she doesn't need to. Agreed?"

Michael nodded, feeling tired once again.

"Okay, now off to bed. Love you, Mikey."

He only smiled in reply, but that was enough, and he went upstairs to end what turned out to be a good day.

CHAPTER TWENTY-EIGHT

Suddenly the road ended. It certainly was not without warning since it was a path he knew so well, but he looked up to see the "Welcome to Ohio" sign, which meant they were less than twenty minutes from their destination. Home?

They had already passed Interstate 275 circling Cincinnati. They would only be about ten minutes from his childhood home. At least there were strangers living there now. If he were to make a family visit, at least the location would be different.

Drew retreated to his usual quiet place, and they rode in silence to a hotel in the northern suburbs. Michael was a little disappointed to hear that the studio had moved. He held hopes of at least seeing the downtown skyline again.

***

Michael quickly discovered that radio stations put up their guests in the nicer suites—probably a deal struck between the hotel and company to mention the amenities. This time Michael had a room with a hot tub and a big screen television. There was also a mini bar, so he poured himself a Jack Daniels on the rocks. He wasn't sure how the hotel charged for that, but he could take care of it all later. Maybe it was complimentary. Now that would make for a first-class experience.

He looked out the window. It did not look much different than any of the other views he'd seen out on the road. Convenience stores, fast food, gas stations, sometimes with all three in the same body. He didn't even see any of the places he'd never seen outside of Cincinnati. But even if he did see a United Dairy Farmers, LaRosa's, or Skyline Chili, it still didn't feel like home. Not anymore.

He poured a second Jack Daniels, no longer thinking about whether the price was included in the room.

Shortly after the radio show, at such an ungodly hour, Michael knew he would be ready to hit the road again. Hopefully fast. He also hoped that one of the late-shift guys at the radio station would have a little pick-me-up. Michael absently rubbed his nose. Not much, just a little. Someone there probably had coke. It was likely in the job description.

Or he could go out and get some now. He didn't have a car, but a bus would get him from point A to point B, and then back again. But if he was going anywhere, he figured he should see some people. Maybe he could add point C to the itinerary. It wasn't even early evening, and if he got that out of the way, then his chances of having a tolerable time would likely increase.

***

After a brief chat with an overly friendly hotel clerk, she said he could take a taxi down to University Village. It would not cost all that much, but there would be little wait. She even offered to call a cab for him, which he accepted. For some reason he was impressed with how convincing his lie about wanting to see a program at The University of Cincinnati was. Given how bent this place was on customer service, he would not have been surprised had she cut up an eight ball for him at his mere request.

"Hope you enjoy the show, Mr. Clover," she said, snapping him out of a daze, and directed him to a yellow cab that had pulled up by the front door.

"Uh, yeah. You too. I mean, thanks."

She only smiled and answered an incoming call with unimaginable perkiness. He wondered if she would share what she was taking.

"University Village?" the driver asked as Michael slid into the backseat.

"Yeah."

"Okay."

As they pulled down the road, the familiarity assaulted him. While it was hard to come home, he feared it would be harder to leave. The first time he left did not feel like it was that long ago.

***

After his second day back to school, after the world as he knew it had done an about face, life did not merely resume to normalcy. It actually felt good.

Ugh didn't even get a JUG for breaking Kent Stapleton's nose. Enough people had reported that he had acted to defend Michael, and since he hadn't attacked after the initial blow, the principal had only given him a verbal warning. Stapleton would be punished, but it had been silently determined that a broken nose was sufficient. As long as all parties remained in low profile, there did not seem to be any need to delve deeper.

Michael even heard Jessie laugh about how that jackass punk had been put in his place and that he was ugly enough even before his nose turned purple and swelled to take up most of his face. She didn't leave for school at such a ridiculously early hour anymore. Still earlier than Michael thought necessary, but there was less to hide from.

Dinner in front of the television halted as well. Trivial conversation with the family replaced trivial conversation on a sitcom.

"So, Mikey," his mother said in the middle of dinner. "I hear the football team really doesn't want you now."

"I thought that was well established."

"Yeah, they're afraid of getting too many personal fouls. Anyway, the world has plenty of athletes and honor students. But not enough who stand up to bullies. I really shouldn't say I'm proud of you for what you did. But I really can't say I'm not, either."

Michael smiled.

"I'll come out and say that I'm proud of you," his father said.

"Me too," Jessie said.

The television was not turned on at all that day.

***

A week later, a note came home from school requesting a parent to meet with the principal. The only thing that troubled Michael about it was that he had no idea why it had been sent. He'd done well enough, kept out of trouble, and had not fallen behind in any of his work. No fights or harsh words. While not the perfect student, he would have considered himself close enough.

Suzie went to the school because Timothy had an Alcoholics Anonymous meeting. She thought it might be better without him. While she wasn't sure what the school did or did not know, she assumed the notice was more an invitation to size up Timothy, and that was really nobody's business. She had long since grown tired of pathetic people using the guise of compassion to simply watch someone suffering.

Father Wilfong sat in for the principal, and Suzie was not able to mask her discomfort. He only smiled. His kind eyes put her at ease for a moment.

"Mrs. Clover, thank you for coming. Please have a seat. Can I get you something to drink?"

She was immediately glad her husband was not there. He undoubtedly would have asked for communion wine. "No, thank you."

"If you're wondering why I'm talking to you today, well, I consider it on-the-job training since I will be taking over as principal next year."

"Oh," she said, not knowing if she was supposed to have some other response. "Congratulations."

"Michael's file shows he's no stranger to this office or unsavory extracurricular activity."

She wanted to say he got it from his father, but she couldn't.

"Now, there is a place for discipline in this school—I don't deny that—but there also needs to be understanding."

Suzie nodded absently.

"We found these notes that he was writing in class." Father Wilfong pointed to wadded up paper on the desk.

"You brought me in here because he was passing notes?"

He paused again, making her even more fidgety. "He was not passing them. He was writing them to himself."

She reached for the paper and flattened it out. *I heard ignorance was bliss. Don't know about all that, but I'm happy.*

With a shrug and a soft laugh, she said, "I still don't know why I'm here."

He handed her another. *The Bible says bestiality is wrong. Do you think God was disappointed the day he actually had to tell his people not to have sex with animals?*

This time she laughed in spite of herself.

"I laughed, too," Wilfong said. "I should probably be a little ashamed of that. But there's this one too."

She opened up the third piece of paper. *The song says* Suicide is Painless, *but I'll bet a botched suicide hurts like a motherfucker.*

While still in the middle of a sigh, she opened the last one.

I hope to be like my father when I grow up. I'm halfway there. I can't hold my liquor either.

Now she was unspeakably grateful her husband was not with her.

"I hope you share in my concern."

She nodded.

"He's a bright boy," he said. "And talented...but wounded, and it breaks my heart to see someone so young suffering. Just keep an eye on him. I will be, and he knows he can come talk to me at any time should he so choose. Now with your daughter—"

"What about Jessie?"

This time his pause was more than she could handle, and a tear betrayed the stoic face. Wilfong handed her a tissue.

"Well," he said. "Nothing."

"Nothing?"

"Yes. And that's the problem. She's stopped speaking in class. Stopped turning in homework. I've asked her teachers to show her a little mercy, and they have. I ask you to show her the same mercy, however."

"Okay." Suzie reached for another tissue.

"They're both good kids. They're just not okay right now. Not sure where you stand on faith, but I pray for your whole family."

"God knows we need that."

"He does."

***

When she returned home, she felt like she held a secret that had already been revealed. No matter how strongly a delusion might take hold of her, she knew her family was in crisis. And she could not separate from it. She could not make anything right, and somehow she believed the lie she told herself—that she was the most stable one. When she saw her own children, she did not even know what to say. Michael knew she had been at the school to talk about him, and the report there really was not all that bad. Unsettling, to say the least, but at least he was not being intentionally bad. For as much as it defied logic, Michael was the easy one.

She had once hoped that Jessie would not say a word. Now that the wish had been granted, it hurt all the more. And what could she say to her now? There had to be a way to make things right.

But that would have to be another plan put on hold. Timothy did not come home that night. Suzie, Michael, and Jessie sat on the couch in front of the blank television screen until after midnight. There was no need for discussion. Everyone had the same thought and no clue what to do. The paperwork on the dining table had all sorts of phone numbers, but calling seemed unfathomable. And what would anybody say? There's a drug addict on the streets, call us if you need the body identified?

One thought kept Michael from sleeping while his mother and sister started to doze on opposite ends of the couch. He remembered his father having a hushed conversation on the phone, and then writing down an address. When Michael had walked in, his father had put that address on top of the refrigerator and tried to act casual. It was a poor acting job, but Michael hadn't thought much about it.

He found it quickly and snuck out without waking anyone. Years of sneaking out could finally be used for some good. He shut his bedroom door first, so if they woke up they might think he had just gone to bed. They would have no idea he intended to play the hero. Somebody had to.

He recognized the street name on the address.

His father had to run some *errands* by there a while back. Rosemont Avenue. It was about a mile and half away. While taking his bike would be the fastest way, opening up the garage door would make a stealth exit impossible. He might as well go on foot. Walking would be too slow, but running would look suspicious. He decided that walking by himself in the middle of the night was bound to draw a few looks, so he should just run. Less time to be seen.

By the time he made it there, he was sweating and out of breath. The house was completely unexceptional and not in such a bad neighborhood, even at night. Maybe his father was in there. Hopefully not. But if he had made it this far, how could he just turn around? If he could rescue his daddy, all could be well once again.

He knocked on the door. Heavy footsteps ran to it. A small man peered through the window at the top of the door and unfastened several locks before opening it.

"What the fuck you think you're doing? Want to wake up the whole damn neighborhood? Who the fuck are you anyway?"

The man was short and as indistinctive as the house. No tattoos or facial hair. Just someone forgotten as quickly as he'd been seen. On any other occasion, that is.

"I'm looking for my father."

"He ain't here."

"You didn't even ask who he is."

The man grabbed Michael by his shoulder and pulled him into the house. He looked outside with several nervous turns of the head before shutting and locking the door again. "Damn, kid. Could you be any louder out there?"

Disinfectant spray lingered in the air. The front entrance and side room, all that he could see, were empty with the exception of a folded up cafeteria-style table propped up against the wall. There was some movement upstairs.

"I'm looking for my father."

"And I told you he is not here. Go." The man started to unlock the door again.

"His name is Timothy Clover."

"Then he definitely isn't here. He was. But the sack of shit didn't have a damn cent on him and still wanted more. Your daddy owes me money, boy."

"Where is he?"

"Not here."

Michael turned to leave when the man grabbed him. "Leave me alone."

"Your father fucked me. He stole from me. Can you believe your old man would do that? I'll bet you can. I trusted him, and he took what didn't belong to him. Tsk tsk."

The hollow tone in his voice terrified Michael.

"Tsk Tsk."

"I'm gonna go now."

"No rush. So impatient. Just like your father. But you can do something really nice for dear old Dad. You can pay off his debt."

Michael ran for the door, but the man, despite his small frame, threw him to the floor. The fall knocked the wind from him, and as he tried to get back up again, he felt the man's knees push him back down.

"Stop! Stop it!" Michael cried, his voice echoing off the barren walls.

The man pushed his head to the ground. His nose thumped and he could taste blood and running snot.

"Pumpkin," a woman's voice said as she came down the stairs. "Pumpkin, what's going on down there? Are you okay?"

"Fine. Go back upstairs. Gotta take care of someone."

"Will you be long?"

Michael tried to scream, but a hand clamping down on his throat stopped him. He tried to kick him, but that only resulted in a punch to his ear. A new wave of dizziness hit him. "Let. Me. Go," he managed to say.

"Be up in a minute, Muffin," the man said.

"Okay. Just don't hurt him too much. The boy just made a mistake."

"I won't. Not too much. In fact, he might like this."

"You might be right. You always are."

Michael felt the fight go out of him as he was punched in the ear again. With his other ear now pinned against the ground, he could not even hear himself cry.

He became too dizzy to think. Too frightened to feel. Yet as hard as he tried to tell himself his pants weren't being pulled to his ankles, he was all too aware of it. And he thought he was fighting back, but he felt closer to operating a remote control of himself as the batteries dwindled down to nothing. A kick here, a flail there, all for nothing.

A second later his underwear were pulled down to his knees, and he couldn't understand why he wasn't fighting harder. A searing pain came as the man entered him, bringing the world back from a gray haze. Another punch in the ear returned the world to a merciful nothing.

***

Timothy came home, startling Suzie and Jessie. He tried a silent entrance, but that failed when he fell face first over the front step.

"Daddy?"

"Hi, Jeth," he mumbled. "Howth me baby?"

"You son of a bitch," Suzie said. "Do you know how worried we were?"

"Dunno."

As she began to storm back to her room and this time really slam the door, the phone rang. "Yeah. I'll bet that's the police," Suzie said as she walked toward the phone. "Hello."

She mocked surprise. "Yes, of course it's the police."

She listened on the other end and her hand began to shake.

"Mom, what's wrong?"

"No. We didn't report Michael missing. He's—"

Timothy got up from the ground and rubbed his knee. "Knew I should have fixed that step."

"He's where?" Suzie screamed. "No. He's right upstairs."

Jessie ran upstairs to check her brother's bedroom. "He's not here, Mom. He's not here!"

Suzie hung up the phone. "I know. I, uh, well, I really, really need you to stay here and babysit your father." She attempted to speak more, but she couldn't even whisper.

"What happened? What happened to Michael?" Jessie asked.

"Something happened to Mikey?" Timothy asked. "What happened?"

"He's in the hospital," she managed to say. "My baby's in the hospital."

***

She was not able to take him home until two days later. He did not want to talk. He did not want to be touched. Instead she just sat in the world's most uncomfortable chair and watched her son suffer hours of restless sleep. She only left the room for the regular ice and dressing change, so as not to invade his privacy any more than it already had been.

His sister wanted to visit, but it was decided that he didn't want to be seen like this. His face was also badly bruised, like his attacker had kicked him in the chin when he was done with him.

"I'm sorry, Mom," he said in the middle of the night. "I was just trying to find Dad and bring him home."

"It's not your fault, Mikey. You tried to be very brave."

"I won't talk to the police."

"Why not?"

"I've got to protect the family. He'll come for us. I won't let him hurt you or Jessie."

She wanted to reply that guys like that needed to be thrown in jail forever and have the same thing happen to them in the shower every night, but all she said was, "Okay. We can talk more about it later."

"No. I never want to talk about it."

"I understand that, too."

"Never."

"Okay."

The room fell into immediate silence except for a nurse pushing a cart down the hall.

"Are you okay, Mikey?"

"No. Don't ask me that again either."

***

In the week off that Michael had before going back to school, he barely left his room. At his request, he had no visitors. His mother dropped off his dinner and homework. He was actually more interested in the homework. At least it was something to do.

He ate carefully. His stomach hurt, and he was not ready to imagine the pain of a bowel movement. He wondered if that would be funny to the outside world. Maybe only if he cried.

But he couldn't do that either. He felt neither happy nor sad. With the shades drawn, there were only varying shades of gray in his room. There was no point in looking outside. What would there be to see? All he would have is an outsider's view of a world that terrified him.

It was not until a couple days later—he'd lost count almost immediately,—that his father came into his room.

"How you doing, sport?"

Michael shrugged.

"Come on, now. Your mom said you've been in here all day."

"And before that, too."

"How about you and me go out to the movies?"

"Not today."

"I can take off work early and we'll go tomorrow."

"Don't take off work."

"I was just thinking we could use a little father and son time. You know, like we used to do."

"Don't want it."

Timothy paused. "Your mother said you snuck out of the house. It's dangerous to be playing outside at night. Just glad you're not hurt."

"Nope. Not hurt at all. In fact, I'm nearly hunky dory."

"That's my boy."

"I'm a trooper."

"Yes, you are," Timothy said with a smile.

"So much so that I wasn't just out there playing like you said. No, I was out on a mission. A mission to find my father. And I knew where to look. Just didn't have the right time. Rosemont Avenue is not the place to be at the wrong time."

"Rosemont?"

"Rosemont."

"Oh, dear God."

"You know it well," Michael said. "And somebody there knows you even better. He said you're even with him now. If that makes you feel any better."

"And it was—"

"Yes. Some guy said you're even now."

Timothy stared out the window. "I'll kill him." There was no emotion or fear in his voice. No inflection.

"No. Stay here. Enough has been done already."

Timothy nodded.

"And I need to get back to sleep. One day things might be normal. Better get ready now."

"Okay, Mikey. Good night."

***

Michael woke up to his mother's screams. He did not hear the phone ring, but he saw her back slide down the wall until she sat on the floor. She let the receiver fall from her hands as piercing screams bounced off the walls. Despite the pain, Michael ran down the stairs. Jessie was right behind him.

Before they could ask her what happened, and before she could think of a way to soften the news, she said, "Your father's dead."

***

The bus driver said he never saw it coming. He was driving along his route when all of a sudden, a man walked off the curb, directly into his path. With the speed limit of 45 miles an hour on that particular stretch of Southbend Road, the driver swore he was going at least five miles per hour slower. None of that mattered to anyone but the driver himself, who saw the man's eyes before he thumped off the front of the vehicle before being dragged half a block.

Other witnesses gave the same account, only a few added that the man was smiling just before he was crushed.

Timothy's wallet was in his front pants pocket, containing his driver's license and other identification. The face was not immediately recognizable after the impact, but there were enough witnesses and few questions that could be asked. The answers to the more pressing issues died along with him.

In his shirt pocket, wrapped in a sandwich bag, was a note with two words written. *You're welcome.*

***

"You're here, pal," the taxi driver said, waking up Michael. "Thirty-five dollars."

Michael handed him a fifty and stepped out of the car. "Keep it."

Without saying thank you, the taxi driver took off. Michael stood on the street corner, looking at the peak of McMicken Hall, the front entrance to The University of Cincinnati. This really wasn't where he'd requested to be dropped off, but it was a short enough walk.

But was that what he really wanted? Right now it was. A little bit later, probably the same answer. But he was new to all this. What would he say? *Hello, fine gentleman. I'm new to this area and was wondering if you might know where I can acquire a decent amount of cocaine.* He would sound like a really bad undercover cop, and if that did not result in a bullet to the head, then nothing would. Regardless, it was no deterrent. Nor was the fact that this, ultimately, was what had killed his father. Well, that and the hefty scoops of guilt he'd piled on dear ol' dad.

Why couldn't he have just keep it to himself? He hadn't needed to go out and be Rambo. He never should have left the house. It wasn't his job. And just one look at himself now showed how deep his hypocrisy went. He'd made his father feel like shit, and that was what had pushed him in front of that bus. Had Michael said nothing, maybe his old man would have improved. Instead, here he was now, a visitor in his hometown, looking to buy drugs just to survive the trip.

What he needed more than anything was a drink. And that was easier, too. Within a three-block walk were several bars, all

186

of them catering to the college crowd and filled with all things Bearcat. He wasn't entirely sure what a bearcat was. The university's mascot probably looked very little like its namesake.

The first place he saw was Uncle Bob's, and that sounded good enough. When he walked in, it looked all the better. It was the typical bar with Bearcat prints on the wall, and in between were countless flat-screen televisions. Not a single one was tuned to anything other than sports. Even though there were no local games on, the bar was about half full.

What he liked most about this place was that he was not the only non-college-aged guy in there. Several people spread throughout the bar, mostly older, sat by themselves. Michael was not there to socialize, nor was he there to nurse a beer. He sat at the bar and ordered Jack Daniels on the rocks. Within two minutes he was ordering another.

He wondered if Ugh still lived in town. For some reason he pictured him growing up to be a foreman at some warehouse. But hell, maybe he was a doctor or an astronaut. He could also be a transvestite hooker working at a truck stop because he liked the diesel smell and company.

He could stop and ask his mother. She might have kept up with some people.

He wished he had not thought that, because it was not leaving his head. The clock on television, just above the continuously crawling scores along the bottom of the screen, showed it was 8:45 PM. He had to be reminded that he was back on Eastern Standard Time. If he caught a cab now, he could be at his mom's condominium by nine. Any later than that, and he might as well forget all about it. And for as good as that option seemed, something just wouldn't let him do it.

He flagged down the bartender. "Gotta go visit Mom. Gimme a shot of Jägermeister and the bill."

The bartender returned with both. "Visiting Mom?"

Michael nodded.

"The shot is on the house."

He slurred his thanks and downed the drink. "Call a cab?"

"Probably a good idea."

Michael nodded and looked at his bill. Fifty dollars would cover it and leave a few bucks for a tip. Not as generous as it should have been, but he'd lost count of how many he'd had. Oh, well. He'd dropped one hundred dollars and he still hadn't accomplished his original goal. He was hoping the whiskey would quench that need.

He didn't realize how drunk he was until he walked to the door. While he wasn't staggering too much, each step required intense concentration. A few people asked if he was okay. Michael wasn't sure if he answered them or not.

The cab was outside when Michael made his way out of the bar. The headlights of passing cars swirled around his head, and he felt fortunate that he didn't throw up on the sidewalk. The nausea subsided as he took in a few deep breaths.

"You all right, buddy?" the new taxi driver asked.

"Fine," Michael answered and got into the backseat. He was glad he had written down his mother's address so he didn't need to say anything for a little while.

The driver read it, nodded, and took off. Fortunately he was one of the silent types. Michael thought it was funny that neither driver fit the stereotype, but he kept that thought to himself. It made him wonder just how Midwestern this town really was.

It wasn't a long ride, but he felt himself drifting off to sleep. While he was on his way to pay his mother a surprise visit, all he could think about was Dana. Why hadn't he taken her phone number? And would he ever see her again? He could go up to Michigan and search all the strip clubs. But it was hard to make such an endeavor sound romantic.

But it was not about romance, and for as strange as it sounded to him, it was not entirely sexual either. Quite simply, he liked her. He liked her a lot. There was some connection. But of course he'd been high at the time and was wasted now as he reminisced about it. He knew that the sooner he forgot about her, the better. Let her become some nameless fascination, and move on.

Plus, he had so much more to think about. Tomorrow he'd be sitting in the studio during Mac and Mark. And the wake-up call would be coming so early. He was probably not going to be on the air, but his name could be mentioned. There was excitement in that alone. What was he doing going out, getting drunk, and then picking scabs? It wasn't like his mother was expecting him, so he wouldn't be disappointing her if he failed to show up. Wouldn't that be the smarter thing?

But just the simple task of telling the driver to turn around felt like too much. Even though it made no rational sense, he was just along for the ride. He had no idea what he would say to his mother. Or Jessie, if she happened to be there. It was certainly a possibility. But he hadn't done as much as send her a birthday card or a phone call. He had meant to restore contact many times, but he never let it happen. There was always some excuse, some reason to procrastinate. Some way to say, "Some other day."

189

As soon as he was ready to put off this meeting with his mother, the car came to a stop. The new condominium looked unfamiliar, but he'd had the same experience the few times he had been there before. It was still better than the old house. Right now, the hotel felt like home.

This time the fare was only twenty-five dollars. He handed him thirty with slurred thanks.

"Need some help?"

"Nope. I'm good," Michael said as he stepped out of the car, facing only mild dizziness. "I'm good."

With that, the driver left. Michael realized he should have asked him to wait and see if Mom actually was home. Otherwise he'd have to get to a phone and call another cab to take him back to the hotel and complete a monumental waste of time.

He rang the button on the intercom marked *Clover*.

A few seconds later, he heard his mother's voice. "Can I help you?"

"Mom?"

"Michael?" It sounded like it was a real question. "Michael, is that you?"

"What other guy calls you mom?"

The door buzzed, and Michael had to pull hard three times before it opened. He walked inside.

"Michael?" she said looking over the second floor railing. "Come up. Come up."

He still felt dizzy, and the steps took a while to manage. "I'm coming."

Suzie stepped back into her condo, leaving the door open for him. When he walked in, she gave him a big hug and a kiss on the cheek. "You've been drinking."

"Yeah."

"A lot."

"Yeah."

"It's still good to see you."

His mother looked exactly the way he'd expected. A few more wrinkles and a handful more strands of gray hair, but what struck him the most was that he saw no bags under her eyes. No weariness whatsoever. She looked well-rested and alert. That in itself was reason not to recognize her.

"Wow. What brings you back here? How long has it been?"

"Very long."

"Well?"

"Years at least."

"No, what brings you home?"

"Work. And by work, I mean dirty jokes," he said.

"Your father would be so proud. I don't say that with any sarcasm. Really. I can picture him laughing at your jokes."

Michael shrugged.

"No. This I am completely certain of. He'd be proud."

"How's Jessie?"

"Better."

"What do you mean by better? Did something happen? What happened?"

"Settle down, Mikey. She is okay."

"Was she ever not?"

"Yeah. Well, she's divorced now."

"Didn't know she was married."

"Don't feel bad. I wasn't invited to the wedding either."

"Oh," Michael said. "When did this happen?"

A far-away look stuck on Suzie's face. "Not long ago. This all happened in such a short space. I thought he was a good guy, but, well, sometimes a mother's knowledge falls short of infinite. Turned out to be a mean drunk. Around their one-month anniversary he hit her. Hit her hard. Put her in the hospital. Then she lied to the police. They knew better. I knew better. Guess the only one who didn't know better was your sister. She didn't leave him, though. Believe it or not, he left her. Apparently he found a punching bag he liked better."

Michael felt his face get hot. "Where is she now?"

"Just a few blocks away. A friend took her in. I offered, of course, but she said she didn't want to be a burden. She wouldn't be. Far from it. But I understand. She's moving into her own place soon."

"I didn't know."

"How could you have? You weren't here, and even if you were, from the looks of you, don't know how much you could've done. You have to take care of yourself before you can do anything for anyone else. I learned that the hard way."

"Wish I'd have learned more."

"I prayed for you to come back," she said.

"I'm answered prayer? Set your sights a little higher next time."

"You are my son. And I'm sorry for where I've failed you. I hope you don't hold that against me. I hope that's not why you didn't come back before." Her eyes began to redden. Either she was fighting back the tears or she was simply that composed now.

"No. Maternal resentment makes for good jokes, but I'm a grown-up now."

"Jessie said I wouldn't like some of your material."

"I don't like some of it either."

"I see a lot of your father in you."

192

He smiled slightly.

"And that scares me."

"Me too."

"The thing about your father was that he was always on display. His life was an open book, even the unsavory chapters. What are you holding back?"

"I don't even know any more."

"Michael, listen to me here. It's not your fault your father died. But if you go out because of that shit, then yes, that will be on you."

He sat speechless. "Yeah."

"Hey, I'm your mom. Mothering is my job. You just haven't let me do that in a long time. And not that I blame you. I hold a lot of regret."

"It's a family trait."

"I'm not much of a host, either. Can I get you something to drink?"

"Just water. And if I can bother you some more, a ride back to the hotel. In a little bit. Not yet. I'm not ready to go again."

***

There was no more important conversation, and that suited them both fine. He got an update on Ugh, who was now a travel agent somewhere in North Dakota. That had to be a goldmine. People must be willing to pay a fortune to get out of there. As she dropped him off in front of the hotel, he realized he hadn't told her he was in town because of a national radio show, nor did he feel like that was of any importance. He was back home, and he had a mother once again. For so long he had been so far away, had held whatever assumptions he'd wanted. There was no one there to talk him out of them.

When she dropped him off, he wished he had remembered what she'd said. All he could think about was how he had every intention of buying at least an eight ball. He was glad he'd decided to booze it up instead. Maybe he wasn't so stupid after all.

He watched his mother drive away and wondered who that strange woman was. He also knew he'd better get to sleep. The wake-up call was coming obscenely early.

CHAPTER TWENTY-NINE

After only a couple of hours of sleep, Michael could not believe how good he felt at 4:15 AM. He had already showered, shaved, and scrubbed his teeth. He was pretty sure that the radio station would have some sort of breakfast table, but if they didn't, he was far from hungry. There was no leftover feeling from the alcohol, and he felt alert. Granted, he would just be sitting on the sidelines, but that was okay.

The car would not be coming for another fifteen minutes, but he went down to the lobby to wait. Maybe Drew would be there already. Talking in front of a couple hundred people in a club was one thing, but being broadcast to millions was something else entirely. Just the thought of it made Michael nervous, and he became grateful for the part he'd be playing, which was none at all.

Not that he ever read them, but it was still too early for the hotel to have the newspapers set out. It was probably something he should do—plenty of current events material to be found there. It would also kill some time right now. He wore his usual stage clothes: jeans and a button-up shirt, long sleeves rolled up to his elbows. It always made him feel the most comfortable. Far from formal, but not overly casual. He'd worn that on his first open mic night, when he'd thought he might as well just give the whole comedy thing a shot. Looking back, he had no idea what had made him try in the first place. If anybody asked him, he normally said that he wasn't sexy enough to be a model, smart enough to be a scholar, or skilled enough to be an athlete. But he could tell dirty jokes, and therefore he was adding something to the world.

Sitting in the lobby made him remember the open mics, which were not all that long ago. There were a bunch of nervous comics with aspirations of, well, he wasn't sure what. But there was always that one who wanted to be the cut up. The one who played like he was onstage all the time. From the very beginning that had struck Michael as painfully amateur.

"You Michael Clover?" asked a guy wearing a t-shirt with the radio station's logo emblazoned across the front.

"That's me."

"Hey, I'm Cartman."

"Cartman?"

"Well, it's my radio name. I do weekend overnights. Real name is Ryan."

"Nice to meet you, Ryan. Haven't heard from Drew yet. He should be here any minute."

"Nope. It's just you."

"What?"

"Yeah, dude. Drew Greene cancelled. He's been puking all night. He just called. You're listed as backup."

"Oh."

"So you coming or what?"

Michael followed him out to the car, which was a Jeep with designer graffiti all over it. He barely looked at it as he hopped into the passenger side.

"Pretty cool ride, huh?" Ryan said.

"Uh, yeah."

The guy kept talking all the way to the radio station. While the drive lasted maybe five minutes, Michael had lost track of when he should say, "Yeah," or nod his head in absent agreement.

***

"Yeah, y'all, I got him," the artist choosing to be called Cartman said as they entered the studio lobby.

The only ones there were a receptionist, who was on the phone, and a pudgy guy wearing a black tie and short-sleeved shirt that was so worn it had become nearly transparent. Outside of the station posters, the lobby looked no different from any other.

"Hi, I'm Charlie Stultz. Stultzie to just about everyone."

The name sounded familiar, and it wasn't because it sounded close to the guy who drew Charlie Brown and Snoopy. He hadn't listened to *The Mac and Mark Morning Show* in quite a while. Michael figured he must have played some side characters. He held out his hand. "Michael Clover."

Stultzie shook it. "Good to meet you. Drew said to mic you up. He vouched for you. But if you fuck up, it's not just on you, but on your meal ticket as well. And I'll be pissed. That's not something you want to do. Trust me on this. We have a five-second delay, but if I have to bleep you, don't bother asking if you can ever come back. Understood?"

Michael nodded.

"Now, I'm doing this as a favor to Drew. Just mentioning that his opening act is in the studio advertises him. Anyone else I would tell to go home and listen on the radio instead of wasting my time."

"Good to know."

The stars of the show walked in without paying Michael a second glance. They entered the studio past the square "on air" sign. Within fifteen minutes it would be lit up.

"All that will happen on your end," Stultzie continued, "is that you will say you're on tour with Drew Greene, then we'll go to archived material of Drew. Mac and Mark will find something to chat about, pick on Wilson Warrick, and there will be pseudo news breaks from Maggie. That's it. That's the magic of the show."

Stultzie led Michael into the studio. Tan walls, brown Berber carpet. A large table that looked to be solid oak was big enough to accommodate twelve should the situation merit. Today was obviously not one of those days. Michael wondered how they'd gotten such a cumbersome table into this small room.

Yawning on one side of the table was Mac Hayes. His on-air personality was cantankerous and anal retentive. From what Michael could tell, he was just playing himself. Next to him was Mark Chase. He played up the skirt-chasing playboy. Perhaps that had worked for him twenty years ago. In person he looked more like a dirty old man. It was a good thing his voice still sounded young.

Sharing a side of the table were Newsgirl Maggie and Wilson Warrick. Maggie was used primarily to make the show sound legit. She read news stories suited for the others to heckle. Being the only female set her up to be playfully harassed. It was a miracle she hadn't snapped yet.

Wilson Warrick was always listed as the sports guy. Instead he played the comic foil. He was a walking id. And even though his name was not in the show's title, he was clearly the star.

Stultzie said, "I think you all know that our guest, Drew Greene, cancelled. I didn't think we had shit for a backup plan, but I was proven wrong. We do have shit for a backup."

Everyone but Mac looked up and gave a kind but brief smile or wave. Apparently there was some truth in advertising regarding Mac's personality.

Michael sat at the empty side of the table. There was no further acknowledgement of him as they all looked over the papers on the desk or checked email on their phones. Wanting to look a little busy, he pulled a scrap of paper out of his pocket and flattened it out. He wrote, *I have ADD, and it takes forever to masturbate*. A smile crossed his face. That was a keeper.

Mac turned to Stultzie. "Can we get a mic check on this guy?"

"Hey, road kill," Stultzie said. "Don't scream. Don't mumble."

"I can handle that."

"You mumbled."

"Okay, everyone. Since we don't have Drew, we can just use his old stuff, mention he's on the road, and then we'll just have other bullshit. Just a regular day. Maggie, anything come off the wire?"

"A ninety-five-year-old grandmother has been pole dancing on amateur night at Déjà Vu in Baltimore."

There was no response from the other four until Michael said, "At ninety-five she's still an amateur? I just hope she doesn't take off her Depends."

There was no reaction. He didn't think it would be possible to feel more awkward.

"So, Clover," Warrick said. "We normally try to get a background brief on newcomers. Anything interesting?"

"Well, I'm from Ohio."

"Fascinating," Mac said.

"Don't worry. We have plenty of archived material," Mark said. "We don't even need to be here."

Maggie sighed. "Why don't we just call it a best-of show and call it a day?"

"Hung over?" Mark asked.

"That's a great idea," Warrick said. "If we get desperate, we can play *Why is Maggie hung over? She doesn't remember.*"

"If we get desperate," Mac said. "And we just might."

Stultzie tapped on the glass, alerting the guy on the soundboard that things were getting started. "Okay, ramblers, we're ready to go live."

The room stayed unnervingly quiet until Warrick was signaled. Stultzie looked disappointed that he actually had to direct Michael to put on his earphones.

"It's early. It's really, really early. And that means it must be time for *The Mac and Mark Morning Show*. And since we cleverly titled this show, the stars of this morning's program are Mac and Mark. Maggie Templeton will have all the news to make this show eligible for a Peabody Award, and I, yes, I, Wilson Warrick, have sports and cunning insights that will make your bookie think you're fixing the games. So now, without further ado, and before I start rambling, I introduce you to Mac and Mark."

"I thank you, Wilson," Mac said.

"Morning Wilson," Mark added.

"So," Mac began, "it's Friday and well, we're sorry we don't have Drew Greene today like we promised. Drew, if you're listening, get better soon. And to all those listening on the Armed Services Radio Network, thank you for doing what you do, and come home soon. So, Maggie, any news at your station?"

"Well, I'm glad you asked. It appears that ninety-five is not too old for amateur night at a strip club in Baltimore, Maryland. Gretchen Banks, who dances under the stage name of—get this—Granny Candy, has been stripping for months now at Déjà vu and is apparently getting good tips."

"Good *tips*," Wilson said. "I'm sure hers are still perky."

"I'm only interested in a cougar that has all her teeth," Mark said. "Although I could see an advantage of none at all."

"Ninety-five and she's still just an amateur?" Mac asked. "I hope she doesn't take off her Depends."

The staff burst into laughter. Michael looked around, but nobody noticed his discontent, much less the fact that his joke had just been stolen.

"So is that all the news?" Mark asked.

"After that I couldn't read any more," Maggie answered.

While Michael could not hear the sound guy and Stultzie behind the glass, their discussion was more than animated. Mac noticed it right after. Mark, Maggie, and Wilson were indifferent.

"I see this as an inspirational story," Wilson said. "In fact, it's like *Chicken Soup for the Soul*. If you all remember, Maggie was asked if she would do some pole dancing, and her response was, well, that she was too old. I think Granny Candy should give you a little motivation."

"I'm in complete agreement," Mark said.

"In your dreams," Maggie replied.

"Oh, yes. That and a whole lot more in my dreams."

Even when Mac wasn't looking, he still forced himself to laugh into the microphone. "Well, it hasn't been a good morning in the history of the show. Featured guest Drew Greene is sick, and so is our equipment. It looks like we won't be able to get to any of your requests for a little while, but we've been promised that it will be resolved shortly. Until then we have the man on tour with Drew Greene. Coming all the way from, well, not all that far, but it's good to have him nonetheless. Joining us in studio is—" Mac said and rustled through the papers. "Here it is. Michael Clover."

"Wow. That was the worst introduction I've ever heard," Warrick said. "He's new to our show, Mac. Don't make him nervous. Because you're not nervous are you, Michael? There's no need to be nervous. Of the millions of people out there listening, some might not be paying close attention, so whatever you do, don't be nervous."

"Wilson Warrick, you may be the worst person alive," Maggie said.

"Just trying to help the guy."

"So, Michael," Mac said. "You've been out on the road with Drew Greene. How's that going? Learning a lot out there?"

"Well, I've learned that America isn't going to run out of corn or orange barrels any time soon. I wanted to go out and see the good ol' U.S. of A., and, well, guess that's what it's all about."

"Sorry to keep asking you about Drew," Warrick said, "But I really do have a man crush. Is he not here because of me? Or is he hung over? You can tell me."

"Well, it's not really a hangover if you're still out from the night before. Drew, if you can hear me, come home. We miss you."

"What about you? Do you partake in the occasional drink out on the road?" Maggie asked.

"She's asking if you can hold your liquor," Warrick interrupted.

"For a little while. Then I have to drink it. You end up looking like an alcoholic if you're always holding a drink."

They all laughed into the microphones. Michael couldn't tell if it was natural or just part of the shtick. Whatever the case, it probably made him sound good to the listeners.

"Since we don't know much about you, are you a married guy, dating, single, straight?"

"I'm in the ranks of the divorcee."

"You're in good company there," Mac said. "There's been a total of ten in this room. Maggie's been four of them."

"It always feels so good to have that fact broadcast."

"Yep, I'm alone and sexually frustrated," Michael said. "So it's like I'm still married. And can I get political for a minute? If gay also means happy, then I will state publicly that I don't believe in gay marriage. I'm not opposed to it, just don't believe in it."

He hoped the laughter was real. It came a little faster this time.

"But no, she was a racquetball enthusiast. And she said the best place for her to train was with her instructor. At his cabin. Up in the mountains."

"Are you sure it wasn't handball?" Warrick asked.

"Something regarding hand and ball is what got Wilson Warrick the job here in the first place, Michael," Mark said.

"Well, if that's his most clever line, it seems like he owes you another," Michael replied.

"I think it's time for my annual evaluation," Warrick said. "I'm hoping for a raise. Better lube up."

"I just threw up in my mouth," Mac said. "Now let's return the focus back to Michael's pain and not yours."

"It wasn't a pain. I rather enjoyed it."

"Anyway," Mac said. "Is it fitting that your wife had an affair with a racquetball instructor, leaving you with blue balls?" Mac laughed, very impressed with himself.

"Well, I made up the part about him being a racquetball coach. It just sounded better than what really happened."

"Tell me he wasn't a fry cook. Those guys never get laid," Mark said.

"No," Michael continued. "She left me for a man who sells Mary Kay Cosmetics."

"Well," Maggie said, "that could be convenient."

Mark answered, "Incest is convenient. Having relations with a Mary Kay man is just unnatural. I got even with her, though. Yeah, now I fantasize about other women, and I stayed broke so she could only take half of nothing."

This time he knew the laughter was genuine. And that was the type of joke Wilson Warrick lived for. Behind the glass Stultzie signaled Mac. Mac returned with a nod.

Michael decided he was going to continue until he was signaled to stop. "Yeah, the biggest problem with the love life right now is that I have ADD."

"ADD?" Maggie asked.

"Yeah. Because of that, it takes forever to masturbate."

He was glad he had just written that joke; it was already paying off. While he'd known they would laugh, it was still good to hear.

"That can be a problem," Wilson said. "I've got an issue with carpal tunnel. Any other problems with you?"

"Well, I have to take a lot of antidepressants. Yeah, thanks to Prozac, Zoloft, Effexor, Welbutrin, and Abilify," Michael began, making his voice slow and sad, "well, I'm just so damn happy."

Only Maggie and Wilson laughed.

"It's gotten to the point where I don't even notice the side effects any longer," Michael said. "Have you ever read the warnings on those labels? Not very encouraging." He began to speak in an announcer voice. "Warning, this product may cause headache, dry mouth, fatigue, constipation, restless leg syndrome, erectile dysfunction, and increased thoughts of suicide."

All four chuckled, not heartily, but that was good because he needed a pause before the punch line.

"You know, I really wasn't thinking that last one before my penis stopped working."

Now they laughed heartily. He was just glad he'd remembered to say penis and not dick. While dick was the better way to deliver the line, this was not the comedy club. Blue material was fine, but profanity would get him in trouble.

"See, now, that right there is just a side effect of the side effect. But what do I know?" Michael said. "I'm just that guy paying three dollars a pill just for those damn things to cheer me up."

They all laughed. Mac even gave him an appreciative nod.

205

"Well, it looks like it's time for a break," Mark said. "Got to keep the advertisers happy. We'll be back with more of *The Mark and Mac Morning Show*."

"And we're out," Stultzie said walking back into the room. "Not too bad, kid. I almost shit my pants when plan B fell through. For plan C, you did all right."

"Yeah, you did good," Mac said.

"We got the technical difficulties worked out, so your job is done," Stultzie said. "Mac, if you can just plug Drew's show this weekend in St. Louis, then we've fulfilled my promise to him."

"Pretty sweet gig," Maggie said. "Your day is over, and the sun may not even be up yet."

"Yeah," he said, not wanting to ask if he could stick around a little longer. "It was nice meeting all of you."

"You too, Mike," Mac said as he stood up and shook his hand. It was the same with all the others as well.

"And see if you can get on our Mac and Mark stand-up tour. Give it a shot."

He nodded and let them get back to work. On his way out he saw all the glossy photos of comics who had been on the air. The picture of Drew Greene was at least a decade old. But it was good to know he could now belong on that wall.

CHAPTER THIRTY

The distance between Ann Arbor and Columbus wasn't all that far, Dana thought, assuming you weren't a college football fan. And it could be nice to take a mini road trip solo. While absently surfing the Internet, she decided to check and see if Michael was performing nearby.

She didn't have to look far. Typing his name into the search engine produced immediate results. *A Night With Drew Greene and, as heard on the Mac and Mark Morning Show, Michael Clover.* It was scheduled to be performed on Ohio State's campus. The advertisement stated one night only. It was on a Wednesday night, and that worked for her. There was more dirty money to be made dancing on Fridays and Saturdays. And maybe the show falling on a Wednesday would mean a lesser crowd, but with so many living on campus, weekend or weekday didn't always mean a whole lot. She decided to buy the ticket now. That way she wouldn't be disappointed if it sold out.

Disappointment was likely to come anyway, but she didn't want to think about that. It was something out of her control, and she might as well just take a chance. She also decided that she was going to make the trip alone. This should have seemed like common sense because there was nobody else to go with. Of course there was Randi, but if she told her where she was going, it would look obsessive and downright sad. Plus, she was okay having time alone.

It wouldn't be a really long drive. But long enough to pick out what music she wanted to listen to on the way. Her iPod had broken months ago, but she had boxes of CDs and could not remember the last time she'd actually just sat down and listened to any of them. And since she was off work that evening, why not get back to that now? This would keep her from feeling too stupid.

But she also told herself that there was nothing stupid about it. All she was doing was taking a chance. Maybe she wouldn't even be able to talk to him. Or if she did, there was always the possibility that he wouldn't recognize her or would pretend not to. That would hurt, and it would take a long time to heal. But sitting alone, doing nothing, would be worse. There could be no healing from that.

She remembered some words of wisdom: It's better to regret something you have done than to regret something you haven't done. Then again, she thought maybe she'd heard it from a Butthole Surfers song. Maybe she needed to look to them every time life got tough. One of the girls back at Alison's Angels used to dance to that. Sadly, stripping had been Dana's connection to most songs for a long time.

That had to be part of her problem. It didn't sum up everything entirely, but it was definitely an aspect of it. It was also a small portion of what she could remedy now.

The first handful of CDs filled her with embarrassment, even though she was alone. She had listened to the hair metal bands from the 1980s long after grunge had knocked the boys in lipstick off the airwaves. But what had compelled her to buy Winger's rousing rendition of "Purple Haze" on compact disc?

It was amazing to see how many years had passed since most of the albums had been released. *Guess everyone's getting old,* she thought. Doing so without a future was even worse, but she didn't even have the energy to hold onto the sorrow. She'd done enough of that already, and the more she did it, the more she talked herself into feeling hopeless. And if that was how she saw herself, how could she expect anyone else to see something different?

She pulled out a classic. Years had passed since she'd last listened to *Dark Side of the Moon.* Pink Floyd sounded like a better choice than Winger, and she'd never gone out and purchased anything by Butthole Surfers. Perhaps that was her loss.

She put in the disc and hit play. As she reclined on the couch, she felt—as long as the music played—like a different person.

CHAPTER THIRTY-ONE

"So I was still drunk from last night?" Drew said as he saw Michael in the hotel lobby. "I'm just glad you didn't say I was with the ninety-five-year-old stripper."

"The thought crossed my mind. Feeling better?"

"Feel good. Better at least. Went back to bed after your segment. Just now woke up." He looked up at the clock. It was now mid-afternoon.

"You're not pissed about what I said?"

"If I offend that easily, I picked the wrong profession."

"Didn't know what I was doing. Thought I was supposed to promote the tour. Didn't really talk about that."

"Doesn't matter. St. Louis, Milwaukee, and Chicago are all either sold out or close to it. Plus we'll do a Wednesday night in between at Ohio State. Not much of a detour."

"*The* Ohio State University?"

"Is there another?" Drew answered. "Just booked it right after your bit. Didn't have a chance to tell you about it."

"Cool."

"Well, you ready to hop back on the road? Hope it was a good homecoming."

"It was. Somehow it was."

***

As the road stretched out, he could not believe how heartbreaking it was to leave. He had not seen his sister, but he was already on such an emotional overload, he did not think he could physically handle anything else.

And now he was leaving home again, but it was nothing like he expected. A few goofy moments on the radio and his boss was happy. Now back out to cross the Ohio border into Indiana, then through the middle of Illinois. He was seeing a lot of the same thing. The giant signs at the state lines didn't change anything.

A little nausea kicked in as he dozed off and rested his head against the rattling window. When he woke up, the discomfort increased. He didn't want to tell Drew to pull over so he could throw up on the side of the road, but doing so in the car, well, it was hard to get worse than that. Even though it was likely Drew that had made him sick, there really was no defense for puking in someone else's car.

Sitting upright with his eyes closed helped for a little while, and the drive promised to be pretty flat. *That should help*, he thought. He just had to be sure to take care of himself a little more. He'd just been on national radio, albeit briefly, but his name was out there. It was keeping him from having to work a *real* job, which was good since he'd never been much of an asset to any employer.

A small bump jolted the car slightly, and the dizziness made his head heavy and sent his stomach into somersaults. He just hoped they got to St. Louis fast so he could just go to bed. No stopping at the hotel bar or having a few in his room. Just sleep. His body couldn't handle anything more. But the more he thought about it, and the more he tried not to, he couldn't help but wonder how much time he did spend at the hotel bars. Since he was not exactly working a nine-to-five, his downtime was different. The only thing he had to do was make sure his checks had been deposited and hit the Laundromat if the hotel didn't have one on-site. He knew he should have spent it writing and improving his act—especially now—but he had found such comfort onstage that he figured he should just run with it. Why modify what was already working?

Maybe just one drink. Loosen up a bit and then jot down a few ideas. After all, he was an adult, on his own, and a couple of drinks were not against the law. It suited him well.

He couldn't wait until they got to St. Louis.

***

He didn't sleep, but he didn't remember most of the drive. The hotel wasn't as nice as where they'd stayed while on the radio station's tab, but it was pretty damn close. It was just outside downtown in Laclede's Landing, where the cobblestone streets added a throwback feel, and there was pedestrian traffic everywhere.

Even though Michael was exhausted and nearly every instinct in him told him to go to bed, he left the hotel for a little sightseeing. His first stop was a little pub. The entire décor inside revolved either around the arch or Cardinals. He ordered a gin and tonic and watched a bit of the game on television. While the Cardinals weren't even playing, a good portion of the crowd watched intensely. The team in the standings behind St. Louis was playing and losing. Michael tried to fit in by caring, and around his fifth drink, he did for a short while. By his eighth he was shown the door by a frail woman who introduced herself as the manager.

She must have really known her job, because by the time he was four steps out of the building, he vomited on the cobblestone. Some must have splashed up and hit someone walking too close, because he thought he heard at least one threat of a severe ass-kicking. He didn't bother to look up from his eventual dry heaving.

All he knew was that he was disorderly in the high-rent district. Cops and judges didn't like that. He was quick to stagger away, muttering apologies to no one in particular.

***

The next night he was amazed at the response he got. The first show could not have gone better, and the audience was even laughing before he got to some of his punch lines. He had never been more on target, even though he'd nearly overslept and got to the club in just enough time to fake through the pleasantries of meeting the management and staff.

The second show didn't start until 10:30. He nursed a Budweiser because his throat was dry, and this was St. Louis. *When in Rome.*

"And as heard on *The Mac and Mark Morning Show*, please welcome to the stage...Michael Clover!"

The second audience of the night clapped, but Michael didn't move until he was nudged.

"You okay there, pal?" someone asked.

He looked up at the emcee who was trying to see through the blinding spotlight. "I'm sure he's here. If not, looks like this is my big chance."

Michael trotted up the steps, much to the relief of the host. "Sorry for the delay, folks," he said as he took the microphone.

"Nobody told me Budweiser has such an effect on the bladder. Broke the seal and I was in the bathroom pissing like a Clydesdale."

The crowd laughed some, a few chuckles perhaps but nothing more. *That's okay. Just go to the routine, but don't let it sound rehearsed.*

"Have you ever been so horny, you fantasized about your own wife?"

While his opening joke normally got him a good response, it just didn't kill tonight. The crowd was quiet until someone answered, "No."

Now that brought the laughter. Especially from the big table where the gentle heckle had originated.

Just keep plugging through, he told himself. Just find the rhythm of the routine and go with it. A little perspiration began to wet his temples. Sweat was nothing new, especially under such hot lights, but it usually didn't begin until he was halfway through the set. Perhaps these lights were set a little brighter. The heat he could handle; the dizziness was something altogether different. It had to pass. It had to.

"Sorry, folks. I'm just in kind of a bad mood. See, my wife left me, and that really hurt." Michael paused until someone gave a sympathetic *aww*. "But then she came back, and that shit was devastating."

While that was never one of his better jokes, it usually got him enough laughs to pause and go onto the next. Tonight he stood on the stage in silence.

"Guys, some of this may sound familiar, but she said I don't communicate. I'll talk more on that later. She said I don't understand the female perspective and that a relationship is a *two-way* street. I told her it would be more beneficial if we made it a *three-way* street. Or a six-lane highway? Dirt road? Roundabout? I'm just trying to understand you better, baby.

"After that, communication only went one way."

There was barely a chuckle coming out of the silhouetted audience. His eyes hurt, and he closed them as the ache in his head continued.

Since he was getting no love out of the audience, he might as well try some new material.

"I was recently called a loser by a guy who is in three fantasy football leagues. Now if that doesn't hurt the ol' ego, nothing will."

His ego was more damaged by the lack of enthusiasm in the crowd. He just had to put his time in, get through the set, and yield the stage to Drew. That was his job. Then he could drink away his misery.

"But these fucking guys who get into these fantasy sports are the same bastards that gave me shit for playing Dungeons & Dragons."

At least a few liked that joke.

"I've actually never played Dungeons & Dragons. I'm sorry to say I was never cool enough to hang out with those kids."

A few more liked that one. A belly laugh from a guy in the back echoed throughout the club.

"Sir, if I could clone you, I would fill this place to capacity with your mutants."

Not even the guy Michael wanted to clone gave more than a chuckle. Oh well. He decided he'd better get back to his routine and return to what was tried and true. The only problem—and he hated to feel these types of complaints enter him,—was that he had been telling the same jokes over and over. It just wasn't funny anymore. And if it was not funny to him, what made him

216

think anybody else would like it? These people had not heard most of his material, and he was just supposed to warm the stage for Drew Greene. The worst thing he could do was think that people had paid to see him. It was a nice delusion but false nonetheless. The only thing that could be worse was to think too much onstage. Just do the routine. He could do it in his sleep.

Sleeping would be better right now, because as he stood on the stage, he forgot his next joke. Didn't even remember how it was set up.

"So, what should we talk about?" he finally said when the silence grew beyond a few seconds.

"Talk about why we paid for this shit," a heckler said, bringing laughter, followed by applause, which was much worse.

"Hey, I already cashed the check," Michael answered.

"Then give us a refund," someone else said.

"I already spent it on drugs." Michael wished he had.

Another person said something he could not hear, but a few others laughed. He'd heard about having a *hell gig*, and now he understood.

"So this is St. Louis. And that means two things. Baseball and beer. I like both. I'm a bigger fan of baseball, though. Don't really have the patience for Budweiser, I'm sorry to say. By the time I finally get a healthy buzz, I'm already down a case and spending the rest of the night in front of the urinal. Not that I have better things to do, but I tend to get a bit dizzy if I'm on my feet too long.

"But, yeah, I love baseball. And it's near impossible to talk about baseball anymore without at least mentioning steroids.

Now, St. Louis, don't worry, I'm not going to mention Mark McGwire."

Finally some applause, even though it was not truly for him. That was okay. It was still good to hear.

"Now, I come from a town that idolizes Pete Rose."

He got some mixed reactions, which he expected.

"Say what you will about Pete. I'm just glad he became a baseball player and not a guidance counselor."

Maybe one or two people laughed. He didn't know why he'd gone with that joke. There was no punch to the punchline.

"What kills me the most about sports is the announcers. Shouldn't you at least have a grasp of fourth-grade English before you become a broadcaster? Like the expression, *This team controls their own destiny*. Whenever I hear someone say that, it just makes me want to kick a puppy. That defies the very definition of destiny."

He stepped back as nobody seemed to be enjoying themselves. And by saying that he was from Cincinnati, he not only embarrassed himself, but his hometown while he was at it. And the talk about kicking puppies did him no favors.

"Another thing that kills me about language is that nobody knows how to use similes and metaphors. See, these are supposed to be a comparison of two seemingly unlike things that are put together to create a more vivid image. But this is what you hear. *Dude, that is cool as hell*. Now my understanding of hell, both Biblical and metaphysical, is that it's a place that is considered damn hot. Heard this one time: *Man, you are smarter than shit*."

Finally a few laughed.

"Have you ever taken a dump, and the turd looks up at you and says, 'I think you should invest in Microsoft. Or be like me and liquefy.'"

A few more laughed, and he thought he just might still get through this.

"This is a common one. *That hurt like a motherfucker.* And that one might be true. I'm not going to find out. And here's an old one. *Ugly as sin.* Now that all depends on who is doing the sin in question. Like if that waitress down there stepped up on stage with me and flashed her tits, well, it may be sin, but it certainly ain't ugly."

Perhaps he had redeemed himself somewhat. And he still had a good while left on the clock. Not as much as he thought he should have. The last bit had taken longer than he'd expected, and that was good news. Leaving the stage ten minutes early was not the worst thing in the world, especially on the late-night show. There was a light at the end of the tunnel. He was almost done. Then he could apologize to Drew and try to make things right again. He was in survival mode, and the sweat was now dripping down from his temples. A couple of shots of whiskey would calm his nerves.

"Now, you know what I find funny? This may sound insensitive, but it's bulimia."

A couple people chuckled. "I'm sorry, but the very idea of a woman trying to increase her sex appeal through continuous vomiting is hysterical. Then her teeth start to rot out and she gets this whole third-world sickly thin thing going on. And the funniest part? Most guys would still tap that, just like when she carried a few extra pounds. Ladies, your problem in life is that you're working way too hard to please an easy audience. And speaking of audiences, you're beautiful, St. Louis. Good night."

Michael stepped off the stage before the panicked emcee could race up there. The applause had halted before he could grab the microphone off the stand. He looked at his watch and nervously said, "Michael Clover, ladies and gentlemen."

Not many followed the lead to clap for him.

"We've got a few minutes before Drew Greene takes the stage. He's not done slaughtering that goat on his Costco altar. The man has the strangest pre-show ritual I have ever seen. Anyway, I was at my in-laws' house the other day, nice place you know, when I had to take a shit. Everybody does it. Don't wrinkle your nose at me, lady. Anyway, it was a floater. Glad you asked. So I flushed the toilet at the end of the transaction, and it kept circling around the top of the water. Then it started to go down, but the water stopped running, so the turd floated right back to the top. So I did what any normal person would do and flushed again. And again it rode around, skimming the top of the water like a California surfer until it was finally sucked down.Then what happened next? Yep, the poop popped right back. Now at this point, what do I do? A third flush raises suspicions. A piece of shit left in a toilet bowl falls under the category of ill manners. So what is the etiquette in such a case?"

Michael walked out of the club as the audience howled. Being upstaged by a poop story hurt a bit, but at least his night was over. Violet circles danced across his vision. His eyes normally adjusted to the bright light, but this evening, everything was different.

There was no commitment at a neighboring bar tonight, but he did walk into the first one he saw. It was a bit more upscale and wasn't covered in sports paraphernalia. The thing that made it most perfect was that it wasn't the same one as the night before. Covering the same sidewalk twice in as many days would be bad form.

He'd heard himself say before that he needed a drink. But tonight he knew he truly *needed* this drink. As long as his hands were steady enough to keep him from spilling all over himself, he should be fine. And the sweat continued to pour from his temples even though he was far from the spotlight.

"Whiskey. Last name Daniels, first name Jack. Straight up," Michael told the bartender.

"Want to start a tab?"

He handed over his credit card. "Good luck with that."

When the whiskey was in front of him, he downed it. He loved the smell of it, and it went down smooth with little more than a kick.

"Want another?" the bartender asked.

"I had a teacher one time say there are no stupid questions. That, my friend, was a stupid question."

"Whatever, dude." He poured another drink, then walked away.

As he drank the second, he found that he actually enjoyed it. His hands stopped shaking. "Going to keep you busy over here," Michael said as he looked at the other patrons who were now watching him. He laughed to himself. The fact that he had stage fright now was ironic.

"I'd put the bottle on the table," the bartender said, "but management doesn't like that. Plus, they want me to work for a living." He poured the glass a little higher than he had before. "Just take it a little easy there."

"Yep, taking it easy," Michael said. Within a minute the drink was gone.

221

The bartender took his sweet time getting back to him. That was okay in the regard that there was no chance of any type of tip. Maybe he would go to another bar, but that felt like too much work. There was probably another, perhaps just across the street, but if there wasn't, he'd be wandering around for a while. By that time, the prick bartender would have stopped playing big brother and returned to his simple fucking job of serving drinks.

"Get you another?"

Michael looked up to see he was back. He made the right decision. "Can you make a Jägerbomb?"

"You got it."

"Good."

He was off making the drink before any type of conversation could begin and was back just as quickly.

"Seriously. It's my ass on the line if I give you too much and some shit goes down."

"I'm not driving," Michael said. He wondered why he was getting raked over the coals. He wasn't even that drunk.

"So everything is just fine then?"

"I just thought that would be your biggest concern."

"Don't be concerned with my concerns. Enjoy your drink."

"Will do."

And he did. He sat at the bar and downed the solution of Jägermeister and Red Bull.

The bartender approached when the drink was gone. "One more?"

"Yeah, one more."

"Just one more."

"You're the boss," Michael said, but as the words escaped his mouth he caught his reflection in the mirror. He had been staring forward the whole time, right where the mirror ran the length of the bar, but had seen nothing. His face was a bright red blotch bordered by a sickly pale complexion and matted hair. "Yeah, just one more. Probably for the best."

It took about as long to finish his last one as all the previous combined. He would find out how many there were when the bartender brought him the tab, and again he had to accept whatever it would say. He was in no place to argue. All he wanted was to go back to the hotel and sleep. Maybe he would wake up with a less horrid face. He smiled briefly when he thought he would need at least another two or three drinks before even considering having sex with himself.

While he was certain that he had a pen and folded piece of paper in his pocket, it just felt like too much work to write down, *You really have to re-examine your life when you're too ugly to masturbate.*

He laughed out loud, a snarling, cackling sound that drew an audible gasp from a woman at another table. Trying to regain some composure he turned around and said, "My utmost apology mad am. I was thinking somethin' in my head 'bout my face being so ugly it made my dick break. Dat's what caused my ruckuss. My upomostest apologies."

"Okay, buddy," the bartender said. "This place would be a whole lot better without you."

Michael stood up. His legs almost failed him, and he held on to the stool for support. He was unable to understand why he was having such difficulty. He really hadn't had all that much to drink. At least he didn't think so. He couldn't remember, and trying to remember gave him a headache.

Once the bill was paid, he walked outside. He wondered why the bartender was making such a big deal about him leaving. There was only a hint of a wobble in his step, barely a slur in his speech. Perhaps he was just trying to be a hero. Whatever the case, he was happy to leave. He could just go back to the hotel, sleep for a while, then wake up the next morning and try to be funny. It was a better gig than washing dishes or selling perfume, so he had no reason to complain. But shouldn't life be better? He was living out what so many would consider to be a dream, yet he still found reason to feel sorry for himself. If it wouldn't have made him look so damn crazy, he would have slapped himself right there. But he knew better, and that had to mean that he was not too drunk.

Maybe he could stop for another nightcap. Part of the fun of going to a bar was the built-in camaraderie. That asshole of a bartender had robbed him of that. Maybe it was just a tough town.

"But where am I now?" he whispered to himself.

Didn't matter. It was somewhere in the Midwest, and there wasn't much to differentiate one town from another. He knew. He'd grown up in what was widely considered "flyover country." For a moment he lamented that this tour with Drew had been done entirely on the road. No airports whatsoever. He could have gathered some material somewhere between security and food stands so overpriced they made Starbucks look reasonable.

All he had to know about this part of the world was that it was founded by *settlers*. These were people who had started from the east, knowing there was gold in California. But they got too tired and lazy along the way, so they had to settle for where they were.

Was that funny? Maybe. And he knew he should write it down, but he didn't feel the pen in his pocket and did not want to look around. Perhaps the thought would still be there later.

"You okay there, buddy?" some guy said to Michael.

He looked up. "What was that?"

"Just making sure you're okay."

"Borderline peachy."

"Need anything?"

"I need you to fuck off," Michael said.

"Enjoy your cirrhosis, asshole."

The only comeback he thought of was, *Oh yeah? Well, you too!* But since that was neither clever nor coherent, he decided to say nothing. At least he had that going for him. And before things got too out of hand, he had better get back.

He walked up the avenue, waited for the light to change, and crossed as soon as the signal changed to the white light walking man.

Whatever happened to the simple WALK? Was the figure there for those who didn't speak English, or for the illiterate? The sound of his laughter frightened even himself. In a very real way, it sounded like it was coming from someplace else.

He turned left onto the next street, certain that he was heading back to the hotel. When he looked up, after walking another two blocks, he questioned this, so he went right up the next street. When he reached the next streetlight, he reasoned this was not correct, so he took another right. That didn't look good either. There were no hotels this way. He stopped, pivoted, and turned around. To his left were some taller buildings and fast food restaurants, the types of places where hotels could usually be found. That had to be it.

After a good deal more walking, he made his way into the Hampton Inn. The number 221 was etched into his memory, and he pulled out the key card. At the time the front desk was unmanned, which was perfect. He had no interest in talking to anyone.

The loud ding of the elevator signaled that the doors were about to open. He only hoped it wasn't one that went from one floor to another at warp speed. Even on his best days, that made his stomach uneasy. Yeah, he'd had a few drinks, but that didn't mean he was drunk. If the elevator made him sick, that would be a difficult thing to explain.

When he got to room 221—after the unnecessarily swift elevator almost made him toss his cookies—the key card refused to make the light turn green. Instead the light flashed reddish orange each time he inserted it.

"Fucking thing. What's wrong with a normal key?"

He made another unsuccessful try."

"Fuck."

"Can I help you, sir?" a hotel employee said as he walked quickly toward Michael.

"Hell yeah, you can help me. Fix your fucking key cards and let me get to sleep. I have to work in the morning."

"May I see that, sir?"

Michael handed him the card.

"This isn't for our hotel."

"What? Well why would you give me a key to someone else's hotel? That's pretty fucking stupid if you ask me."

"Has it occurred to you that you might have the wrong hotel?"

"No."

"Come on downstairs. Let me help you sort this thing out."

"Don't need your help," he said slowly, careful that his voice would not sound slurred.

"You scared the woman in that room half to death. Wouldn't be surprised if she's called the police. Don't you hear her on the phone right now?" the man asked, pausing for just a moment. "Let's go back down to the lobby."

Michael nodded. Once they got off the elevator, which was much worse on the way down, he noticed that the man was holding him up and leading him to a chair.

"Think she called the cops?" Michael asked as he sat.

"Yeah, and that means a lot of paperwork. Let's get you out of here fast."

"Okay."

"Do you remember what hotel you were staying at?"

"Thought it was this one. Still do, but I may have to admit to being wrong about that one."

"What's your name?"

"Michael Clover."

"Hold on," the man said and disappeared into an office behind the front desk. A young woman who looked to be just out of high school stood there, following obvious orders to keep an eye on him. She did not return the wave that he sheepishly offered.

After what felt like half an hour the man returned. "Not finding anything."

"Try Drew Greene. I'm on the road with him."

"Seriously?"

"Yeah."

"He's in town?"

"Yes. And I'm with him."

"That's pretty damn cool," the employee said. "Hold on."

The young lady, whose demeanor managed to sour further, stared at him as her suddenly impressed co-worker left once again. He returned a few minutes later.

"Dude, you're two miles off course."

"Guess that's not too bad."

"Yeah, Mike, you're staying at The Hilton. I talked them into sending one of their shuttle buses over. They're on their way."

"Cool."

"But so are the cops. I'm betting on it. So look for the bus outside that Cracker Barrel next door. That will work best for all parties involved."

Michael just stared back blankly.

"It's not like you're a fugitive or anything like that, but life would just be a hell of a lot easier for you if you got on that bus."

Not needing any further nudging, Michael left. It had been years since he'd had to deal with anything police-related, and this was not a good time for them to resurface. The outside air was warmer than he'd remembered, and within a few minutes he saw the shuttle bus. Without saying a word, he stepped onto it. A police cruiser pulled into the hotel lot. There were no sirens or lights, and the cop didn't even seem to be in that much of a hurry. He guessed he wouldn't see himself on *America's Most Wanted* anytime soon.

He was happy in that moment he didn't have celebrity status. The security tape from the hotel certainly would have made the rounds on gossip shows and the internet. For now, as he was driven back to the correct hotel, he found happiness in obscurity. The veil of darkness covered him as he fell asleep on the short ride back.

CHAPTER THIRTY-TWO

The shrill ring of the hotel phone woke Michael from a very deep sleep. He didn't remember getting off the bus, much less going to his room. As long as there were no police officers on the other end, he could deal with it.

"Hello?" He didn't know why it sounded like a question.

"Rough night?"

"Drew?"

"Yes."

"Oh. Hi."

"Hi."

"What can I do for you?" Michael asked, knowing well that his attempted nonchalant voice was failing miserably.

"Ready to go?"

"Yeah."

There was silence on the other end.

"Where?" Michael finally asked.

"Well, I was hoping you might, oh, I don't know, want to do the show tonight. I mean, that is why you're out here, isn't it?"

"What time is it?"

"Close enough to show time that the butterflies should have already started."

"Oh," Michael said, looking around for a clock.

"I was going to just knock on your door but was afraid I'd find you dead, and that would be a killjoy for tonight."

"Might be a bummer."

"Yeah. Meet me in the lobby in ten."

The phone was silent. Michael held onto it for a few seconds before safely assuming that Drew had hung up. He brushed his teeth as he looked in the mirror. It was a good thing he was in the comedy field. Not many other professions would make allowances for such an atrocious appearance.

Within a few minutes he was ready to go, still wearing the same clothes from last night. Might as well just get to it. Being funny, he realized, was beginning to feel like a job.

CHAPTER THIRTY-THREE

It was a good thing last night's crowd hadn't passed along their reviews of the show to this gathering. No matter how bad he felt, he could at least make it through a half hour. If that was a day's work, then he had no business crying about anything.

"I'm so glad you're an accepting crowd. I actually just got in from last night's show. They drove me to drink. If anything, I'm a victim."

There wasn't all that much laughter, but Michael could sense that the crowd was enjoying themselves. Sometimes that was enough for a little while.

"Now this is what I love about comedy. I can tell you that I came in from a night of drinking and a game of Twister with a disfigured homeless man, and this actually helps me in this career. Don't judge me. I wanted to play Scrabble with him, but since he was paying me, well, I just gave in. But if you heard that from your insurance salesman or therapist, you might not be filled with the same type of confidence.

"Embarrassing stories are not out of line here. In fact, sharing them with you is a form of professionalism. Like the other day, it was a Tuesday afternoon. While most of you were at work, I thought it would be a good idea to have sex with a chainlink fence. Don't tell me you haven't tried it," Michael said as he looked in the first row. "Ma'am, I believe I saw your video on the Internet the other day."

He paused and took a drink of his Budweiser. "But I must confess. The only reason I stick my dick in fences is because I'm a lonely, sensitive guy. Just looking for a little love. Nothing too expensive. A woman who doesn't mind if I leave the seat up, and I don't care if she does the same. That's what love is all about. That is also why I love strip clubs."

A few guys cheered.

"I take it that those in favor here are dateless. That's okay. Fear not. I am here to remedy that. Because this is the part of the show where I like to give the audience something back. No, I don't have free CD's or eight-by-ten glossy photos. I'm giving you something of much greater value. For free, I'm going to tell you how to fuck a stripper."

Those same guys cheered. A few laughs were thrown in as well. He had been comfortable going off the cuff, and now that it was time for the set part of his routine, he felt himself shifting to autopilot.

But he also had to laugh to himself that he'd had a real shot with a pretty cool exotic dancer, and all he'd done was talk like it was a late-night game of truth or dare. And he didn't know where to reach her. He could call all the titty bars in Michigan, but that seemed impossible. And even if he did reach her, what would he say? *Hey, just in case you weren't weirded out enough before, I'm calling you at your job because I can't harass you any other way. For your trouble, I'll mail you a couple of singles.*

If he had just asked for a phone number... If she had seemed willing enough to sleep with him, she likely would have also welcomed a call. But maybe that wasn't how things worked. Maybe this fantasy girl was only that. *And holy shit*, he thought to himself, *I'm daydreaming on stage.*

Somehow the audience was laughing, and he heard himself, mid-joke, saying, "Your job here is to outsmart the stripper. And I'd like to think you're at least capable of that much."

Michael was relieved. The horror of standing witless onstage might rival other nightmares. It also became clear to him that if Dana didn't consider him a complete asshole, that was a character flaw on her part. Probably best to let the fantasy die. He also realized how much sweat was pouring off him again. Once the show was over, he was going back to bed. Maybe he'd try to get intimate with a chainlink fence for real and make his show more legitimate.

He smiled to himself as he got back to work.

CHAPTER THIRTY-FOUR

Michael had forgotten about the one-night show at Ohio State until they were halfway to Columbus. He wished he could have said that the majority of his time was spent daydreaming, but instead he was thinking about the real dreams that were coming back to him. Like he had brought it on himself, he had a nightmare of being onstage without knowing who he was or why he was there. And it did not work with the audience. Instead of booing or holding their own conversations, they stared at him. And it was not simply a blank gaze. It was an empty, hungry look that made him afraid to walk away.

He found himself dreaming about his father again. It had been a while, and he was not ready to start again. But he knew the harder he tried not to, the more pervasive it would become. Like putting a mound of sand in his palm, then tightening his hand into a fist, he knew that no matter what he did, his mind would outthink him. And why battle the mind anyway? Why even think of it? But in the silence of his own world, that was all he could do. There was no more running, but he was still going to try. He closed his eyes, but all he saw was the blood spilling out of his father's broken body and flowing down the street.

He also knew that the image wouldn't still be haunting him if it hadn't been his own damn fault. Kids could be stupid, but he should have known better than to run out and try to be a hero. All it had done was put him in a very dangerous place where he was violated and humiliated. That had put so much guilt in his father that the oncoming bus had to feel close to a warm embrace. Looking back, Michael really couldn't blame his dad.

Even if he had managed to get his life straight, feeling responsible for getting his son raped because he was out looking for him while on a bender would be a pretty damn bitter pill to swallow. Or he could simply blame his stupid son for going out and putting himself in harm's way. That would make sense as well. Instead, he'd just checked out permanently.

Michael also found himself dreaming about Dana. She had to be someone who understood violation. Hell, she put up with it every day. Maybe he would just have to call all the gentlemen's clubs in Michigan, ask for Angel, and see if she eventually came to the phone.

It was also hard for him to accept that he was broken-hearted over a one-night stand that didn't even happen.

As he closed his eyes, that familiar dream returned. *On a warm day, he walks on impenetrable ice. Somehow there's fire. There are also the footsteps coming from behind him.*

Any psychoanalyst would tell him that the steps came from either his mother or father. If he was Freudian by nature, then the answer was almost always the mom.

As he drifted in and out of sleep, all things made sense while his brain shifted gears. Maybe it was a call for him to take the same way out as his father. There had to be some merit to that. Michael also knew that he should feel more guilt. Sometimes he felt guilty for not feeling guilty, but he reasoned that was not the same thing. He didn't feel bad about himself when he got wasted like his father. Since he hadn't reached the same extremes as his dad, it only served as a reminder.

There was no doubting that if Michael was not the scum of the Earth, he was at least close enough. And if he were going to die, he should at least experience it to the fullest. He thought about the fire. There had to be no worse way to die than by burning alive.

Although there was also drowning. Maybe that was what the water was all about. Then his fevered mind began to take a few more turns. Maybe, just maybe, this dream was telling him he should do both. If he were to stand on a frozen lake and set himself on fire, he would eventually burn long enough to melt through the ice. And by that point he would have no strength to pull himself out. Likely the only thing he would be able to do would be to hold his breath for his last minute alive. Then the fight would be out of him, his lungs would fill with frigid water, and his burnt, lifeless body would submerge to the bottom.

Since there would be nobody looking for him, he would be Thanksgiving dinner for the fish and therefore serve some purpose. At least his life would not be a complete waste.

He pulled himself from the thought with all the self-preservation he had. Drew didn't look over, even though he must have seen Michael shivering. That was good. This was not a time to talk.

Instead he realized he should think about the show. Was it tonight or tomorrow? Whatever the case, he should be ready. He didn't want to think about being funny, but he couldn't remain where he was either. This could be an easier show, but his opening needed some tweaking. He could interchange the words *wife* and *girlfriend,* but that didn't always have the same effect. If nothing else came to mind, he could at least fall back to that.

The rules would be a little different. For one, he didn't need to be overly original. He just had to relate to the audience. All he could think about Ohio State University was that the student body loved beer and hated Michigan. He could toss in some old stuff to warm up the crowd.

Did you hear about the University of Michigan linebacker who graduated? Yeah, me neither.

It was a cheap joke, and the old expression about people in glass houses came to mind, but he thought it might be something to toss out there.

Yeah, I'm an Ohio boy, too. And in school I had a 4.0. Blood alcohol content, that is.

That one might be too old, but it was a classic.

How many University of Michigan football players does it take to screw in a light bulb? Just one, but he gets three credits for it.

While that was another old one, he still liked it. He couldn't believe he would get paid for this type of thing.

With his mind semi-clear he gazed out the window. More of the Midwest. There were no road signs or billboards. He wasn't even sure if they were back in Ohio yet.

After a few minutes passed, he asked, "So, uh, is the show at OSU tonight or tomorrow?"

"Tonight."

"Okay."

Since that was apparently the end of the conversation, Michael stared out the window, hoping he'd find some bearing.

"Yeah," Drew finally said, startling Michael. "Show is in about four hours. We'll be there in two."

"Cool."

"They'll have dinner for us. Probably something simple out of the student common area, but hell, that's good enough for me."

"Me too."

"Oh, and I should probably let you know, sometimes they ask for a faculty-only show, before the real one. I did it last time and hated it. So if they ask, I'm volunteering you."

Michael shrugged. "You're the boss."

Since Drew agreed, he didn't say anything else for about another mile. They passed a sign, but Michael missed it. "You should also be careful on these campuses. They might just be kids, but kids can be dangerous."

"Okay," Michael said, his voice trailing off.

"For one, a lot of high school kids like to feel like hot shit and roam the campus. As an entertainer, you can overcome the stigma of a DUI, but statutory situations, well, it's harder to put a good spin on that."

"I'll ask for ID first. But you know, it isn't fair. When I was in high school, the girls hadn't developed like that. If they did, then I'd have been ignored by some chicks with big tits."

"That's not my big concern, though."

Michael just stared at the open road.

"There are other temptations. Don't want to see you fall victim to any of them. Do you understand?"

"Um, I think so."

"Sometimes it can be as simple as just showing up at the wrong hotel."

"Uh oh," Michael said.

"Yeah. I was in the lobby when they brought you in. They wanted to call the ambulance. I told them you just needed sleep. I should have let them. You really didn't look so good."

"Oh."

"I called the next morning. You didn't answer. If you didn't answer before the show, the next call would have been to 911. Then it would have been my fault and your death on my conscious. Glad you picked up."

"Feeling much better."

"Apparently. But as I said, there's a lot of temptations out there."

"Yeah, happens to the best of us," Michael said. He always thought that joking with a comedian should have been easier.

Drew opened a console in the dashboard and held up a coin. "Alcoholics Anonymous, eleven years." He handed it to Michael. On the back it said, *To Thine Own Self Be True.*

"Good for you."

"Yep. I'm a coin collector now. Before that, well, it wasn't so pretty. It cost me my wife, house, and a hell of a lot of money."

Michael nodded absently.

"Go to a lot of meetings while you're still asleep. They aren't hard to find. You can always join me if you want. But that's all I'm going to say about it."

And that was all Drew had to say for a while. He went back to his usual quiet place, and Michael back to his. They passed another road sign and Michael saw that, as always, Drew was correct. Columbus was one hundred and seventeen miles away. He stared out at the open road, trying not to think, trying not to dream, and just mentally shutting down.

CHAPTER THIRTY-FIVE

The venue at Ohio State was much bigger than any comedy club. It was also better lit, so he could see the entire audience without having to squint. And the place was packed. He couldn't call it sold out since it was free to students and only five dollars to anyone else. Everyone he saw looked like a student, so he would have been surprised if the ticket window collected more than fifty dollars. That was okay. He was going to have fun with it, get paid, and then head back out on the road.

"Ladies and Gentlemen, are you ready to laugh? It's comedy night, and Ohio State University brings you the best. Starting off this evening, fresh from his appearance on *The Mac and Mark Morning Show*, it's Ohio's very own Michael Clover!"

Michael jogged to the microphone, gave the emcee the half-handshake, half-hug, and stared out at the audience.

"Ohio State, eh?" he began. "Understand this little institution has a football team. Did I hear that correctly?"

There was some clapping, enough for him to pause.

"Now it's also my understanding that there's another school up north, in a town with the macho name Ann Arbor, who thinks they play football too. Ever heard of it?"

A woman up front said something he couldn't understand.

"Honey, please tell me your major is not communications because I couldn't understand a damn thing you said."

That warmed up the audience pretty well.

"What I think she meant to say was The University of Michigan."

Some people booed, but he held up his hand, and they immediately stopped. *Good crowd*, he thought.

"I was going to let you know that I dated a girl from Michigan. Yeah, apparently they don't sell Epilady up there. I don't want to say she was bushy, but I now know why they're called the Wolverines."

The laughter echoed in the room. It was his best opening in a long time.

"But they do have academics up there. By the way, a school talking about their studies means that their team is not bowl eligible. That's just a little code they use. Any idea how many University of Michigan football players it takes to screw in a light bulb?"

He paused for a few seconds.

"Just one. But he gets three credits for it."

Since he had the audience on his side, he felt comfortable going into his set routine.

"So, have you ever been so horny you fantasize about your own girlfriend?"

Even with the word change, which he didn't like as much, it was still working tonight. Giving up the clubs and playing strictly in colleges started to sound like a good idea.

***

When Michael finished his set, he looked at the clock and realized he had gone over by six minutes. This was a cardinal sin most of the time, but he hoped the setting would be a little more forgiving.

"Let's give another hand for Mister Michael Clover," the emcee said, and the crowd obliged.

Michael waved to the crowd as he saw Drew waiting for his turn.

"Good show out there. Good pacing."

"I went over by six minutes."

Drew shrugged. "Then I'll finish up six minutes early. Cool with me."

"Now, Buckeye nation," the emcee began. "We bring you another veteran of *The Mac and Mark Morning Show*. Please join me in welcoming a legend. Ladies and Gentlemen, Drew Greene."

The applause was loud, but Michael wondered if the response he'd gotten was not even greater than Drew's. Possible. After all, he did play to the crowd pretty heavily. Even if he was milking it, it was good for the ego. Laughter was laughter. It was his job to get it, and he did exactly that.

Since he was still feeling a rush from the show, he was entirely too antsy to sit and watch Drew. He walked outside, where a kid barely old enough to grow peach fuzz handed him a beer.

"Killer show, man."

"Thanks, pal," Michael said and opened the beer.

"I could never do that, you know, stand in front of all those people and tell jokes and shit."

"Stay in school and you won't have to."

The kid nodded. "You get high?"

"Well, no. I should probably—" Michael began, looking over his shoulder. "No. The one thing I've learned in life is that it's hard to smoke weed, then later act and smell like you didn't."

"Got a little powder."

"Then you, my friend, are okay with me."

***

Michael was back before Drew's set was over. The bitter numbness made its way down the back of his throat, and he felt infinitely more fidgety than before. Another beer would help with both. He drank it quickly and nursed another. He understood at that moment why some people smoke. Sometimes the most difficult thing in the world is to stand there and do nothing.

"Hey," Michael said to the kid. "Owe you anything?"

"Nah, man. Got it free myself."

"That happen a lot?"

"You should register for classes."

In his head Michael began to wonder if paying for tuition and books and getting free cocaine might be a wise investment. Probably not. At best he would break even. It sounded insane in his own thoughts, but he didn't really like the drug all that much. Even though he jumped at the opportunity to do some, he would have been okay without it as well. And it wasn't like he did it often. He'd only done it a few times now, and yeah it was cool, but he knew he wasn't addicted.

"You know what, Ohio?" Drew said as he looked up at the clock. "The east and the west coasts may consider you to be flyover country, but I consider this to be the heartland. And if America has a heart, it also has an asshole. But really, we've

244

talked about Michigan enough. Thank you very much. My name is Drew Greene. Good night."

At this point Michael was definitely sure that he'd gotten the loudest applause for the night. It would be victory to keep to himself, of course. He couldn't be that stupid. And, even if he had topped him for the night, Drew was still the name people paid to see. Michael was still riding in his car and on his coattails. There was no reason to be cocky. Just enough confidence for tonight and going into the next show, wherever that may be now. It didn't matter. All these places started to look the same. He was out seeing America, but there was a lot of redundancy in doing so.

"First you make fun of my profession, then you hate on my home state. I'm glad I didn't tell you about my grandmother, or you could blast her from the stage as well."

Michael spun around and gave Dana a big hug before even saying hi. It clearly took her by surprise, but she was okay with it, even welcoming. "It's so good to see you. I never got your number, and calling you at work would have been, well, awkward. And on top of that, I didn't even know where you work, so I thought about calling every possible, well, establishment, but then I would have seemed like a stalker and scared you off and—"

"I thought you said women talk a lot."

"I'm just saying that I'm happy to see you."

"Good. Glad someone is."

"Hey, Mike," Drew said, running up to them. "I somehow got talked into doing an interview for some paper. I hate this stuff. Anyway, enjoy yourself. Your bags are already in your room. One of those student counsel kids can lead you to it."

He stopped and turned to Dana, extending his hand. "Drew Greene."

"I know. We've met twice previously."

"Oh. Sorry."

"It's okay. It meant a lot to me, too."

Drew took a half-step back. "Oh, yeah. Wow. Looks like Mike has a fan. Devoted one at that."

"Yeah, he's okay," she said.

"Okay," Drew said. "You kids have fun. We'll hit the road late morning tomorrow. No rush."

Michael nodded as Drew started to make his way out. Several students stopped him, likely looking for another joke or trying to deliver one.

"I feel old here," Dana said.

"Yeah. Me too. Let's leave."

There were people in every direction. Many shook Michael's hand as he passed. He returned pleasantries with each one, but was also brief and quick to get away.

"It's like I'm with a celebrity," Dana said.

"No, celebrities are rich and famous. I told dick jokes to a bunch of college kids."

Within a few minutes they were away from the pedestrian traffic and only saw kids walking to and from the library. Those weren't the stereotype Ohio State students, Michael thought. He also wondered what they thought of the group he'd just left.

"Do you know where we're going?"

"Nope. You're the one from Ohio," Dana answered.

"Different part of the state."

"Like there's a difference between parts of Ohio."

"You beat me to the punchline."

Michael had grabbed Dana's hand at some point. He didn't remember doing so, and he couldn't imagine letting go. It felt natural and, perhaps a first for both of them, wholesome. Eventually they passed a bar.

"Want a drink?" Dana asked.

He almost answered yes and was surprised that he didn't. There was a small diner across the street, as well as a coffeehouse and used book store.

"Have you eaten?"

"Before I left for the show."

"Which would have been hours ago," Michael said. "And I'd like to take you someplace fancy, but seeing as how we're in Ohio, may I treat you to a fine Midwestern greasy spoon?"

"Well, aren't you a Casanova?"

"On a budget," he added. He didn't want to throw in how things didn't end so well the last few times he'd gone into a bar. And how he'd been thinking about her. He thought about her a lot, and maybe she had done the same. Either that or she just wanted to come to a comedy show, even though she had already heard most of the material.

They crossed the street, and Michael held the door for Dana as she walked through. The place was old, probably a staple in the community, but it looked clean enough to pass the health inspector's test.

"This place doesn't look too bad," Dana said.

"Yeah, it wouldn't deserve to be called Bed, Bugs, and Beyond."

"You going to write that one down?"

"Would you mind?"

When Dana shrugged Michael pulled a wadded piece of paper out of his pocket and scribbled down the thought. Then he folded it back up and put it back.

"It's like watching Picasso paint," she said. "I don't understand him either."

Michael smiled. He felt like he should say something. He wasn't comfortable in silence, but he feared saying anything stupid. The waitress approaching was an unfathomable blessing. She also fit the stereotype of a diner waitress, which brought an equal smirk to Michael and Dana.

"Getcha all something?" she asked with a slight southern accent and heavy smoker's rasp.

"What's this establishment's specialty?" Michael asked.

She sighed. "We have a fried cod, french fries, hush puppies with coleslaw. You can also get breakfast all day. It's all on the menu. Need a minute?"

"Would you mind?" Dana asked.

"No," she answered, sighed again, and left.

When she was a safe distance away, Michael said, "She must live on the sunny side of the street."

"I sadly relate to people who have been burnt out for years. Not everyone can tell jokes for a living."

"This should be paradise. Shouldn't it? But you don't want to hear me bitch and moan."

"Can I tell you a joke?"

He nodded. "Can I steal it?"

"It's not mine."

"Let's hear it."

"So this guy is talking to his doctor, and he says, 'Doc, I don't know what's the matter with me. I can't eat, I can't sleep.

I feel like crying all the time. Nothing has any meaning any longer. I'm just so depressed that I don't know what to do.'

"Then the doctor says, 'What you need to do is to change things up a little bit. Go out and have fun. In fact, you should go downtown to the circus. Paggliachi the Clown is there. He's funny. He will certainly make you laugh. Things will start getting better then.'

"'That's all well and good,' the man says to his doctor. 'The only problem is that I'm Paggliachi.'"

He started to laugh and wasn't sure why he stopped. She was telling him something, and everything in him wanted to play dumb. It felt like a very rare case where laughing at a joke would be rude.

"Like it."

"So what's on the menu?" she said, changing the subject.

"According to our waitress, they have cod and pancakes."

"You could order both and get fish in a blanket."

He thought about just ordering coffee, but he was already so damn jumpy. She could tell last time that he was coked up. Could she tell now? He'd only had a little, not much at all, really, but she knew about these things.

The waitress returned to the table. Neither of them had taken much of a look, causing another raspy sigh. "Decided?"

"Yeah," Michael said. "Is it possible to get fish wrapped up in a pancake?"

"Honey, I've seen some of these kids order some things on a gross-out contest. Made me sick just to carry it to them. And the Mexican dishwasher will eat anything."

"Mexican dishwasher?" Dana asked.

"Yeah, what other types of dishwashers are there?" Michael answered.

Dana just shook her head. "I'll just have a normal turkey club and a Diet Coke."

"We have Pepsi products."

"I guess I can make that work."

"So Diet Pepsi then?" the waitress asked.

"Yeah, I'd consider Diet Pepsi to be Pepsi's answer to Diet Coke," Michael said.

"Some people have a strong preference."

"With all the things that divide people, the world really comes down to two categories," Michael said. "Coke drinkers and Pepsi drinkers. And Mexicans of course."

"Have you decided, sir?"

"Since I haven't really looked at the menu, I'll do the turkey club as well. But just water. I'm Switzerland when it comes to the soda wars."

Effectively ignoring him, she continued to write as she walked away.

"I really don't hate Mexicans. She just set that joke up."

"You are a comedian after all. But you're off the clock."

"Good, because it's been a tough week."

"Want to tell me about it?"

"I had this dream, and I think I know what it means. But I don't like where it's leading."

"Was I in it?"

"Don't think so. I've had it since I was a kid. But it scares me. And—" He paused. "Well, you don't want to hear all this."

Michael looked over to see if the waitress would come and offer some relief from his discomfort. Instead, he guessed she was out smoking.

"Sometimes a dream is just a dream and your mind is a Petri dish growing something unnatural and frightening."

"Wow, you're pretty smart," Michael began.

"For a stripper?"

"No. You're pretty smart, period. I was just guessing nobody tells you that very often."

She shrugged.

"But what's even better is that you have this—this insight. Did I tell you I thought about you a lot?"

"Yeah."

"So I can tell you what group of people I really do hate. Can you guess?"

"I'm afraid to."

"Eskimos."

"Eskimos?"

"Yep. They don't seem organized enough to mount up a counterattack. And, really, you do have to hate someone. Am I right?"

"Well," she answered. "It does seem like a safe group to bash. Want to know who I hate? As long as you promise not to take it personally."

"I never looked up my family tree, so feel free to wail away."

"Men."

"So you're against roughly half the population? I'll bet Eskimos are under one percent."

"Not quite all. But I don't see the best in them. And, Mister Comedian, to cut you off at the pass, I'll tell you that I am not a lesbian. I don't know what I am. I know I'm angry. That has to count for something. But yeah, I'm fed up with most men."

"Yet you're here," he said.

"Yet I'm here."

"And I haven't shown you anything close to chivalry."

"I don't want that. I want someone to be real with me."

"Can I ask for your phone number? Before I forget. And I won't be one of those typical men folk who never calls."

She reached into her purse, and then wrote down what looked to be more than just a name and number. He wasn't ready to look at it yet, so he tucked it in his shirt. He didn't break eye contact.

The waitress returned with the drinks. "Your food should be out in a little bit."

They both nodded.

Michael finally said, "Can I tell you something about my hometown?"

"Sure."

"In just about every restaurant there, it's perfectly legal to get a three-way. And it doesn't cost much."

"You don't look like you're from Thailand."

"No, Cincinnati's much more conservative than that. But the signature dish there is called a three-way. It's spaghetti topped with chili and cheese."

"I'm just a little concerned about the combinations of three-ways and cheese."

"That's way better than my punchline."

"Maybe you should take me on the road with you."

"Yeah, maybe I should," he said. "Huntington, West Virginia, is nice this time of year."

"I've survived decades of Michigan winters. The good news is I'm not afraid of hell anymore."

***

Before they realized it, the clock registered one in the morning. The delightful waitress stood at the cash register, slowly losing her charm.

"Sorry," Dana said. "Time just kind of got away from us."

"Must be nice."

Michael paid and gave her a twenty-dollar tip. That brightened her mood a little. She waved when they left. She also looked happy to flip the sign on the door over to "Closed."

"Okay," Michael said. "How do I say this without sounding creepy? Here goes. You probably don't want to drive home tonight. I'm leaving in the morning. And, well, it would just seem rude not to invite you back to my room."

"You really aren't very good at this whole proposition thing, are you?"

"I thought I was playing it smooth."

"You get an A for effort."

"How about execution?"

"You failed miserably. But, yes, you can show me back to your quarters."

"One problem," Michael said.

"And what's that?"

"Not exactly sure where that is."

***

They had walked farther away than they realized. Once they got on the campus, it took half an hour to find someone who had a key to Michael's room. That person had to be woken up, and she made no effort to mask her contempt over it.

The room was a simple dorm with a bunk bed. There were only a television and towels. Michael was glad that there were at least two towels. His bag had been put on the top bunk.

"Not as ritzy as your last place," Dana said.

"So much for the rock star treatment."

Dana looked at the bunk beds. "You like top or bottom?"

"Never been asked that before."

"Guess you really aren't a rock star."

She sat on the bottom mattress, the only place to sit, grabbed the remote control and turned on the television.

"You know, I've seen Drew Greene many times on the comedy channel. Is it cool to be on the road with him?"

"I wish I could be coy about this, but yeah, it's actually really cool."

"Have you taken any other girls back with you?"

"Just you."

"That sounds like you're giving me a line."

"It does, doesn't it? But no, I don't have much game."

She laughed. "Was I a fool to come all the way down here?"

"Was I a fool to be excited that you did?"

Michael knew this was his time to make a move. Everything was in place. This should have been every man's dream. But there was a smile on her face that looked so sweet, so genuine. And what was better, she probably didn't even know she was doing it. She put her head on his shoulder as they watched some movie that was probably pretty popular, but he had not followed any pop culture like that in quite a while.

He definitely knew the moment had passed when he heard her breathing change, and it soon became a very faint snore. That was okay, too. It felt normal, natural. If he thought about it too much, his mind would go to a strange place again. But he just liked to watch her, this strange woman, and maybe his only fan.

He'd never sat with his wife and watched a movie. At least not that he could remember. There was a lot that he couldn't recall, but something like this would have stuck in his brain. Maybe if only he'd spent more nights like this, he wouldn't have divorced so quickly. Maybe if only he'd spent a little carefree time with her, they wouldn't have split at all. But Michael also knew a lot of his life story started with *if only*.

After a little time passed, he figured Dana would be better off lying down. She said something he couldn't quite understand as he lowered her onto the bed. He figured she was talking in her sleep, because he heard nothing else. Bending slightly, he kissed her forehead.

"Good night," he whispered. He thought about calling her his angel, but that would have been the worst thing he could have said.

A smile crossed her face. "Good night, Michael."

Just hearing her speak his name was a thrill. There was something special about her. Something he'd never felt before. She was now sound asleep. He tried to watch the television, but whatever was on just couldn't hold his interest. He kept looking over at her. But if she were to wake up to his stare, that would redefine creepy and she would be out the door, never to show up again. Yes, this was definitely an opportunity.

The best thing would be for him to step outside, get some fresh air. Hopefully he would tire, then he could climb up to the top bunk and take her to breakfast in the morning. He knew a place that served breakfast all day. Maybe he would be able to find something even nicer.

Silently he closed the door and went outside. The campus was quiet. The only other person he saw was way on the other side. Not even his own thoughts disturbed him. He couldn't remember the last time that had happened.

"Hey, are you that Mike Clover guy?" someone said, running up to him. "Yeah, you are. Man, that show was fucking hysterical. Dude, you're funnier than a public fart."

"Wow. Don't know if I'm deserving of such praise."

"I actually heard you on Mac and Mark. Funny as hell."

"Thanks, pal."

"I really thought you were funnier than Drew Greene tonight. I mean, you gotta love Drew. He's a legend and all, but you brought it tonight."

"Really?"

"Seriously. His jokes are classic, don't get me wrong. But you know, classic is just another way of saying old. Your shit was fresh. Can I buy you a beer?"

"No, I'm good. And it's late."

"I know. We only got about forty-five minutes before last call. And how many times do I get to have a drink with a famous person?"

"I'm famous?"

"You were on coast-to-coast radio. You go around the country because you're funny. That counts as a celebrity. My name's Nick by the way."

Michael thought about it. Did people out there really know who he was? Would more very soon? Had this dream morphed into reality without him realizing it? One thing he knew was that he would not be able to sleep now. And since he didn't like beer, he would just have one. It would settle him down, and he'd be able to function once again. He'd be no good to anyone completely sleep-deprived.

"Okay, Nick. You drive a hard bargain. You really think I'm funnier than a public fart?"

***

The bar was a typical dive, poorly lit, which was beneficial because it masked how dirty the place probably was. There were old televisions up on corners, and not the flat screens that were all the rage in most establishments.

"What are you drinking?" Nick asked. "I'm a Guinness man myself."

"I could go for a chewable beverage."

"Yo, Tommy," Nick said to the bartender. "Two Guinness."

A minute later the drinks were delivered. "Who's your friend, Nick?"

Nick stood up and announced to the bar, "This is the very funny and famous Mike Clover, on tour with Drew Greene and hanging out in Columbus tonight."

"Oh, yeah," Tommy said. "Drew Greene, eh?"

"I'm just his opening act."

"But he takes you out on the road with him? Sweet gig you got there. Sweet fucking gig."

"It's fun."

"Well, the drink is on the house."

"I thought Nick was buying for me."

Tommy looked over at Nick, who shrugged. "Well, your second drink is on the house then."

"Okay, but after that I'd better get back. It's close to last call. Don't want to get you in trouble or anything."

"Hell, it's my bar," Tommy said and flipped the sign to mark that the place was closed. "Ain't no law against hanging out with my friends. Got any jokes you want to work out on us?"

Michael shrugged. "Yeah, I'm always writing. I may have something."

CHAPTER THIRTY-SIX

He'd always known Ohio State was a big place. But at 4:30 in the morning there was nobody wandering around. Michael wasn't even sure if that was indeed the time, but he guessed the big clock on campus was probably accurate. His world was desolate, like he was the last man alive. He should have asked Nick for some help, but the poor guy had long since passed out. Probably a couple of hours ago. Oh well. He was just a kid.

But even if he did see someone, he really didn't know what any names were. The best he could do is ask where the dorm rooms were, and he knew that if he couldn't find a dorm room at this school, he couldn't find boobs on the Internet. The thought amused him. He would have written it down, but that was simply too much work. Hopefully he'd remember it later, though that was the least of his concerns.

By the time he found his room, he realized he'd left his key inside. It was too late to knock, and there was a possibility that he'd picked the wrong room. That would set off a panic, one that would likely get back to Drew. A disaster would be averted if he just waited in the hallway. Dana would wake up and, well, what would she do?

He tried not to think about it as he slid his back down the door and eventually fell asleep.

***

"Michael. Michael, what happened?" Dana asked as she opened the door. His head fell into the doorway when she opened it. The rest of his body sprawled out in the hallway.

Slowly he opened his eyes. "Dana?"

She shook her head. "Get up. You don't want the impressionable youth to see you like this."

He tried to stand, but just getting up on his elbow brought on dizziness and nausea. He remained in the position until he got onto his knees. It took at least a couple of minutes before he could stand. At that point, however, he had to go into full sprint so he could throw up in the bathroom.

When he had finally finished retching, he realized his toothbrush was still in his bag. He wiped his mouth as much as he could with a washcloth and stepped back into the room. Dana was standing in the room, her purse on her shoulder, her eyes swollen and red.

"I really need to brush my teeth," he said.

"And I really need to go."

"I was hoping to take you out to breakfast. I know this place that serves breakfast all day." He put his hand up to his mouth and breathed out. "Wow, I need a hell of a lot more than Double Mint."

"I really need to go."

"Can I take you—" he began.

"No. Don't. I have to go. It just breaks my heart that I was right about you. I've been wrong about so many other things. Why did you have to be the one I got right?"

"What are you talking about?"

"Look. I know you weren't exactly clean when I saw you last night. But you were still so sweet. And then you leave and end up in the hallway too fucked up to stand. Even I deserve better than that."

He nodded.

"At least for a short while I was able to pretend. For that I thank you. But for everything else, well, I've got to go."

Michael didn't try to stop her as she walked out the door. She barely looked at him. He wanted to tell her that while she may have been right about him, she was terribly wrong when talking about herself. She deserved the best of the best. The only problem was that she didn't know where to look.

Even if he could tell her anything, it wouldn't have made a difference. He'd had a chance. She was in his room, and he'd chosen to spend the night with drunken strangers. How could she not be upset?

When she was gone, he still stood in place. Maybe, just maybe, she would come back. It wouldn't have been a wise move. If he ever got the chance to talk to his sister, he'd certainly tell her to run from a guy like that. Run and keep running.

He knew he should talk to Jessie. But she was lost to him as well. Dana had just left, and she was long gone. Calling home and talking to Mom didn't seem as painful as before, but he couldn't bring himself to actually pick up the phone. He could do that later.

If he didn't brush his teeth, he wouldn't be able to stand himself any longer. That should have been a shorter leash. He'd given himself way too much slack. Perhaps a shower would help clear his head as well.

***

It took him much longer to get ready than usual. Physically he felt okay, a little queasy but not bad. Everything else, however, was terrible. He felt like he should cry, but he simply felt too vacant.

He was on time to meet Drew. At least he still had a job, and a good one at that.

"Ready to hit the road?" Drew asked.

Michael nodded. He had never been more ready.

CHAPTER THIRTY-SEVEN

There was some comfort back out on the open road. All the towns looked the same, every horizon only lead to another horizon. It wasn't long before the pain was less than a speck in the rearview mirror. He just hoped that the next stop, wherever that might be, would be a long distance.

It felt sad to him that he did not know where they were going. He certainly was not a big enough star to be indifferent to people who just might call themselves fans. But soon he would be entertaining them. Soon the road would take him far from here. There he could be safe.

Drew was back to his usual quiet self. Hopefully he hadn't seen the latest fiasco. It had been so late that there probably wasn't anybody around to see.

He was exhausted and hoped for dreamless sleep, but his mind raced too frantically. While he tried not to think about Dana—and he was certain she was going to be doing the same—she'd said some things that made him wonder. Had he told her about the dream? Just because the mind told something in a dream, that didn't necessarily make it prophecy.

Even in his younger years, he had never been good at keeping his thoughts still.

Dana had also said she'd been wrong so many times in her life. She was a smart woman, but sometimes smart people tended to make the worst decisions. Maybe he was just a victim of bad choices, but it sure felt like more than that. What was worse was that he was left with a lot of time alone with his thoughts.

CHAPTER THIRTY-EIGHT

The middle of America, Michael decided, was home. He knew what to expect and he liked it. His humor worked, and he never had to venture far out of his comfort zone. It pained him that the tour with Drew Greene was coming to a close. More than anything, he wanted to beg Drew to take him out again. This was the good life, and he didn't want to give it up.

After doing shows in Kansas City, Omaha, and Tucson, Drew knocked on Michael's hotel room. There were only two more stops left—Aspen and Denver, both big shows—then it was back home, whatever that meant. The show the night before had gone pretty well. He'd closed the bar next door, but he'd done his job by playing friendly with the locals. If he didn't know better, he thought he might have made himself some new fans. This was probably the time to start asking about the future.

Drew had waited until early afternoon. He might not have appreciated Michael's method of rubbing elbows with the fans, but it was part of the job after all.

"I didn't order room service," Michael said.

"I'm just glad you have clothes on."

"I'm wearing a thong under this."

"I'll take your word for it. Here, take this." Drew handed Michael a folded-up piece of paper. "Call this number."

"Who is it?"

"Just call and tell me about it."

Drew left and Michael looked at the number. He didn't recognize it, but he couldn't think of any number he would recognize off the top of his head. There was no name on it, so he went ahead and dialed. After three rings, someone picked up.

"Yeah, this is Charlie."

"Uh, hi. I'm Michael. Michael Clover. I was told to call."

"Hold on."

There was no hold music, but Michael was sure he recognized the voice. A second later he was back.

"Yeah, sorry about that, Mike. How's the road with Drew?"

"Interesting."

"But it's coming to an end, right?"

"Well, yeah. It is. I think."

"It is. So anyway, if you didn't know, this is Charlie from a little dog and pony show called Mac and Mark. We got some calls about your little bits here, so we've been replaying them every now and then."

"Cool."

"Glad you approve. Well, the reason I'm calling is this: Wilson Warrick is going to emcee some shows to kick off a tour. The Mac and Mark Comedy Tour. Interested?"

"Me?"

"Yes, you. I need to fill the opening act. It will be fourteen dates, starting in Boston and heading down the east coast. This will start about two months after your last show in Denver. Guess it's more like ten weeks. If you want to be on it, you need to tell me."

"Yes. Yes, of course."

"Okay, you're on. I'm sure you'll know some of the other names on the tour. I'll get them to you when they've confirmed."

"Sounds good."

"Yeah. Yeah, it is. Now, if I understand, you don't even have a cell phone, so I'll send the information through Drew for now."

"Uh, okay."

"Yeah," Charlie said. "That's okay for now, but for your own sake, get a cell phone. Even homeless people have them."

"Will do."

"See that you do. We'll be in touch, no matter how roundabout the method."

Charlie hung up and Michael sat in silence, wondering where this wild ride would take him next. And how odd did it feel to call a famous comedian to tell him he was set to take off with more?

CHAPTER THIRTY-NINE

Colorado was just as magnificent as promised. No wonder so many beer commercials were filmed here. The scenery was breathtaking, Michael sometimes wondered if the mountains were real and not just some elaborate painting stretching up to the stratosphere. As the car wound up and down the terrain, Michael gazed out the window. He wished he had a camera, just to remind him that such places really did exist. The people were just as friendly. As long as he didn't make fun of the Denver Broncos or drink anything other than Coors, he would find himself in a good place.

"Ever been out here?" Drew asked.

"No. And I've been missing out."

"Yes. Yes, you have. I'd play this place for free, but let's just keep that our little secret."

"It's safe."

"Speaking of secrets, you didn't tell me Mac and Mark were re-airing your little segment."

"Yeah. Pretty cool," Michael answered.

"Pretty cool? Don't downplay that shit. If that happens more and you get back on there, which with the tour and all is pretty much a guarantee, then you're on your way to headlining."

"Seriously?"

"To coin an old phrase, I'm as serious as untreated syphilis."

"Wow."

"You must understand syphilis. But yeah. Better keep writing, and get used to the spotlight. You'll be under it longer."

"I know I said it before, but wow."

Drew paused. "How's your biggest fan?"

"Talking about my dead father might be an easier conversation."

"Ah. Sorry."

"Don't worry. There's more out there. Comedians don't get rock star groupies, but you'll do okay. That's the extent of my pep talk."

"Get right back up on that horse, right?"

"That's kind of gross, but if that's your thing, then so be it. You are from Ohio after all."

"Yes," Michael nodded. "But I was from a poorer part of the state, so when we resorted to bestiality, which was quite frequent, especially during the holidays, we had to settle for stray dogs or the occasional dead raccoon."

"I've done worse. Reminds me of a waitress in Wisconsin. But you do have to be careful out here. And it looks like women is something else that needs to be added to your vice list."

"There was something different about Dana," Michael said, wishing he could make himself stop talking. "But I'm sure there will be something different about the next one. And the one after her, too."

"Then you'll stop noticing."

Michael wanted to ask Drew if he was being sarcastic, because his voice betrayed nothing. While that was part of his demeanor, he just hoped for a straight answer. "Yeah, I guess I will. That will keep things from getting too complicated."

"Sometimes life is better complicated. Just because I couldn't handle it doesn't mean that there isn't something to it. I may try again somewhere. Someday," Drew said, his voice trailing off.

This easily could have been the end of the conversation, but Michael couldn't seem to stop talking. "She told me a joke."

"One to keep for the act?"

"It was a very direct one. And I don't think she was joking."

"So let's hear it. Maybe I can steal it."

"Okay, here goes. So a guy walks into a psychiatrist's office and says, 'Doc, I'm just so depressed. Life just hurts too much. I can't take it anymore. I don't know what I should do.'"

"And the guy turns out to be the clown himself?" Drew interrupted.

"Guess I've got to get up awfully early in the morning to get a joke past you."

"Not so much that. But I had thought about telling you that one. Just a little more free mentoring advice that I'm not so good at. So, as my profession might indicate, I resort to telling jokes."

Michael gazed out the window. The spectacular view didn't feel so magical any longer. "Wow."

"Guess you shouldn't have let that one get away."

CHAPTER FORTY

In an attempt to make some change in her life, Dana stopped dancing to Rob Zombie in favor of a mix of Lenny Kravitz and Soundgarden. Maybe if that went well, she could move on to a combination of Perry Como and Motörhead. Nobody would notice, or if they did,they wouldn't care, so she might as well be amused.

She almost laughed to herself, thinking that she was back to the daily grind as she thrust herself against the stripper pole and was rewarded with a few dollars tossed her way. At least the rent was getting paid. At least she knew what she was doing.

As her second song ended, Elijah, filling in as the voice of Whispers, said, "Gentlemen, get those hands out of your pants and put them together to clap for Angel, that classy lass with the dynamite ass."

Dana acknowledged the coerced applause and started to walk toward the back when she saw a figure that disgusted her. Even in the poor light, she could not help but notice the pervert who'd touched her crotch and made even a dirty girl feel impossibly filthy. Her first thought was to wonder why he'd been allowed back in, but she'd never said a word before. She'd just let it all go. Instead she only hoped he wouldn't show up. But she should have known better than to hope for something like that. If she wasn't stupid, she certainly was a slow learner.

Troy. That was the rat bastard's name. She couldn't believe she had forgotten, but there were a lot of things she couldn't believe that had proven themselves to be true right before her eyes.

"So guys," Elijah continued, in love with the sound of his own voice, "if you appreciate what a good job Angel does, let her show you in a closer setting. Just ask her about a private dance. Not recommended for those with a pacemaker, or women who are nursing, pregnant or may become pregnant, or for guys with a history of stroke leading to carpal tunnel syndrome." He was not able to finish the last sentence without a laugh that led to a smoker's cough.

Troy briefly looked over, but her face, in no uncertain terms, told him that it would be the death of him if he took a step closer. She also would have been lying to herself if she said she didn't want to do a dance for him. As soon he tried his perverted hijinks, she would be justified to jump up, kick him under the chin, watch and listen to his head snap back at the same time, and let the paramedics deliver him with a story to tell the emergency room doctor as well as his unsuspecting wife. Now that would be entertainment. That would feel good. But instead he was talking to Cinnamon. He whispered something in her ear, something that clearly unsettled her, but still she returned a hesitant nod. Dana wanted to run up and scream at both of them now, but it would do no good, and at least Cinnamon knew what she was getting into.

Nobody asked Dana for a dance, and it was hard to see that as anything positive. Finding a silver lining was just going to have to remain impossible. She could use a break, adjust the makeup, maybe take up smoking or something else equally productive. For now she was just happy that people were leaving her the hell alone.

CHAPTER FORTY-ONE

The hotel and the club in Denver were better than he could have asked for, even if he were a real celebrity. He was given star treatment, and when he got a phone call from Charlie, the attendant at the front desk called back to verify that he had indeed received it. Apparently he was a fan of the show, therefore a fan of Drew of course, and now Michael. Since he was a nice kid, Michael listened to a few jokes, and laughed politely. In truth, they weren't so bad.

Charlie was just calling to say that Michael was slated to do a half-hour set. While he still wouldn't say much about the other comedians, he did assure him that their credits included late-night national shows, one of whom was veteran enough to have been on Johnny Carson. Others, outside of Mac and Mark of course, had Comedy Central specials as well as CDs and videos.

So instead of heading out and seeing the sights, Michael stayed in the hotel to work on a few ideas. If he didn't know better, he might have just confused himself for a professional. Plus, in all the thin air, he had heard that it didn't take more than a drink or two to start a buzz. After the show, he could experiment to see if this was indeed the truth, but for now he had work to do.

He felt that he had made the right decision for a change, because his first show went really well. The material worked with the audience. His pacing had certainly improved.

"So I'm guessing that when we aren't talking about the Broncos in these parts, we have some Rockies fans."

Just about everyone in the club clapped. When there was enthusiasm even before the joke, he was confident the rest would go well.

"Yeah, I'm a baseball fan. But now, it's gotten to the point where you can't talk about baseball without at least mentioning steroids."

The grumbling in the audience came from agreement. He was still okay.

"I'm guessing with the thin air up here, there's no need for performance enhancers. Hell, with a combination of juiced players and a city that's a mile high, the fucking ball might end up in Utah. That is a border state, right? I never was so good at geology. But yeah, the whole steroid scandal just doesn't bother me. Apparently some of the players were going to step up and address the issue, but nobody had the balls."

Even that throwaway joke got a good laugh, even though he was certain it had been done before, probably countless times.

"Although it does get to be a bit of a problem when you flip on the television and realize that what's on ESPN is also being shown on C-SPAN. Yeah, they've got these players up on Capitol Hill, swearing on bibles that they indeed did not take steroids.

"And now they start talking about charging these players with perjury? Can someone here please explain to me *why* it's a

278

crime to lie to Congress? Is that not just the ultimate hypocrisy? Seriously. You lie to Congress, you get arrested. You lie *in* Congress you get re-elected."

Michael was not expecting the applause and laughter to come before the joke ended, but if that was his biggest problem, then life was pretty damn good.

"I tell you, the very idea of being charged with lying to Congress is like being charged with wearing a mullet at a NASCAR race in West Virginia. It's a when-in-Rome type of thing here, people."

The laughter was intoxicating.

"And now the baseball commissioner is stepping up to say that this whole fiasco is going to hurt the players' Hall of Fame chances."

He paused to switch gears.

"Could you imagine if The Rock & Roll Hall of Fame kicked out anybody who has ever taken an illegal substance?"

The laughter came in waves. He had not experienced that in a while,and he loved every second of it.

"So suddenly, MTV and C-SPAN are being simulcast."

Michael put his index finger up to his ear to imitate a reporter.

"Dateline: Cleveland. After months of investigation, it has been determined that shamed rockers like Jim Morrison, Janis Joplin, and Jimi Hendrix have indeed behaved badly. Their displays are being dismantled to make room for the new wing featuring The Osmonds, The Cowsills, The Doodletown Pipers, and Frankie Valli and the Four Seasons."

He put his finger back to his ear.

"This just in: it's now Frankie Vail and the *Three* Seasons."

He was ready to go back to his more rehearsed material, but it felt good to have some new stuff to work with.

***

Michael stuck around for all of Drew's set before talking with some of the people. Most people wanted to meet Drew, and that only made sense. He was the one who had been telling jokes for a living for a long time now. But Michael got quite a few compliments, and more than one flirtation from a woman who was well out of his league. Who knew dick jokes could take him so far? The secret to success was much easier than any self-help guru's book would ever say.

"Wow, who would have thought that my brother would become a professional goofball?"

Michael nearly jumped when he saw Jessie. She didn't look any different than, well, however long it had been since he'd last seen her. He tried not to think about that. Her face just looked a little tired. Her shoulders, however, were not stooped over. She stood tall without being instructed to do so.

He ran over to Jessie and gave her a hug. Even though it was only a few steps, it felt considerably longer.

"It's so good to see you," he finally said.

"Well, I was nearby."

"Really?"

"No, but I saw you'd be in Colorado, and since I've never been here, nor have I seen you onstage—or for that matter, seen you at all—it seemed like as good a time as any to rack up some frequent flier miles."

"So you came out here to see me?"

"No," Jessie said. "I came out here for me. I needed a break. But I also needed something else. It's good to see you."

Michael could only nod.

"And it's so nice out here. Even though I don't know anybody out here, it would just be nice to go somewhere I can just completely start over."

"I've thought that before," he replied.

"Dad would have thought you were hysterical up there. He would have been really proud. Really proud."

"Yeah, he liked this type of thing. Maybe I got something good from the old man after all."

Jessie nodded. "Dad wasn't all bad."

"He wasn't."

"I miss him, too."

"I even miss the sitcoms. Damn, that man had some deplorable taste. So," Michael continued, changing the subject, "you came out here on a vacation?"

"No. I was running away. Got divorced. I married an asshole. I can't believe things didn't work out. Ultimately, he's paying for this. I should have flown first class."

"You deserve it. And my ex-brother-in-law, whoever he is, deserves to get the bill. It only seems fair." He would have to remind himself to write on a scrap-note, *I'm divorced, but that's cool, since that's the only thing about me that's remotely trendy.*

"Some things never balance out. Not looking for them to."

"Well, you should," Michael said, then began to stammer. "I'm sorry I never contacted you."

"It's okay. What would you say? What would I say? Anything you would have said would have reminded me of something I was trying to forget. So if it makes you feel any better, I didn't want to hear from you. But that's not something for you to take personally."

"I was thinking about you."

"I know. Clear your conscience. And be careful. I don't believe everything I see on the Internet, but what I've pulled up on you, well, I wish I could say I'm full of greater doubt."

Michael stared back, his mouth gaped open. He wanted to ask what she'd read and where, but he probably didn't want to know. The idea that he was important enough to have gossip written about him momentarily filled his head.

"Mikey, the biggest problem with this world is not how few good guys there are out there. And trust me, the pickings are slim. The tragedy is that there are some good men who refuse to play the role. And another thing I do know is that you are one of the good guys."

"Well, I don't know about all that."

"You can learn from your little sister."

"I've got another show tonight. I'd invite you to stay, but you're just going to hear the same jokes again."

"If a joke is funny the first time, it's funny every time after that."

"You quote a wise man."

"Right or wrong, he'll always be Dad."

"What happened? You sound all grown up now," Michael said.

"It happens. It should happen to all of us, but I digress. And Ugh isn't Ugh anymore. He's Mr. Uggla. Somehow he's a travel agent. I called him, and he set this up for me."

"A person named Ugh should never grow up."

"I know you have another audience coming in," Jessie said. "I hope they love you as much as the first one. But remember that you can still be loved when you aren't making someone laugh."

"Did someone put you up to this?"

"No. But, really, for a man who makes his living off his wits, you can be awfully dense. I'll meet you here when the show's over. We'll catch up. It's been too long."

Michael was hoping to say more, but Jessie left and a few guys came up to say they liked the show. Most of the time that was good, but he was finding it hard to just smile and say thanks. By the time he was through with the pleasantries, his sister was gone.

He didn't see Drew walk up behind him.

"I liked the Rock & Roll Hall of Fame bit. Keep that."

"Uh, thanks, Drew."

"Listen, I'm going to grab a bite with an old friend. I was going to talk to you about expanding your set when you hit the coast, but guess I don't have to. And who told you Hendrix used drugs?"

"I have my sources."

"Okay," Drew said and patted Michael on the back like they were longtime buddies. "I'll see you in a bit."

Once Drew had left, Michael looked around. The only people left were the staff busing tables.

"Can I get you anything, Mike?" one of the waiters asked.

"Yeah," he replied, trying to think if he had ever known this guy's name. "Yeah, buddy. I feel like celebrating. Crown Royal?"

Before Michael realized it, the waiter had returned. "Get you anything else?"

He shook his head no and sat down with his drink. He had forgotten just how damn good it was, and he asked for another. The second was just as smooth, just as refined. His third finally relaxed him, and he took the drink into the back when he saw the first of the late-night crowd start to wander in.

It did not take long for the club to fill to capacity, and in what seemed like seconds later, the emcee was onstage. Michael asked for a bottle of Coors so he could play nice to the crowd. After the Crown Royal, the beer was like eating a gas station hot dog after being accustomed to filet mignon. But it was only a prop since he didn't plan on doing more than just nurse it.

The bottle was a little more than half empty when he was finally summoned to the stage. He had forgotten to write down the idea of divorce being trendy, but if he were to get stuck, he could fall back to it. He also figured that the myth of getting intoxicated easier in the light air was indeed untrue since he barely felt a buzz. Instead he was filled with a new confidence. It was a good time to examine his act. The big shows were coming up, and that would be no place to tinker around. He'd thought he had hit pay dirt when Drew Greene, seemingly out of nowhere, took him out on the road. Apparently, that was only the beginning.

When he shook the emcee's hand, following up with the ever-popular half hug, he realized he had forgotten the guy's name. That didn't fill him with panic any longer.

"That's a funny man right there," Michael said when he took the microphone. "Great kisser, too."

A few people chuckled, but he knew he shouldn't have expected more out of an old joke.

"Now, guys, have you ever been so horny you fantasize about your own wife?"

His opening line worked well enough, and he was ready for the show to begin again.

CHAPTER FORTY-TWO

Even though the audience for the second show was not as enthusiastic, Michael still felt like he hit his marks and put on a good performance. The crowd was at least warmed up for the headliner, and that was ultimately his job.

The emcee jogged back up onstage and said, "Michael Clover would be a much better kisser if he didn't always have dick on his breath. There are some things Mentos just can't cover."

Michael looked up onstage, wondering what the hell this guy was talking about when he remembered the joke about him being a great kisser. At least he didn't have to worry about not knowing his name any longer. As far as anybody knew right now, they were pretty tight.

Drew would be onstage shortly. His set went about fifty minutes, so that meant Jessie would be by in roughly an hour. He still couldn't believe she'd come all the way to Colorado. Clearly she had talked to their mother, and she would have told her about his visit. He wanted to see her, he really did, but he was already so overloaded with feelings he could not control, much less identify, that he could not handle anything else.

"Good show out there, Mike," the waiter said when Michael made his way to the back of the room. "Can I get you another Crown Royal?"

"Oh, I could just kiss you if the taste in my mouth wasn't so, well, distinctive."

He just needed a drink and a moment to relax. If there had been another ultra cool waitress with a small bag of cocaine and a big heart to share it, that would have been all the better. But for now he could have a good drink and hope the next hour would go quickly.

The audience applauded loudly, meaning Drew Greene had just been announced. Maybe he could watch his show, get some pointers, and be a better comedian by night's end. It was a job after all.

"Damn, it's good to be back in Denver. I asked my travel agent to send me to the mile-high city, and after four and a half months in Amsterdam, I realized I was in the wrong place."

Michael couldn't tell if they loved the joke or if they loved Drew. Whatever the case, he wondered how he could get them to love him. Before he forgot, he pulled out a slip of paper and wrote down the divorce joke, finding it less amusing now.

The waiter put down an empty glass in front of him. Before Michael could give the standard everyone-is-a-comedian line, he saw that there was a nearly full bottle of Crown Royal in front of him. Damn was show business ever a good thing. Before he could thank him, he was gone.

He poured a glass almost to the top. Since he was pretty sure he shouldn't have the bottle, it was bound to be taken away soon. He didn't want to appear too greedy, so he should just sip and enjoy. When he looked at the clock, he saw that Drew was about halfway through his set, and that meant he would see Jessie very soon.

"Now is it just me, or is Republican Party a contradiction in terms?" Drew said. "A bunch of Republicans hanging out does not make for a good time. But don't think I'm leaving out Democrats, because I've been to California, and that's a breeding ground out there. Yeah, the Dems have the support of Hollywood, but is that really the ringing endorsement you want? *Yes, we have the backing of science-fiction religions, career transvestites, and millions of people who think it is a good idea to live on the San Andreas Fault Line.*"

Michael finished one last drink, spilling just a little on the tablecloth, and walked outside to wait for Jessie. The crowd burst into more laughter as he left. He knew he should have remembered what that joke was, but he had to leave. There had been too much laughter for one day.

The air might have been clean except for the cigarette smoke wafting his way. He barely noticed. Even if he had, it wouldn't have bothered him. He hadn't smoked since he tried to look cool back when he was a kid. Since he was sure that never worked for him, he never picked it up again. But he always hated when someone took an artificial higher ground over someone with the vice. There had to be some sort of joke in there about some areas being so polluted that a cigarette may actually increase the air quality. Los Angeles came to mind, and since everything except tobacco was legal there, it seemed like a joke would just write itself. Not today, however.

He walked down the sidewalk a bit and leaned against a tree. Then he sat. Waves of familiar nausea hit, and the last thing he wanted was for Jessie to see him throwing up. She'd traveled over one thousand miles for this trip. The very least he could do would be to not puke on her. It was only polite. He realized part of his problem must have been the thin air. Since he hadn't had all that much to drink, that was the most likely reason.

Once he closed his eyes, the awful feeling intensified. But after keeping them closed a little longer, he found comfort in the darkness. He apparently lost all track of time, because he heard people walking past him. He knew it must have been the crowd from the comedy club, but he also felt like he was in a controlled dream. If he really had to, he could wake up.

"Mikey."

It was Jessie. And it was definitely time to wake up.

The job proved more difficult than he had originally thought. By the time his eyes stopped fluttering, his legs had gained at least seventy-five pounds apiece. His arms, however, had become weak, uncoordinated and completely incapable of moving his cumbersome legs. As he looked up, he saw that his sister was not exactly inclined to help out. Her eyes just looked sad.

"Hey, Jess. It's the thin air up here. It makes everything different. Colorado is the perfect place for the alcoholic on a budget."

"What are you talking about?"

"Oh. Nothing. Just that I can hold my liquor most of the time, but see, at these higher altitudes, it's a different world. So I must apologize for this rather unseemly sight."

"Once again the Internet was correct."

"Was I on Wikipedia?"

"Come on, get up."

Michael looked up to see that Jessie had her hand extended to help this time. He also realized that somehow, he was now lying on the ground instead of leaning against the tree. Once he had taken her hand, he was surprised at how easily he was back on his feet. While he was not exactly stable, at least he was standing.

"Where to, sis? Sounds like you know the neighborhood better than I do."

"I just called for a cab. It's going to take you back to your hotel room first, then me back to mine. That way I can feel a little more confident that you'll live through another night, and I can get back so I can pack and go home. It's been a good vacation, but I'm ready for home."

"Not sure what home means."

"Don't know? Maybe, well, home is where the heart is."

"Home is where all your stuff is."

"It's just an apartment, but I miss it. Imagine a place you can go and feel comfortable. A place to think, feel, and be happy. Do you know what happened when I walked past the old house the other day?"

He shrugged.

"Nothing. I thought I missed it. I mean it was a decent house. There was nothing wrong with it. But what made me sad was what the place should have meant to me, but didn't. So all that happened was that I walked past a house."

"But you weren't the one that destroyed it."

"No. And it wasn't you either. That said, you sure are doing a great job imitating the person that did. You're doing comedy; Dad would have been proud of that. You should know that by now. But he would be screaming at you right now for all the right reasons if he were here. I believe that."

"He would also be screaming since I was the one who killed him."

"Fucking stop it, Michael. This is not about you. Dad was a good man. He was a sick man, but he was good, and I sure as hell will not sit here and listen to whatever fucked-up viewpoint you want to take on the worst day of my life. You can let whatever guilt you've got inside you form whatever image you want, but it's stupid, wrong, and dangerous. If holding onto Daddy's failures makes you feel better, then so be it. But know this: being some sort of hotshot right now does not mean a damn thing. That's because more people will have mourned Daddy than you. If you die, yeah, sure, it will make the news, but we're not talking front page story here. Then something else will happen, and people will forget. Hell, I might forget because I don't even know you."

"Damn. I thought you were here so we could catch up."

"Mikey, it's your job to make people laugh. That sounds good, but when is last time you laughed? When is the last time you were happy?"

"Well—" Michael began.

"And I know you are going to give some smart-ass answer here, and right now, I don't want to hear it. I'm going to go back to the hotel so I can go home, be content, be real. You can go on to whatever city is next, be whatever it is you are up there, and move on. I just hope the next time I read about you, it won't be a tragic story that will make people momentarily sad."

"How'd you know it was going to be a smart-ass answer?"

"Because it's what I would have done in your place. What was your answer going to be?"

"The last time I was happy was just before they shut down the massage parlor."

290

"See, Mikey, that was kind of lame. You may have some funny stuff sometimes, but you're not ready for improv."

"Damn, you got harsh since we last talked."

"Beware of people willing to kiss your ass. Be thankful for those who care enough to kick it."

Michael laughed. "Thanks. I needed that."

"The laugh or the kick?"

"Both equally."

***

The taxicab pulled up to the curb, and Jessie waved that they were coming. Michael's feet shuffled along, but he did speed up ahead of Jessie so he could open the door for her. She scooted over so he didn't have to walk around to the other side.

"What hotel are you staying at?" she asked.

"Oh," he said, slurring slightly, and leaned forward to talk to the driver. "It's a Marriott. I know there are a bunch of those, but it's only a few blocks."

"Wow, look at you," she said.

"And this time, I know which hotel it is. If you get that wrong, it can make for a lot of confusion. And a lot of walking."

"Seriously?"

"Sadly, about this I'm not joking."

"Now that is a real shame. How can you show up at the wrong hotel?"

"There have been times when I didn't know what city I was in. When I found out, I didn't care."

She laughed. "That I can believe. Any good stories from the road?"

"I met some really cool lady. She was awesome, and, well, rather easy on the eyes. And get this. I think she liked me."

"That's good."

"It was. At least it was until I scared her off. She gave me her number, but I lost it. I don't think she would want me to call even if I still had it."

"Should I ask?"

"You don't need to. I'm guessing you already know."

She shook her head. "There's more out there. Stop scaring them off. Stop scaring me."

The short drive was already over.

"Is this your hotel?" the driver asked.

Michael nodded even though he wasn't sure the man was looking in the rearview mirror. "Yep, for now it's home."

"Come home again. If just to visit."

Again, he only nodded, this time because he knew that if he started crying he wouldn't stop, and that would probably require that he tip the driver more. With that in mind, he reached for his wallet.

"I'll pay for the cab. Go inside and sleep in a bed, not outside where people have to step over you. When Mom asks about how the visit went, I won't tell her about that part."

"You're a hell of a gal," he said and reached over and hugged her. "And thank you. We'll talk soon."

He hopped out of the car and paused to turn and wave but only saw the taxi pulling out of the parking lot and onto the street.

There was still so much more to say, but at this point, he didn't know what. And if he did, he likely wouldn't know where to begin or why he was doing so. Sometimes leaving things unsaid was simple wisdom. It was good to see her, good to know she was okay, but it was more than that. It was a hell of a lot more than he could imagine. He belonged. He had family.

No matter how reprehensible he had become, there was still a door open.

But Jessie had done something else. She'd challenged him to grow up. Perhaps she was just dreaming, because that felt like a pointless task. After all, what was the point? He was lucky enough to make a living off of being immature. Not many were that damn lucky. If he had a business card, which would probably be a good idea down the line, it could say *Professional Goofball*. Now that definitely would have made dear old dad proud.

Maybe if he just started making subtle improvements like flossing his teeth or attempting a sit up every now and then, he would at least be accomplishing something. Eating the occasional fruit or vegetable sounded like something else to go on the list. And, of course, he could call home. Once he finally got a cell phone and joined the rest of society, that would be the first call. Nobody was meant to grow up in a single day.

Inside the hotel, the bar was empty. He didn't even see anyone working there, so he figured he might as well just go up to his room. Few things were more pathetic than having to beg someone to pour a drink. And an overpriced one at that.

His room had a nice desk with a view of a shopping center. That was much nicer than the usual freeway just outside his room. He also knew that it was an ideal time to write. Just a few thoughts here or there that could be polished at a later time.

Some of his best jokes worked that way. First he would cut out a chunk. From there he would chisel until it was funny. Sometimes it wasn't, and he ended up forcing it, but it was his method.

Instead he turned on the television and watched someone else's work while sitting on the bed. He was not tired at all. A nice, crisp gin and tonic sounded comforting, and the lime could help put him on the road to better nutrition. Might as well have a buzz while nourishing against scurvy. But to do so, he would have to leave the hotel again, and that was just too much of an obstacle.

Before long he found himself watching *Family Ties*. It was probably the most sophisticated of his father's favorite shows. Of all the character defects that man had, his taste might somehow have been the most egregious. Michael smiled. Watching the idiot box with the family had been such a good time. All the memories didn't have to be bad; Jessie knew that. There was no point in taking what had been bad and making it worse, either. On the television, wacky neighbor Skippy said something that triggered the laugh track. After the show's run had ended, Marc Price, the actor who played Skippy, wound up doing stand-up. How cool would it have been to introduce him to his father? While certainly that might not have been impressive in most people's minds, it would have been a connection, some silly timeless moment they could have laughed about later.

Only it was too late. He had said goodbye to his father years ago. Thinking too much about it now just kept the wound from healing.

But he'd never said goodbye. Not that he could remember. He must have gone through some of the ritual, but that was so long ago.

He got up to flip off the one light that lit the entire room, then turned down the volume, leaving the screen to flash images that reflected in the darkness. As he moved to sit back on the bed, the view outside the window caught his attention. He stood again to peer outside.

There was nothing interesting going on. He envied being in a place where he could be quiet and boring.

"Dad, I'm sure you can't hear me," he said to the empty room. "And I know this is stupid, me just talking to myself, but I want you to know that I miss you. Jess said you would be proud of me, but I'm not so sure. You shouldn't be, and if you see any of this shit going on down here, well, I'm sure you're anything but happy. I kind of fucked some stuff up. Maybe if you can't hear me, you'll read about it in the newsletter."

Michael turned from the view and sat down on the bed. "Guess I'm still talking. See, Dad, part of my problem is that I don't know when to shut up. And I am talking to myself, right? Since there's no sign, I'll take it that I'm right."

He looked around and saw nothing in the room. He wouldn't look at the television, afraid that instead of seeing Skippy or Michael J. Fox playing their characters, he would see them staring right at him from beyond, speaking some direct message like a cliché from a really bad horror movie.

"I knew I was right. I just had some complimentary whiskey with free refills a little while ago, and since there aren't many people in my life I can drunk dial, I thought I would try to extend into another world and see how you're doing. Yeah, I know. I sound pretty stupid. If you're up there next to Solomon, and you can both hear me, he might suggest to you that you cut me in half. He was wise like that."

He stood up again and turned off the television, being careful not to look at the screen and leaving the room in near darkness. "Dad, what I think I am trying to say here is that I'm sorry. And that I forgive you."

His legs began to wobble, and he sat on the bed. There was no way he could even think about sleeping. As soon as strength returned to his body, he left the room to go out and have a drink.

CHAPTER FORTY-THREE

Michael slept the entire drive to the tour's last stop. He didn't even remember where he was when he got there. Drew had to get him up so he didn't miss the final show. Between Drew pounding on the door and the foul taste in his mouth, Michael was finally able to get up.

On the ride from what looked to be a nice hotel to the comedy club, Drew remained silent. While not uncommon, it certainly felt different. And since Michael could barely remember the shows from the previous two nights, he just hoped he didn't fuck up onstage badly enough to ruin his chances for the next tour. But he was confident enough in his routine. After basically telling the same jokes over and over, he could at least do it with little thought or faculty.

***

"Well," he said, looking at the clock and realizing he was about to close his last set of the tour right on time At least that was going for him. "Before I go, I thought I would share with you something that I find funny."

He took a sip of his nearly finished beer and tried not to think about the fact that he would be off the stage for a while. This was it for more than two months, and what would happen then? He could do some open mic shows to keep fresh, but that wasn't the same. And a show on a Wednesday night didn't quite hold the same luster.

"I know this might sound insensitive," he continued, "but it's bulimia."

He waited for at least a few to laugh. Some were much louder than he expected.

"I'm sorry, but the very idea of a woman trying to increase her sex appeal through continuous vomiting is, well, hysterical. And then her teeth start to rot out and she gets this whole third-world, sickly-thin thing going. And the funny part? Most guys would still tap that, just like when she carried a few extra pounds. Ladies, your problem in life is that you're working way too hard to please an easy audience. And speaking of audiences, you all are beautiful. I love you all. My name is Michael Clover. Thank you."

He put the microphone back in the stand, shook the emcee's hand, and his show was over.

"Keep clapping for Michael Clover," the host said as Michael was already nearing the door.

At this point Drew would have been primed to take the stage, but there was no way Michael could even think about staying for it. Besides, the bar next door was having drink specials for anyone who went to the show, and it would only be polite to stop in.

The bartender barely looked up when Michael sat down. "You go to the show next door, pal?"

"Sort of."

"Got a ticket?"

"I don't think they give out tickets," Michael said.

"You don't think? Sure you were there?"

"I was the opening act."

"Really? You're a funny man? Tell me a joke."

"I'm off the clock."

"Want to hear one?"

"Bring me a drink first. Gin and tonic, extra lime. I'm kind of on this health kick right now."

"Okay," the bartender said, not laughing at the joke, causing Michael to scrap it permanently. "Here goes. A Greek man walks into a bar. Backwards."

"You should've given me the drink first."

"Fuck you. I think it's funny."

Michael held up his drink. "I agree. Just got a lot on my mind right now."

"I make a hell of a mind eraser."

"May test you on that," Michael said.

"You party?"

"That's a word with many connotations."

"Nah, I'm not Greek. Got a deal from a buddy. Going to share with my roommate later, but he won't notice if a line or two is gone. You ain't got to pay, but just tip big."

"Oh. Tempting," he said. And it was. Just a line or two would pick him up. Then he would have his wits back about him, and he could think about going back home.

"Give me a minute."

The bartender left through the back door. Michael just hoped he would hurry. Not that he needed it so badly... He just didn't like feeling so awkward. A little boost would lift him out of this post-show depression. He did not want to think about his empty apartment, or if his car had any hope of starting when he got there.

"Sorry, pal," the bartender said. "It's already a little light. And if it's too light, then I owe him money for rent. And you know, I've got other bills. It's tough out there."

"Don't sweat it." But Michael found himself sweating. His left arm was twitching, and he felt like the temperature had just dropped twenty degrees. He could find someone else. Certainly one of the trust-fund skiers had more than enough. He wasn't going to ask for much. But what bothered him all the more was how confident the bartender had been about Michael's propensity to say yes.

"Want to hear another joke?"

"Multitask and make another drink, too."

"Mind Eraser?"

"Only if it lives up to its name."

"Yeah. How is a hot dog like a vagina?"

"I give up," Michael said.

"If you knew what was in it, you'd never eat it."

Michael shook his head. He couldn't tell if it was funny or not. Since he was able to fake a laugh, it didn't matter. It didn't hurt that the guy wasn't overstating his drink-making abilities. But if he was going to call himself a comedian, shouldn't he at least know what was funny?

"Good drink."

"Thanks, pal," he said and disappeared behind the bar again.

Michael guessed he was going to make his roommate's light stash a little lighter. But it was probably bad form to complain about what was not his. A few minutes later he was back. And Michael was certain his suspicions were correct.

A few other people entered the bar. Michael hadn't realize he'd been the only customer until now. He hoped they would be the type that played the Golden Tee video golf game with a bizarrely intense passion that always lead to screaming and chest bumps. Pride over video golf had to be comedy gold. He'd have to work on that later. He reached into his pocket and pulled out a scrap of paper.

"Hook me up with another," Michael said when the bartender was close.

CHAPTER FORTY-FOUR

He woke up in Drew's car as it pulled to a stop. They weren't speeding past cornfields and cows this time. They were heading toward the airport. Since he was just getting dropped off, Michael thought he should probably say something, if it was only a simple thank you.

"End of the road, kid," Drew said. "Feeling any better?"

"I've never flown before."

"Afraid?"

"No. I just won't sit by one of the emergency exit rows. If the plane crashes, those people are expected to be heroes."

Drew nodded.

"I kind of fucked up near the end. Sorry."

"Yeah. Yeah, you did."

"I was hoping you were going to downplay that."

"Well, you did fuck up. You missed some of your punchlines last week, forgot a whole segment, and went ten minutes short."

"Damn. I've never had a premature problem before. Honest."

Drew nodded again.

"Did I ever thank you? You know, for this whole experience."

"Probably."

"Don't think I don't know how lucky I am. I never really paid my dues. Next thing I know, I'm on the road with someone famous."

"Famous?"

"By my definition."

"Not really, but thanks. I think. Don't worry about this whole paying dues bullshit. I heard your stuff, laughed, and that was enough. I don't like to fly, and since I've been doing this long enough, well, I just kind of do what I want. I feel more comfortable in the middle of the country. Don't know why, just always felt that way. Guess if I keep driving, I'll forget what I should have forgotten years ago. Doesn't always work that way. So, kid, when you talk about fucking up, know that I fucked up too. Somehow I learned."

"I didn't quite grasp all that. I'm sure it was wise."

"It wasn't. I'm tired, and I ramble when that happens. But I made mistakes out on the road. I just stopped making them as often."

"But I'm going home. That's more dangerous than the road."

"You can never escape yourself," Drew said. "You can hide for a while, but you know that already."

The car stopped in front of the terminal. Michael looked at the itinerary that had been folded up in his wallet. If he had any trouble, he could just ask what plane was headed for Cincinnati. He doubted many people wanted to leave Colorado for Ohio.

"Thank you, Drew. Thank you."

Michael extended his hand, and Drew shook it.

"Hope you're still alive the next time I see you."

"Well, that does fall under my immediate plans," Michael answered. Then he grabbed the few bags containing most of his possessions, put them on the curb, and waved as Drew drove away.

***

If he had been looking for comedy material about long lines in security or delays, he would have been sorely disappointed. Everything went smoothly. He had to ask only one person for direction, and the next thing he knew he was on the plane waiting for takeoff. At least the plane was less than half full, so he could sit by himself.

One glass of wine to celebrate the end of a life-changing adventure, then he hoped to sleep. From there he would try to make his drab apartment look borderline respectable. That way, when he came back from the Mac and Mark tour, he would have a place that almost looked like a home.

There really were no nerves, but just to be safe, he ordered a second glass of wine. It was box-quality, but he didn't consider himself a connoisseur. It was a fine complement to the free pretzels.

He listened through the safety announcements but held little interest in writing new material. Airline humor had to rank in the top five for most used material, perhaps somewhere between wife and dick jokes.

Just as soon as he began to doze, the plane accelerated. If there had been an announcement, he would've missed it. He felt the cabin pull up, nothing greater than an elevator, and then they were up and away. Back home.

He couldn't complain about coach accommodations. There was enough foot room, and it took nothing more than the slight recline of the seat to put him back asleep.

***

"Is Dad coming home soon?" Michael asked his mother as he sat at the table. "It's been a long time."

His mother only stared at him, mouth agape, and shook her head. She looked around the house that Michael's dreaming mind knew was his, yet none of the details remained consistent. "Mikey, we talked about this. He's not coming home. You killed him."

"Shucks, Mom, sometimes I forget these things. Should I ask Dad about it when he comes home?"

"Not a good idea, seeing as how he's dead."

"Oh, yeah," Michael said.

When the door opened, Michael turned slightly to the right, but the door was no longer there. He turned all the way around. From somewhere else came the sound of an audience applauding.

"Hi, Dad."

"Timothy, you shouldn't be up. You know what the doctor said."

"He's just a coroner. What does he know?"

Canned laughter echoed in his ears.

Suzie nodded in perfect agreement. "You're right. Go on. After all, are things really going to get worse?"

"Oh, Suzie, you kill me."

"No, that was Michael."

All three laughed instantly but stopped in unison. All smiles faded.

"Suzie, I'm just going to take Mikey out for a walk. That's okay with you, right?"

"Just get him back home."

"I'm not ready to take him full-time just yet." Canned laughter rung out again.

Suzie nodded as Timothy took Michael by the hand and led him out.

For several blocks, neither spoke. The neighborhood was the same, except that the space between each house had tripled. He couldn't remember any of the names of anyone inside the houses either.

"Where are we going?" Timothy asked.

"Don't know. Thought you were leading."

"I was following."

"Lead, Michael. Lead. I'm not the only one following."

Michael turned to look behind his shoulder, but his father stopped him.

"Don't turn, Mikey."

"Okay."

Silence remained for what felt like only a few steps, but when he looked up again the neighborhood had fallen far behind. No need to look behind again. The ground changed with each step, not quite slippery, but the footing became more cautious.

"Why'd you take me here, Mikey? Why did you take me back here?"

"Where are we?"

"Please tell me you don't know this place."

Michael had not realized his eyes were closed. As he opened them, he saw a place he knew. Back on the frozen pond, he saw the flame as well. He still heard the echoes of their footsteps.

"Don't turn around, Mikey."

"Didn't realize I did."

"You do that a lot. That's why you brought me here."

"What is this place? Did you take me here?"

Timothy looks sadly at him. "I hope not. With all my heart, I pray it's not true."

**

The skidding tires woke him. He was home. The long flight was supposed to be a buffer between there and here. Instead, it was practically a warp-speed journey. For some things there could be no preparation.

He tried to listen to the announcement welcoming him to Cincinnati and the accompanying information about the local time and temperature, but he could only stare outside at what should have looked like home. All he saw were other airplanes being taxied into the gates while baggage cars zipped left and right.

Once the rest of the passengers had exited the plane, Michael stood up before he had to be nudged.

CHAPTER FORTY-FIVE

Michael knew his apartment was practically empty, but when he finally walked back into it, he became homesick for the hotel rooms. At least there he knew he was surrounded by other people, even if they were just the front-desk clerk, the housekeeping staff, or the bartender. Here, at what he should have called home, he didn't even know the name of his next-door neighbor. If he had ever been interested enough, he could have looked at the lobby mailbox, but all that would have done is tell him the last name of someone he didn't care to meet.

There was no food in the refrigerator. At least he hoped not. If he had left something in there, he had no idea what it might be, and he was afraid to even check.

Cable television was a luxury in which he had never considered indulging. He'd never made much money before, and what he did have did not need to go toward finding that there were hundreds of channels of nothing. But after spending so much time in hotels, where he always had all the extras, he found that cable television was another thing he missed.

Sitting on the couch, only watching his distorted reflection in the blank screen, he knew he could not stand to be alone any longer. Plus he was also hungry. He never saw shame in dining alone, even if it was a weekend, but he was almost certain that it was not.

LaRosa's had always been a Clover family favorite, and he couldn't remember the last time he'd had it. At least he still knew where his car keys were. Whether the damn thing would start became another question. He also hoped he wouldn't get lost on the way. Since he had neither driven nor navigated anything for quite a while, he held little confidence that he would be able to get from one point to the other without a wide variety of assistance.

**

He saw it as a minor miracle when he turned the key and the engine turned over, starting right away. While it sounded more like a tinny rattle, it might as well have been the purr of some foreign luxury car. He pulled out of the parking lot, and he was back out on his own.

Not getting lost was another victory, even if he was in his hometown, and he was pretty sure he could get back home. LaRosa's sign had changed since his last visit. He didn't like the new look but still went inside.

The waitress, who immediately identified herself as Christina, was cute but so young it made him feel dirty for noticing. She was also way too upbeat, which irritated him, so he ordered a bottle of wine instead of a glass. And since it was a red wine, he ordered the lasagna. Might as well look sophisticated. He had missed the taste of the sauce anyway. People outside of Cincinnati tended to be less enthusiastic about it.

By the time Christina brought out the entrée, he had nearly finished the bottle. He took three bites, which were as good as he remembered, but asked for the rest to be boxed up.

"Everything okay, sir?"

"Uh, no. I mean yes. Yes, it was good. Darn tasty, I must say. Just have another engagement."

"Okay," Christina said and placed his bill on the table. "Come see us again."

It would have been great to stay and have someone to sit and talk with, but there weren't many people who were interesting enough for that. He wondered what Dana was up to.

He nodded. Now if only he had a place to go. The only thing he knew was that he could not go back to the apartment. He wasn't ready to visit Mom or Jessie either. He could stop at the bar across the street, have a few drinks, then go home and be ready to make a plan for whatever should happen next.

After paying the bill, leaving a hefty tip driven by embarrassment, he drove across the street to the bar. He was certain he'd been in this one before, but he didn't know anyone there. The bartender didn't look like much of a talker, so Michael ordered Jack Daniels on the rocks and was left alone to watch SportsCenter with the volume off.

While not loquacious, the bartender was quick enough to fill the glass again without prompting. That was enough to keep him happy and there until the bar closed. He paid the bill, along with a generous tip *not* fueled by shame this time, and walked out to his car.

With the late hour and the short distance, he felt confident enough to get home. This time the car did not start immediately. He dropped the keys onto the floorboard. By the time his trembling fingers picked them up, he realized he had sweated through his shirt.

He took a deep breath and looked at himself in the mirror, adjusted his hair, and successfully started his car. Taking his time to back out of the spot, he sighed and stopped for nearly a full minute before he shifted gears and drove out of the lot.

The trembling in his hands intensified, became violent. Keeping the car in a straight line required a white-knuckled grip on the steering wheel, and in being cautious, he kept the speed ten miles an hour beneath the thirty-five limit.

But he turned the wrong way—at least he thought he did. It had been so long since he'd traveled these roads that he wasn't sure of much, especially at night. He knew if he were able to see, he'd be able to get back with little difficulty.

He turned right where it seemed appropriate, followed by another right and then a left. None of these, however, looked even close, so he turned around and tried to retrace his path. When he turned back onto the main road, flashing blue lights reflected in his mirror and engulfed the car just before the deafening siren prompted him to pull over to the side.

The siren seemed a little excessive to him since there was nobody else on the road. How could he not see the rolling blue lights when the rest of the street was fast asleep? He might as well plan what he was going to say. There was no chance in hell that he would escape without a breathalyzer, and that would lead to a free ride to the police station. It was still late. There could be no doubt that he would spend at least one night. He had no defense, so there was no point in putting up a façade. He believed the term for his condition was *officially fucked*.

This could place his position on next month's tour in jeopardy, he realized. While it wasn't like he would be the only one who'd ever gotten into trouble—hell, he was sure several had some arrest record—Michael was not in the position to play around. He was living a wet dream and had still found a way to ruin it.

He put his car in park and nearly shit his pants when the cop sped past him, right through the flashing red stop light at the intersection, and disappeared down the street. He sat silently for a few seconds before pulling back out onto the road and turned back into the LaRosa's parking lot. He'd been given one reprieve—no point in pushing his already stretched luck. Anyway, he felt more confident of directions while on foot. He realized then that he'd left the remainder of his lasagna in the restaurant. That would have made for a nice breakfast.

His pace was slow, but he didn't need the same concentration to walk as he did behind the wheel. And now he was finally eager to get home.

CHAPTER FORTY-SIX

Dana walked into Whispers with every intention of quitting. She found herself making less and less money, and she could practically taste the bile build up in her throat every time she called some disgusting putz sugar or sweetie. And if the money was going to fall short, she might as well work at some fast food joint. At least there she wouldn't get fired when her breasts began to sag.

A bachelor party quickly changed her mind when the best man took a liking to her and, in an attempt at impressing her, dropped five hundred dollars her way on a single tip. That type of thing didn't happen often at Burger King. Might as well stick it out. And while she thought of it, if the best man was trying to show off, well, it worked. She was impressed.

"So what's your story, darling?" she asked as she sat next to him after her stage time ended. She noted that he wasn't wearing a wedding ring. While very few ever did, there was no indention where it would have been. He looked young, but not too young. *A girl can dream*, she thought to herself.

"Just trying to show my friend a good time while he still has the freedom. My name's Jason."

He extended his hand and she shook it.

"Angel," she said.

"Really?"

"No. Not really. But it is here."

"I told you my real name," he answered.

"How do I know that?"

"I'll show you my ID."

"No need, Jason. So what do you do for a living?"

"Sales. Pharmaceutical. Not very interesting."

"It doesn't sound so bad. And you don't need to have an interesting job to be a fascinating person. I've known people with great jobs who just suck."

"Is that a proposition?"

"Sorry, I meant that in a figurative sense."

"Bummer."

"Didn't mean to get your hopes up."

"Or anything else," he said, laughing at his own joke. "So I can't know your name?"

"No. Some things will just have to remain a mystery."

He shrugged. "Hard to get. I understand. My buddy, the poor sap we call the groom, well, he has a thing for Asian women. I don't know if his fiancée knows about this or not. Her name is Molly, and, well…"

"The name indicates she's not Asian."

"Got any back there?" he asked.

"No Asian women back there. We're a domestic establishment."

"Too bad. That girl with the dark hair is close enough. Can I pay for his private dance?"

"Destiny? Sure. She's kind of a bitch, though."

"Yeah, but she's hot enough."

"True. She is. And she thinks she is Queen Silicone."

"But you're hot with personality. Ain't many like you."

"Whatever, dude."

"Seriously," Jason answered. "You're the best of both worlds. And I don't even know your name."

"It's Dana."

"Dana is way sexier than Angel. Yeah. Dana is hot."

"I think I'm blushing."

"You are. And by the way, my name really is Jason."

"Jason is sexy too."

"I would love to believe you."

"You can trust me."

"Even though you didn't even tell me your real name when we first me?"

"That was before I trusted you."

He nodded and looked around the room. Cinnamon was on stage, getting some attention in the form cash being thrown her way. Business was good all-around tonight.

"Okay," he said. "I'm going to hook up my buddy before his life ends. You here all night? May have to check out one of those private dances."

"Yep. Any time."

He left, armed with an impressive bankroll to keep his friend busy with adventures about which he would likely never tell his future wife. Dana began to walk around, and before she knew it, she was up another two hundred with a couple of private dances and appreciative tips.

The bachelor party continued to pump money into the place with pitchers of beer and shots of tequila. It had been quite a while since she'd made so much money, and there were still a few hours before closing time. Time usually slowed down when she had to work, but tonight she found herself wondering where the time had gone.

Jason was talking with one of the other guys in his party when she walked in behind him. Many of the other patrons had left, but it was still a decent crowd. Maybe he was ready for that private dance. If he had exhausted his funds for the night, she would make it a freebie. After all, he had already paid her month's rent.

"Almost ready to go home?" she overheard Jason's friend say. "Did you get that blonde's phone number?"

"I did, but just to see if I could. It's part of the fun. Like a video game. But hell yeah, man, I'm ready to go home. You can get an STD just by talking to any of these whores."

Jason noticed Dana behind him and turned to her. "Am I saying something that isn't true, skank?"

She shook her head, fighting the urge to cry. His buddies laughed heartily. Even though they looked like they felt bad about it, there was no hiding the malice.

"Thanks for shaking your ass at me, but I need to go home and get a shower."

The tears came out, fast and loud, and she raced back to the dressing room in search of a place to hide.

CHAPTER FORTY-SEVEN

The walk home was much farther than Michael had anticipated, but he was right about being more certain of himself while walking. This way, if he careened into someone, it would simply be irritating, not fatal.

When his apartment was finally in sight, he reached in his pocket for his keys. They weren't there. He felt his other pocket. Not there either. After searching every possible place, he knew where they were. He'd never taken them out of the ignition. While he was pretty sure he had turned off the engine, he couldn't know for a fact. He was already embarrassed, and if he'd left the car running, he would border on humiliation.

Unfortunately he had remembered to lock his apartment door. He had also forgotten to bring a sweatshirt with him. The walk home was pretty cold. Standing still became unbearable. A slight breeze caressed him, but while it was far from frigid, he felt chilled beyond belief. He sat on the edge of the porch and leaned against the building. Hopefully he would get a little sleep, then he would be able to go back for the car.

As soon as he felt himself drift off to sleep, he heard a voice say, "Gone so long you forgot how to get in?"

He looked up and saw his landlord standing by the porch.

"Sorry, Alan. Locked my keys in the car."

"Ah. Done that many times myself. Heard you on Mac and Mark by the way. Funny shit there."

"Thanks. Can you let me in?"

"Yeah. Just got to go back to my apartment and get the key. Come with me. One of the neighbors complained that a bum was sleeping in front of the door."

"They might not have been that far off."

"Eh. Come follow me. I'll get that for you."

Michael got up behind Alan, hoping he wasn't going to be all that talkative. After the long walk, and the whiskey of course, Michael was exhausted.

When they got to the landlord's apartment, Alan said, "Come in, got a bunch to go through. This could take a minute."

Michael walked in and plopped down on the couch while Alan opened a drawer and flipped through several keys.

"So it must have been exciting out there, telling jokes, seeing the country."

"I saw a lot of corn."

"Congratulations, Mike. Cool gig out there."

"I suppose," he answered and found himself sinking deeper into the couch. "But yeah, it was cool."

"Was it wild out there on the road?"

"I may have made it a bit too wild."

"You're young, though. I was too. That was a long time ago. A long time ago."

"But you're not old."

"I got real old three years ago," Alan said and held up a key. "I can let you in now if you want."

"I don't know if I can move."

"No hurry. I'm nocturnal."

"But what made you old?"

Alan gave the saddest smile Michael could imagine. "You don't really want to know."

"Perhaps. But I'm guessing you want to tell me."

"I spend a lot of time talking to this empty apartment."

"I understand. But, well, you aren't one of those people who brings people in, and then cuts them up piece by piece and tosses them in the dumpster, right?"

"No. That would be too much work. I just bore them with my stories."

"Then go on. If I doze off, it's because I'm drunk, not bored."

"Three years ago this past January, my wife skidded off the road and into a frozen pond."

"Alan, that's not a boring story. That's, well, fucking awful."

"Yeah, she wasn't drunk or anything."

"Well, the slippery roads—"

"Carolyn was driving because I was drunk. I made an ass out of myself at a party, she brought me home and dropped me off. Not wanting to stick around with me, she went back out and never came home."

"That's terrible."

"That's the second-to-last time I went drinking. I don't remember her funeral. I don't even remember where she's buried. I lost about a month of my life after that. Felt guilty for living. I did some stupid stuff, stuff that dishonored her memory, which was the only thing I had left."

"It's not your fault."

"We'll never know that. Back then I didn't know any better. Now I do. The question is, what am I going to do with it? All I have is myself now. And to thine own self be true."

Michael remembered that vividly from Drew's coin. He desperately wanted to go home but did not want to be alone either.

"Every night, I picture that frozen pond, just waiting for a miracle," Alan continued.

"Don't know why I'm telling you this, but I have always had this dream about walking on a frozen lake. And there's a fire coming out of it. Maybe it's just the booze or the sleep deprivation, but do you think that maybe there's something to it?"

"No," Alan said. His voice was not overly firm but was certainly direct. "Did you know that fire and water is a euphemism for suicide? I spend a lot of time reading. I try not to dream."

Michael no longer felt comfortable on the couch. His father had been so upset in the dream in which he'd taken him to the lake. He'd asked why he was taken *back* there. Dear God, how long had the dream gone on? He felt his cheek and realized he was crying.

"I didn't mean to upset you," Alan said. "I'm not all that good with people. And I know you need to get back to your apartment and get some sleep."

"No," Michael answered. "I need to wake up first."

***

When Alan let Michael back into the apartment, it was nearly dawn. He still had to get his car, assuming it had not been stolen hours ago, and bring it back home. If he got a couple of hours of sleep, then he would feel confident behind the wheel again.

He looked around the empty room. Some of his clothing had spilled out of the suitcase, as had several scraps of paper. He had no idea what he had written on most of them. Chances were, most were not worth the paper they were written on. Hopefully a few would turn into something. That would be for another day, though.

Alan asked him if he partied. His immediate answer was yes, but it never was a party. Pity party perhaps, but nothing to celebrate. It was always Michael by himself. Except for the few times he got to hang out with Dana, but that didn't turn out so well. He just hoped everything was well with her now.

As he sat on the edge of the bed, he looked at the scraps of paper. He picked up one that read, *How did the apple ever make the kosher list? It did a hell of a lot more damage than any pork chop.* Michael laughed a little in the empty room. He did kind of like that joke. But the whole pile that looked like trash was his life's work. There was nothing wrong with telling jokes, but some things would have to change.

He picked up a pen and wrote on a crumbled piece of paper, *I choose to live.*

***

After several hours of dreamless sleep, he felt good, energetic. It didn't take him long to get to his car this time. The keys were still in the ignition, but thankfully he hadn't left the engine running. At least he'd done that right. He hadn't lock the driver's side door, and under normal circumstances that would have been a bad thing. Today, however, it was a blessing.

He started the car and turned off the radio. Being alone with his thoughts didn't feel like such a bad thing. As he adjusted the rearview mirror, he looked at his reflection.

"To thine own self be true," he said, and he drove away.

CHAPTER FORTY-EIGHT

Dana returned to work again. She realized that dreaming about quitting was foolish, if not irresponsible. At least here she knew what she was doing. And to be fair, she'd only had a few bad days. Most days didn't end with her crying to herself after being groped or verbally humiliated. Most days were just a routine, and she knew it well.

In fact, in the weeks following that horrible bachelor party, she simply stopped caring. Dana could not believe what a relief that was. She'd never thought that feeling nothing would feel so good.

It was a Thursday night, and she had already cleared two hundred dollars within her first forty-five minutes. The money could make anything tolerable.

After her second dance, she put on her robe and walked off the stage, where Elijah waited for her.

"Dancing real nice lately, kid. Starting to make some fans."

"Really?"

"Yeah. Some guy is waiting for two private dances. Go get dressed so you can, well, get undressed for some cash. Raking it in tonight."

"Looks that way."

She went into the back, added some lipstick, put her outfit back on, and was ready to go. Leaving money waiting was never a good idea.

When she got back out to the main area, Elijah pointed to VIP section.

"Second one," he said.

She nodded and walked in. Before she looked down, she said, "So you're interested in two dances?"

"Well, I guess that's what I'm paying for."

Dana looked over and saw Michael sitting on the chair.

"What are you doing here?"

"This is the only place left where I can listen to Whitesnake."

She started to turn away.

"Lost your number. And even if I had called, I wasn't sure you'd talk to me."

"So you came all the way here? What the hell are you doing?"

"I knew what you did for a living, and in what city, so I looked everywhere until I found the right angel."

"I don't want to dance for you."

"Don't blame you. You didn't exactly see me at my best. But you saw me at my most consistent."

"That's why I left."

"That's why you should have left."

"So why are you here? Why are you doing this?"

"Aren't you happy to see me?" Michael asked.

"Well, I am. I really am. But I feel—" Dana began but stopped.

"Awkward?"

"Incredibly."

"So let's get out of here."

"I have to work."

"No, you don't. Come with me. Leave with me."

She looked at him. It began with a glare, but immediately softened. "I don't think I can."

"Can you stay here any longer? You don't belong here."

"It pays the bills."

"You don't belong here," he repeated.

"You're wrong."

"No. I've been wrong, well, more than anybody ever. But I'm seeing things a little clearer now." He reached into his pocket. "Do you ever accept coins here?"

"Change is for the vending machine."

He put something in her hand. She looked down at large coin cupped in her palm. "What is it?"

"I may not always work really hard for the dollars I make, but a lot of struggle went into getting that coin. Thirty days clean and sober."

Dana just stared. "Seriously?"

Michael nodded.

"I'd hug you if I were allowed."

"All the more reason to leave. You don't belong here, Dana. Nobody will ever call you Angel ever again."

"I've been called a hell of a lot worse lately."

"You don't deserve that. Did I say you don't belong here?"

"You may have touched on that. But aren't you on tour?"

"Not for more than a month. It was just over a month ago that the shows with Drew Greene ended."

"Sorry about that."

"I'm not. I wouldn't be here right now. I wouldn't be able to be here right now. "

"I'm glad to see you." She smiled and looked at the coin. "And this may be the greatest tip ever. You go to a lot of meetings?"

"Meetings? Do I look like someone who wants to listen to someone else's bullshit?" He laughed at his own joke.

"You cracking yourself up there, funny boy?"

"This may be a bad idea, but leave with me. You don't belong here."

"And do I belong with you?"

"Yes," he answered. "But even if you don't leave with me, leave for yourself."

"You said you've been wrong before."

"I have been. But you belong with me."

"Now that you say it again, it's starting to sound pretty damn good."

"You could always come back here if things don't work out."

"No," she said. "No. I don't belong here."

"Where have I heard that before?"

"But what will we do? Where will we go?"

"I don't know," Michael said. "It won't be an ordinary life, but I do promise you it will be a life. That's all I can offer."

"You may have more to offer than you will ever know. Can we start now?"

"I think we already have."

Dana got up, ran to the dressing room, put on her sweatshirt, pants, and gym shoes, grabbed her purse, then with equal speed ran to Michael and screamed to the rest of the club, "I don't belong here! I quit!"

Before anyone could say anything in response, she and Michael had walked out the door. She was overcome by giggles as she got into the car.

"I've never made anyone laugh like that before," he said.

"Maybe you've always had the wrong audience."

He smiled and turned the car out of the parking lot, back onto the open road.

ABOUT THE AUTHOR

Gregory Petersen is a writer, editor, comedian, coach, husband, and father of two beautiful daughters. He was born, raised, and still remains in Cincinnati, Ohio.

www.ingramcontent.com/pod-product-compliance
Lightning Source LLC
Chambersburg PA
CBHW071528260626
47170CB00002B/554